P
Grand ...

"Linda Sands has delivered a non-stop, leather clad, hard-boiled and hard-knuckled, kick in the groin actioner. If you were looking for a cozy mystery, this ain't it. This is a Texas thriller with narrative and dialogue as sharp as the blade on a truck driver's pocket knife. This is a great first book in a new series and I look forward to reading more."

—Patrick Kendrick, award-winning
author of *The Savants*

"A relentless, hard-driving Kenworth ride with a gorgeous truck driver. You'll be crying with terror and laughing hysterically at the same time as Cajun princess, JoJo Boudreux, delivers hard-assed wisecracks and bullets. One caution: do not begin reading at night as you're going to be very sleepy the next day."

—Les Edgerton, author of *The Genuine,
Imitation, Plastic Kidnapping*

"Linda Sands knows how to tell one hell of a story...replete with clever dialogue and colorful characters, and a plot that speeds along like a Freightliner. Strap yourself in before you start to read this one."

—Baron R. Birtcher, award-winning
author of *Rain Dogs*

"Linda Sands takes murder and mayhem on a fabulous road trip with Jojo Boudreaux, a beautiful truck driver who is a woman of many a man's dreams. But hurt the people she loves and Jojo transforms into your worst nightmare...a high-speed thrill ride with enough crashes and explosions to keep your heart racing from the first to last page!"

—M.K. Gilroy, author of
the Kristen Conner Mystery Series

GRAND THEFT CARGO

ALSO BY LINDA SANDS

3 Women Walk Into a Bar
Simple Intent
Not Waving, Drowning

for Michelle —

LINDA SANDS

Enjoy the ride!

GRAND THEFT CARGO

W Sands

DOWN&OUT BOOKS

Down & Out Books
3959 Van Dyke Rd, Ste. 265
Lutz, FL 33558
www.DownAndOutBooks.com

The characters and events in this book are fictitious. Any similarity to real
persons, living or dead, is coincidental and not intended by the author.

Cover design by JT Lindroos

ISBN: 1-943402-79-5
ISBN-13: 978-1-943402-79-3

For Salena, Eddie, Steve and all of the other drivers who keep this economy running. If you bought it, they brought it. Thank a truck driver today.

"Nothing behind me,
everything ahead of me,
as is ever so on the road."
—Jack Kerouac

When the road is a ribbon of moonlight over the purple moor,
A highwayman comes riding—
Riding—riding—
A highwayman comes riding, up to the old inn-door.

Over the cobbles he clatters and clangs in the dark inn-yard.
He taps with his whip on the shutters, but all is locked and barred.
He whistles a tune to the window, and who should be waiting there
But the landlord's black-eyed daughter,
Bess, the landlord's daughter,
Plaiting a dark red love-knot into her long black hair.

—an excerpt from "The Highwayman" by Alfred Noyes

Chapter 1

We were parked on the shoulder of a busy highway in Sulphur, Louisiana, red reflective triangles set out like an SOS, in case you missed the blinking hazards on our custom Peterbilt or the double rows of orange chicken lights running down the side of a fifty-three-foot-long trailer.

"Remind me again, Jojo," Boone said. "Why do we love this so much?"

I stepped out of the sleeper unit's shower, drying my long hair with a towel, and slid up behind my boyfriend. He was sitting at the dinette/office staring at the blank screen of a phone we were hoping would ring, signaling the arrival of road service. I wrapped my arms around him and nuzzled his neck, inhaling the scent I loved so much—pine and man.

I said, "Well, Tyler Boone, it sure as hell isn't because of predicaments like this."

"Predicaments, huh?" He laughed and reached for me, managing to both kiss me and capture me on his lap in one sweeping motion.

"Well, maybe it is...a little," I conceded, leaning in to the kiss and wondering whatever we would do to pass the time until help arrived.

"I like being the boss," he said, running his finger down my arm. "And all the benefits that come with it."

It was my turn to laugh. "Wait. *You're* the boss?"

* * *

1

Outside, cars raced past on the highway, four-wheelers changing lanes without a care in the world, winding in and out at seventy miles an hour, like dots on a video game, except these drivers would not be given second lives with a "Restart" button.

I climbed off Boone's lap and cleared the dinette area as he dropped the table down and pulled out our bed.

"I'll tell you why we love this life," I said. "Why we don't own a house or a car or a lawn mower and patio furniture. It's because we love freedom. Driving long haul is more than a job, it's a lifestyle. We're *road cowboys.*"

Boone kicked off his shoes, rolled onto the bed beside me, and closed his eyes. "Road cowboys. I like that. Go on."

I put my head on his chest. "It's the way the sun rises over the hood right after you've shined and waxed Old Blue. The way it glints off that silver pig hood ornament, those fat chrome pipes."

"Thought you hated my silver pig," Boone said.

"Oh shush," I said, kissing his neck, tucking my hand inside his shirt. I thought about the best part of driving: the rumble of the engine, the hum of the highway, the way I felt like God, riding high in my hydraulic seat. "It's the sight of clear blue sky peeking through as we climb a mountain pass, and the relief we feel making it safely down the other side."

Boone sighed.

I said, "It's the image of steam coming off wet asphalt, as if Hell itself might be rising. It's the shimmer of black pavement, a dreamy false oasis."

I ran my hand from his stomach up to his chest and laid it on his heart. "But mostly, it's us together experiencing the weathers of three seasons and the climate of two countries in one working day, then pulling over, drawing the curtains, locking the doors, and getting ready to do it all over again with no expectation of what tomorrow will bring."

It was my turn to sigh. I tilted my head to see Boone's face—slack, relaxed, asleep.

I whispered, "That's why we love it."

Boone had fallen into trucking the way I had fallen into him—hard and fast—with no regrets. He was from a small town like me, and even if he was a Texan, I forgave him. You can't pick your momma, or your birthplace.

Southeast Texas had enough Louisiana in it that we could understand each other. It wasn't like a Yankee and a Southern Belle, or a Scotsman and a Brit. We drank our beer ice cold, craved the same spicy seafood, and enjoyed mixing our classic rock tunes with some Zydeco.

Boone might have gotten a head start as a trucker, with his father bringing him into the family business at eighteen, but I was a quick learner. And now? There wasn't much he could do on the rig that I couldn't. Old-school truckers still gave me shit at truck stops and loading docks and, hell, whenever they could—granted, it would trail right off when Boone stood up beside me. He was an impressive figure; a muscular six-foot-five, almost too broad-shouldered for the driver's seat, with tattoos in all the right places and a face that might have appeared in a magazine, grimace and all. He was just the kind of bad-boy pretty that I liked—a lot.

My father, Manny Boudreaux, wasn't sure about Boone or this lifestyle for me.

When I called him to tell him we were on our way home to Louisiana, planning on taking a few days off, he'd said, "You tell that man of yours it's time to think about settling down. You could make a nice home here on the plantation. I'll even put in a pond for fishing. What do you say, Shâ?" he said, sinking his point home with the Cajun endearment.

I lied to the first man I'd ever loved. "That sounds great,

Père. I'll talk to Boone about it."

Sitting in the cab, sipping coffee and waiting for the road-service crew to finish changing our blown tire, I told Boone what my father had said and how I couldn't keep putting him off forever.

"Is that what you want? To get off the road and build a house back in Bunkie?"

"Sometimes," I said. "I'll admit, it sounds nice. Not dealing with DOT, dispatchers, the rising cost of diesel. Not to mention all these new rules and regulations."

"Change is everywhere, babe."

"I know. But it's not always for the best. Remember what happened to Stroker?"

"Hey, he never should have parked overnight there."

"C'mon, Boone. No one deserves to get the crap beat out of them for pulling over to sleep. And then they steal his truck too? What the hell?"

"Is that what's worrying you? We'll be fine. Trust me, Jojo."

"I trust *you*, Boone. It's those other people out there I'm not so sure about."

Doubt. It was the one thing that kept me from being perfect.

I was saved from his hero speech by the ringing phone. I checked the display, then tapped the speakerphone key as our dispatcher's name flickered across the screen.

"Hey, Charlene," I said, "How are you?"

"Oh, Jojo, you know what they say. Same shit, different day."

I laughed. "You know that's the truth."

She chuckled, deep and throaty—a sound that turned into a wet cough. A few seconds later she said, "Sorry to do this to you, honey, but you and Boone are the only ones close enough with the clearances for the job. I know you asked for some time off. But, I'm in a bind here."

I looked at Boone, who shook his head. I rubbed my fingertips together, making the universal symbol for money.

He gave me the dejected-puppy look, then nodded.

I smiled. "Okay. What you got, Charlene?"

"I'm sending it to you now. God bless you, Jojo. You saved my behind again."

"You remember that someday," I said as I took the phone off speaker and went into the sleeper, where my laptop waited on the kitchen table.

Boone climbed down to have a word with the road-service guy while I completed the paperwork, checked the weather, and searched the route for traffic issues before I went back up front. Boone handed me more paperwork, then buckled into the driver's seat.

I mashed my cheek up against his scratchy one and hung my arms around his neck.

He kept both hands on the wheel.

"Are you mad at me, baby, for taking that job? I know how much you wanted time off. I promise, I'll make it up to you."

He shook his head, made a sound in his throat.

"C'mon. It's Texas, baby," I said, moving in closer, running my hands down his chest. "You know how you love Texas."

He mumbled, "Everything's bigger in Texas."

I grinned. "That's right."

He pulled me in and kissed me, hard and long enough that I forgot about Texas. Until he pulled back and asked, "So, what's the deal?"

It was Boone's way: maintain control, and as always, leave me wanting more of him.

I said, "Driver left the warehouse in Michigan two days ago. No one's been able to reach him by radio or phone. He

5

wasn't carrying a priority shipment, nothing perishable, but..."

"Yeah?"

"Destination is a pharmaceutical warehouse in San Marcos. Charlene says they're concerned."

"As they should be."

Early on in my training I learned that some places are more strict on shipping than others, but whether you were in charge of a load of organic carrots or millions of dollars of computer parts, you needed to treat the contents the same.

Boone asked, "Who is this joker?"

"Guy named Edwin Dorsey. From what I've heard, his claim to fame's winning a bacon-eating contest at The Waffle Shack a few years back. Not the most reliable driver. Charlene says he's got a habit of disappearing and won't GPS his company rig."

This news earned me a headshake from Boone. He was all about adding the latest and greatest to our truck whenever he could.

"Apparently," I continued, "the guy has quite a few habits—none of them good. Anyway, Charlene's had everyone out looking for his Kenworth—finally found it this morning at a small truck stop in the Houston area. Missouri City exit, place called Southland Freeway Truck Stop."

Boone nodded. "Yeah, I've been there. What does she need us to do?"

"Get there as soon as possible, disconnect the trailer, and take it to San Marcos. Keys are at the truck stop. We'll have enough time to drop in on my father and see if we can leave our trailer in the barn."

Boone stared past me. "He's not going to be happy."

"I know," I said, sure of two things: Manny Boudreaux would not be happy about our change in vacation plans or about having a bulky trailer in his pristine barn. But he would, as he always did, manage to work things out to everyone's benefit.

People who say you can never go home again did not spend their childhoods on a big-ass plantation outside of Bunkie, Louisiana.

As soon as we turned onto the long dirt road leading to the house, I relived the best parts of my youth—something I wished I could capture, bottle, and pour over myself at will. Especially since our stay would be much too short, with only the time to eat a meal seated at a real table, secure our trailer in the barn, and hear about the latest with Manny and his fiery girlfriend, Pilar.

"Père," I said, "do you really think it's wise at your age to go eco-camping in Brazil?"

"Oh, Shâ, you think no one is as strong as you. Remember where you came from," he said, reaching over and pinching my cheek.

Boone grinned at seeing me reduced to a surly teen in my father's eyes.

We said our goodbyes, promised to be in touch, then climbed up into Old Blue and rattled down the dirt road under the shade of live oaks.

We made good time, driving light without a trailer. Bobtailing. For a trucker it was like going outside without your pants. You might feel light and free, but you knew you were missing something.

We found the truck stop just off the Interstate. The dirty white Kenworth was right where Charlene had said it would be. Boone pulled into an empty spot nearby and shut down Old Blue.

From the outside, Southland Freeway Truck Stop looked like any other gas station convenience store, except for all the semis at the pumps. Inside it smelled like diesel and donuts and looked like a mini Walmart meshed with a Korean bathhouse. You could get a shower, wash your clothes, play arcade games, catch episodes of your favorite TV show, buy a new shirt or some thicker socks, enjoy a cappuccino, or reheat your grandma's special chicken potpie in the rows of microwaves.

Boone jerked a thumb toward the manager's office. "I'm going to get the Kenworth key. Meet me at the truck?"

"Sure," I said, scanning the row of gum and candy at the front counter. I grabbed a chocolate bar, two packs of gum, and some chewy mints and waited for an old-time trucker to pay for his coffee and newspaper. He was the kind of guy who thought flannel was a color. I imagined the interior of his rig: it would include a cigarette-laden ashtray, a well-used CB with mic dangling, and on the passenger seat a tattered atlas with dog-eared pages for Idaho.

I watched him leave, then stepped up to the counter.

The girl at the register said, "Is he in trouble?" her eyes darting toward the manager's office.

"Who?" I asked, thinking she meant Boone.

She leaned in and whispered, "Edwin."

She must have mistaken the confused look on my face for concern, because she kept talking.

"Not that anyone calls him Edwin. He only lets his woman do that. She'd beat the shit out of me if she heard me."

"Edwin?" I said cautiously.

She tapped my hand. "Yeah, The Baconator. Is he in trouble?"

She said "The Baconator" so seriously that even though I wanted to laugh I leaned in to meet her and said, just as seriously, "Trouble? What makes you think that?"

"Well, the last time you TSA people came around, that driver was screwed."

"TSA?" I said. "I think there's a misunderstanding. I'm a driver and we're—"

"*You're* a driver?" she scoffed as if I'd told her I fart sunshine.

I smiled. "Yeah, I am. And, I'm sorry, but 'The Baconator'? Really?"

In retrospect, I could have played the whole thing a little smoother. I mean, bursting out laughing probably wasn't that cool.

She rang up my candy, looking at me sideways the whole time. It was easy for her, with those wide-set reptile eyes.

I searched for the right thing to say, some snappy comeback, a way to win her over, but her body language said she was done with me. I'd seen that same posture in a hundred bars.

I added up the candy cost, checked the numbers on the register readout, and threw some bills on the counter.

The girl kept one eye on the money and one eye somewhere east of my right ear. She hesitated long enough that I turned to look in the same direction, the way you do when your friend tells you some hot dude is checking out your ass but don't look now—too late, you've already looked.

There was a guy at the postcard rack. I wondered how long he'd been standing there. He was big and bald in a sideshow strongman way and wore sunglasses. Inside. On a cloudy day. He snatched a card from the rack and walked toward us, whistling a country tune. I should have known the title, but I never remember stuff like that. I could tell you who I'd been dating when a song came out, or even which hairstyle I'd been wearing, but not song titles or lyrics. My brain didn't work that way.

I thought about asking the whistling guy what it was

called, but when I turned around, I changed my mind. It wasn't how he looked up close as much as how he made me feel when I looked at him—like I was one of those big plastic toys the keepers toss into the gorilla pit at the zoo.

"Thanks," I said to the girl as I grabbed my bag of candy and change, then scooted to the door.

I made my way through the parking lot, turning down the last row of trucks just in time to see Boone backing our truck under the strange trailer. I was close enough to hear the king-pin slide into position.

He waved as he climbed down to verify the hookup, couple the gladhands and electrical line, raise the landing gear. There was nothing left for me to do but get in the truck and look pretty. Like a truck driver should.

Five miles down the road from the truck stop, Boone said, "Someone's awful quiet. You okay?"

I told him how I was offended when the girl at the register said I didn't look like a truck driver.

He looked at me, raised a brow.

"I'm serious," I said. "I don't want to have to gain thirty pounds, start parting my hair down the middle, and go around in Velcro sneakers and elastic-waist jeans from Sears. I thought people were more open-minded these days."

"You're in the South, pumpkin. Don't expect too much. Besides, that description sounded more like someone's grandpa than a trucker. You'd need some steel-toed boots in there." He motioned to his own booted foot on the gas pedal.

I stared out the window.

Boone reached over and grabbed my hand. "Listen. I love you, Jojo. I love the way you smile. I love that little dimple. Yes, that one," he said as I touched the side of my face. "I love your long legs and those beautiful green eyes. But more than that, I love who you are inside, the part I'm just getting to know. You might have hidden it from everyone else, but I know you have a soft spot, even if it is for every stray dog in Bunkie. You can't feed them all, you know."

"Well, not all," I said, blushing.

"I don't care if you don't look like someone's clichéd idea of what a truck driver should be. You know what you look like to me?"

I shook my head.

"You look like the kind of girl that could make a man happy for the rest of his life."

Boone had never talked like that before. He was a man of few words, and usually those involved food or engine parts.

"What are you saying, Boone?"

He stared out the windshield, gripped the wheel a little tighter, then turned to me and said, "Nothing. Just, I love you, Jojo Boudreaux."

I leaned over and gave him the best kiss I could while still strapped into the passenger seat.

"Me too," I whispered.

We rode in comfortable silence the rest of the way, me calling out the route until Boone made a slow left turn, rode the Pharmco fence line—high, barbed, wired—then pulled up to the guard shack. I muted the GPS and noted the miles in the logbook as Boone handed the paperwork and our credentials to the guard. We both had to answer whether the vehicle had stopped within the first two hundred miles of trailer transfer. We said no, followed by an "of course not, we know the rules." I was about to tell the guard how our GPS and any trailer we hauled were monitored, but Boone shushed me. After a minute, the guy waved us through. The second stop was shorter, the guard barely rising from his chair to give us the once over. Maybe the first guard had already cleared us or maybe this guy was too interested in his lunch to be bothered. He pressed a button that opened the interior gate and went back to his sandwich.

We rolled away, gaining speed as we approached a hub of buildings where dark-suited workers rushed through parking lot rows looking like busy ants. Farther down the road, a construction crew hammered, cut, and hauled prefab pieces, erecting what looked like a modern four-story metal-and-glass structure.

I was trying to take an artsy picture with my phone of a yellow crane dangling a sheet of reflective metal when two black SUVs marked "SECURITY" came up fast beside us, running on the right shoulder of the road. We'd done nothing wrong and weren't planning to, but I still got that nervous twang—the one I get when there's a cop driving behind me for a long stretch of time. It's an instinctual fear, or maybe something born of experience. Usually, when you mix power and weapons, you get abuse.

"You see that?" I said to Boone.

"Yep."

He was so cool. I almost hated how nothing rattled him. It wasn't normal.

In a synchronized move, the drivers gunned their vehicles and swerved onto the road in front of us.

"Always in a damn hurry here," Boone said.

"Have we been here before?" I asked.

"Don't think you have. I used to run this route before we met, when I worked as a company driver for Enahel. These guys are sticklers about time."

I looked out at the window at the clear blue sky, sharp beams of sun cutting through the row of trees. A hawk made lazy circles in the sky. I began to whistle the song that had been in my head since I'd heard it at the truck stop. Boone chimed in, adding lyrics about a highwayman, a sailor, a dam builder, and a single drop of rain. He sang so nice with his pure, honest voice, that by the time we'd backed into our dock to offload the cargo, I'd almost lost that nervous feeling.

I got out with Boone, partly to stretch my legs and get some air, and partly because I'm nosy. Some drivers take pictures on the road, landscapes, sunsets, or road kill. I like to get people shots. Usually of other truckers or warehouse workers—something funny. We caption them and send them to Charlene. She posts them in the break room at DTS, where other captions are added. It's good clean fun—well, mostly.

But at the Pharmco warehouse they were all business, giving me the evil eye when they saw me hold up my camera phone. A white-haired guy in his air-conditioned office smacked on the glass and yelled in my direction.

"No cameras!"

The forklift driver dropped his load and retreated, saying, "Sorry, miss, but this is a camera-free zone."

Before I had a chance to give him any shit about what exactly I could and would be doing, I heard Boone.

"That's it, guys. Come on, Jojo, we're out of here."

The dock gate dropped as Boone pulled on his jean jacket and rolled up the sleeves.

"Damn, that was quick," I said as we secured the trailer doors.

"Yep. Told you," Boone said, putting his arm around me as we walked back to the cab. I looked around, unable to shake the feeling we were being watched.

In the next bay, two guys in Pharmco uniforms got out of a white van. One guy wearing a beanie and wraparound sunglasses used a key card to open a door near the dock. A skinny dude followed him, checking the area, then dragged over a rock with his foot and wedged the door open.

Boone draped his arm over my shoulder. "Sure be glad to drop this ugly thing."

I smacked his arm. "What the hell?"

"I'm talking about the trailer, Jojo." Boone laughed.

"Oh."

He gave me a peck on the head, then held open the door to Old Blue.

"I'm going to use their restroom," he said, tipping his head toward the warehouse. He seemed apologetic, but whether it was for making me wait or because he had to go, I wasn't sure. I was going to yell some smart-ass remark, thanking him for thinking of me and our confined quarters, but I didn't. Instead, I admired the receding view.

As Boone slipped through the propped-open door I thought about the guys I'd just seen. They were overdressed compared to the other warehouse workers. Sunglasses, hats, and gloves? This was Texas. In summer.

Distracted by chiming tones coming from my phone—someone's baby news blowing up my feed—I climbed up into the cool interior of the truck and quickly forgot about the men. By the time Boone returned, my mind was on tiny fingers and toes.

"That song of yours must be playing in a loop on some radio show today," he said, climbing into the passenger seat. "Even the guy in the bathroom was whistling it."

"Is that right?" I said, barely listening. I punched in a call to our leasing company's office in Houston as Boone grabbed us some cold waters from the fridge.

"Hey, Charlene. Just wanted you to know we delivered the load in San Marcos."

"Thanks, Jojo. No problems at Pharmco?"

"Nope. They sure are busy, though."

"You're telling me. I got a truck out there every other day it seems."

"And who says the trucking business is dying?" I asked.

"Not me," she said. "Thank God."

I smiled, imagining Charlene in her little wood-paneled office, the fan blowing her permed hair while she crossed herself north and south, then making a wide left-to-right pass over her enormous breasts.

"Hey," she said like she'd just thought of it. "I've got a special load for you guys. Consider it a thank you for saving my ass. That is, if you want it? You'll have to move on it right away."

Boone shook his head, but when I heard what it was paying, I saw dollar signs that translated into chrome and chicken lights—or *maybe* a well-deserved vacation.

We agreed after some discussion to use The Baconator's trailer for the run. We'd pick up the load at a paper warehouse near Corsicana and drop in Dallas. Easy-peasy.

Boone stripped off his boots and jacket, tucking the shoes under the seat and the coat over the back of my chair. He yawned and stretched. "I need a nap. You got this, right?"

"Yeah," I said, driving away from the warehouse.

Boone pulled down the bed in the sleeper, clicked on his iPod, and inserted his headphones. I took a minute to admire the lump of man on my bed, hugging the pillow. Boone would hate that I thought he was cute. He preferred to be called hunk, stud, or beast.

True to form, the interior gate guard barely gave me the time of day, opening it before I even got close. The second one was better, doing a cursory look-see before letting us leave. Pulling away from the guard shack, I adjusted controls to send cool air into the sleeper, increase the volume for the radio, and dim the dash backlighting. My hand brushed the knob for the ashtray we used as a change collector. Something rattled. I slid the drawer open, reached in. If Boone hadn't been wearing his headphones, he might have woken when I squealed.

A diamond ring.

It looked like the one I'd admired in an antique shop in New Orleans.

Boone.

I quietly returned the ring to the ashtray and accelerated to the highway entrance, trying to keep my focus on the road, not the sudden appearance of jewelry in our ashtray. It wasn't easy.

The paper warehouse's loading docks were lit up and bustling as I drove in. No dogs or gate guards here.

Backing Old Blue into the bay, I might have been a bit distracted by all the activity. I had to be directed in twice before getting the green light. I hopped down and handled business with the receiver, exchanged some pleasantries, and was assured I'd quickly be on my way. Two forklifts waited to load the trailer with pallet upon pallet of paper, and an automated ramp stuck from the dock like a metal tongue. I headed back to the cab to wait for them to finish.

Inside, I glanced into the sleeper, resisting the urge to wake Boone and have a little chat. Instead, I clicked on the GPS and began searching the delivery route for road changes or construction. The chat could wait. After all, he wasn't going anywhere.

When the dockworker waved his arms, letting me know they were done loading, I slipped on Boone's jacket and hopped down to lock and seal the trailer. I thanked them before driving off.

It was a straight shot to the highway. Not even a stop sign. It was almost too easy. I merged onto smooth asphalt and settled back.

Heading north at this hour, traffic was mostly big trucks or happy-hour drunks. I preferred the company of trucks— like the long orange semi out of Arkansas two lanes over. We kept enough space between us to be safe, and to allow for passing, but the road cleared out after two exits, and it was just us. Until the Hummer.

I was used to seeing all sorts of overgrown vehicles in Texas—as if the residents felt obligated to personally uphold the state's claims regarding size. If everything was bigger in Texas then that included this guy's attitude. I didn't care for the way he jockeyed with my rig, nosing the big Hummer forward, falling back. I couldn't see into his windows, but I didn't try too hard, thinking giving him attention would be tantamount to giving him power.

Guys who drove big cars could be dicks. As could guys who drove fast little cars. But that was a whole different kind of dick.

I hit the gas, checking out the vehicle as I passed: chrome wraparound grill, shiny roof rack and spotlights, big-ass wheels with big-ass tires. The driver was either a serious off-roader or a failed rapper.

The Hummer hung back, running even with the end of the trailer. There were three open lanes and plenty of room for him to pass, but he seemed content to inhale my exhaust. I mumbled the little forgive-the-driver-for-he's-an-idiot prayer known to all truckers, then reached into the ashtray, pulled out the ring and slipped it on my finger. Cool metal, glittery stones. I tapped the steering wheel, quietly singing along with the radio.

A vehicle came up on the passenger side, pulling out of my blind spot. No telling how long he'd been drafting on my tail. It looked like an ambulance at first—white van with red markings—but there was no light bar, no wailing siren as he passed, just the throaty roar of a souped-up engine.

A clanking sound coming from the trailer caught my attention. Damn. I hadn't noticed anything in the road. I leaned forward and squinted into the side mirror. The

Hummer was still on the driver's side, closer than before—and gaining.

The van and the orange semi I'd been paralleling had shifted into the exit lane.

The Hummer took off like a cop on a call. His headlamps lit the empty road ahead, bouncing off the huge curving cement wall on my side of the highway. I had never understood the reason for a three-story wall on this section of road. Boone said it was designed to hold back the earth and preserve natural surroundings. I thought that was a load of shit. Developers were probably too cheap to level the land.

It took me a second to register that the red lights that appeared suddenly in front of me were the brake lights of the Hummer. His big tires squealed and smoked as he skidded across two lanes and pulled a one-eighty—something I would have thought impossible. He flipped on his high beams, then the spotlights on top of his truck.

"Fuck!" I yelled, blinded. I pulled hard to the right and felt the trailer fight back. I stood on the brakes and felt a tug, then a snap as the trailer rotated ninety degrees. Then it broke in half. Forty thousand pounds of steel and paper headed right for me, while the weight and momentum of the rest of the trailer pulled in the opposite direction. The more I tried to downshift and brake, the closer the Hummer and the cement wall seemed. *How could that be?*

It only took a few seconds, but in the slow-motion way that bad shit tries to rationalize with your brain, I saw it all too clearly.

The breaking back end of the trailer, taillights of the exiting orange semi, fire leaping from my brakes igniting the paper, the tipping of the sleeper, the wrenching and popping of riveted steel. Then Boone was there, one hand on the steering wheel with mine, right before we flipped, as if we could control the laws of physics if we just tried hard enough. When Boone flew through the air I thought about gravity. Then I thought, *Where's all that red paint coming from?*

The cement wall acted as a guardrail as Old Blue dragged her load. The screech and scrape of metal against asphalt, metal against concrete, was deafening. Sparks flew, glass imploded.

I never felt the final impact.

Everything was sideways. Pinned to my chair by the seatbelt, I hung a foot above the ground, smelling fire and gasoline. The radio might have still been playing, but the crackling, miniature explosions and whine in my ears were too loud to let me hear anything else. Every bone in my body ached. I shook my head to clear it.

Boone.

Through the broken windshield, I saw him on the highway. He looked like an acrobat in the Chinese circus, the ones who bend themselves into small, clear boxes. I wanted to curl up just like him and take a long nap.

Someone approached. They stood over Boone, a shadow man caught in the lights of the Hummer. He looked in my direction, at Old Blue tipped and broken, at the burning load of paper, at a river of flammable fluids, then turned away. Sirens wailed in the distance.

I clawed at the seatbelt digging into my chest and neck. It took two tries to get it to release. I didn't figure on the fall. Broken glass, twisted metal. My head pounded a thudding, nauseating rhythm. I squeezed my eyes shut, willing it away as I dragged myself out of the cab. Shards of glass ground into my palms and elbows as I pulled my legs clear of the steering wheel, then the dash and the hot metal hood. Every movement sent a sharp stab of pain. Every stab of pain cleared my vision a bit more so that I could see Shadowman bent over Boone, touching him. I tried to yell. Nothing but a low moan. The sound of a wounded animal. Not me. Blood ran into my eyes. Sirens grew louder. Shadowman dropped Boone, ran to the Hummer, killed the lights, and drove off.

I tried to stand. My leg gave out beneath me. I screamed. Double Boones wavered in my vision as I rose to one knee and made my way to him, part limp, part drag, part scoot-and-crawl, like a zombie marathon.

I collapsed beside him. "Boone?"

My hands searched his face. "Baby?"

I put my ear to his mouth then his nose, seeking his breath. "Don't you die on me, you hear me, Tyler Boone? Listen, they're coming. Help is coming. I need you to hold on."

He moved his lips. A hissing sound came from somewhere. He was leaking.

He whispered, "Love you always," and then what sounded like "highwayman."

I kissed his face again and again. "I love you, Boone. It's going to be okay. You'll see. It's all going to be fine."

I patted his chest, abdomen, his hips where his pockets were inside out. His body seemed smaller, weaker—none of his limbs were in the right places.

He smelled wrong too, not like my man, not like pine and sweat, but like piss and copper.

He smelled like shattered dreams.

Chapter 2

When I woke five days later, a large man was sitting beside my bed hunched over a glowing tablet. I ran my eye over him long enough to note the chiseled jaw, tan, muscular arms, dark, tight, denim, top and bottom, and a reminder that I was still in Texas, a pair of well-worn alligator boots.

"Stop fucking tapping," I whispered, my throat raw, mouth parched.

The man kept typing as I closed my eyes against the brightness of the room.

He said, "Well, good morning to you too." More tapping, then a sigh, the sound of a magnetic cover being slapped shut.

I woke the second time to the tightening of a blood pressure cuff around my bicep.

A deep-voiced woman said, "Hello there, sugar. You ready to greet the world?"

I managed one word. "Uhhh." *Why did nurses have to be so perky?* I don't like perky. I opened my eyes and scoped the room, targeting my gaze on the pink plastic water pitcher. The cowboy was quick on the pick-up.

I sipped from the straw he held to my lips. I felt like we were playing a game, one in which the person who spoke about the accident first loses. I like to win.

Besides, there were things I already knew. Things someone had told me while I was in and out of consciousness, things my mind had already come to terms with: My leg was jacked

21

up. Old Blue was wrecked beyond repair. Boone was dead and buried. I had failed, in so many ways.

"How's the pain?" the nurse asked.

I attempted to shrug, but my eyes must have told the truth. She fiddled with the IV near my bed, and in a few seconds sweet, cool pressure filled my veins. Morphine.

"I'm Caryn," the nurse said, stroking my arm. "Your father's on his way. He wanted me to tell you. Now, if you need anything, just press that button on the bed, okay?"

I nodded. She turned to the man, told him he had ten minutes, no more, then closed the door behind her.

"Spill," I said, reaching for the bed controls, maneuvering myself somewhat upright. I'd already figured the guy was here on some sort of information hunt, why make him wait?

He ran a hand through his hair, then dragged the bedside chair closer and sat, pulling aside his blazer revealing the bulge of the weapon in his shoulder holster.

"Shit."

I have this thing about authority. I don't like it. And generally speaking, it doesn't like me.

He pulled a stack of business cards out of his pocket, shuffled through them, then handed me one, a slick blue and white number with his name, Al "Gator" Natoli, PI, in the middle followed by the abbreviation, T.A.L.I. and the credit, *Distinguished Member*.

Distinguished? I looked at the guy with his long hair and namesake boots, in his blazer, white shirt, pressed jeans, then back at the small print on the card: Texas Association of Licensed Investigators.

"Gator?" I said. "Really?"

He shrugged, then ran his hand through his hair again. Not like he was fixing it, or even that he cared, more like it was habit. I liked that. Even if I hated what the guy stood for.

He said, "Ms. Boudreaux, I should start by saying, I'm sorry for your loss."

I half raised my hand, shook my head.

Gator cleared his throat. "Right. Thing is, I was on the scene of your accident. Well, kind of. I was following this loser and finally found his car pulled over on the bridge above I-45. Guy had passed out at the wheel, radio blaring, puke all over him—"

"Ew. You can spare the details."

"Yeah, well, the job isn't always so glamorous."

"I know what you mean," I said, thinking of all the non-glamorous parts of trucking: waiting, traffic jams, fast food, dirty hands, disrespectful people, and more waiting.

I concentrated on staying awake. The morphine was making me loopy.

Gator smiled. It was a nice smile. One that could make you do foolish things. I thought about girls swarming tattoo parlors, swearing they weren't Florida fans, of women wearing jewelry made from alligator teeth, of the TV shows filmed in my home state of Louisiana, glorifying that same prehistoric looking reptile.

"So, anyway," he said, "I heard your truck approaching, saw the other semi take the exit. I don't know what caught my attention, must be the Trooper in me—ex-Trooper—but when I saw that Hummer on your tail—"

"I know. What the fuck, right? So, wait," I said. "You saw everything? That weird white van? And you told the cops—"

"No, sorry. I did call it in, but the guy in the car woke up and tried to run me over."

"No shit?"

"No shit. By the time I was able to climb down to the highway, you were in the road, the rig was on fire and Troopers were on their way."

I turned my head to the wall, hoping it would swallow me up as vivid memories came rushing back. I tried to curl myself into a ball, forgetting about the cast on my leg. "Ah!" the lovely morphine haze dissipated.

"Hey, Ms. Boudreaux, are you okay?" Gator asked, rising from his chair. "Do you want me to get someone?"

"No."

"You sure?"

I nodded. "Just keep talking. Distraction's good and call me Jojo."

Gator sat, man-style, cowboy boot across his knee.

"So, Jojo, how much do you remember?"

"Of the accident?"

"That, and the whole day, things leading up to it."

"Most of it I remember," I said. "With a few blank spots."

"Yeah. It can be like that for a while."

It can be like that forever, fine by me, I thought.

He tapped his fingers on his leg. "Thing is, I'm not so sure it was *an accident.*"

He looked at me long and hard. I blinked first.

I got that prickly neck feeling that usually happens right before a fish tugs my line, or a fat flock of doves rise from a cornfield. The image of the man bent over Boone on the highway flickered behind my eyes.

"What are you saying, Mr. Gator?"

"It's just Gator."

"Okay. Just Gator."

He braced himself on the arms of the chair and leaned back. I couldn't help but notice the width of his chest, how the white shirt stretched almost uncomfortably across it. A hint of metal shone at his throat. I wondered if a medallion would be at the end of it. St. Christopher, maybe?

He said, "After I gave my report to the cops, I was asked

some routine questions by your insurance provider."

I opened my mouth, but he raised a hand shushing me.

"They'll pay your claim, and settle with your leasing agent, the shipper and receiver. This isn't about that." He paused, then lowered his voice. "What do you know about the recent cargo thefts on your route?"

I shrugged. "I only know what Charlene told me. She said that in the last six months, she started having problems with loads coming out of Pharmco, either the driver went missing or the load did, all or some of it anyway."

"Is that right?"

"It's nothing new to trucking. Loads get stolen, trucks get hijacked, sometimes, even drivers disappear. It's part of the job. And when you're carrying pharmaceutical cargo there's probably even more of risk. Last I heard, the reported financial loss to cargo theft in the U.S. is over ten billion dollars a year, and that figure is probably fifty percent lower than the real deal."

"More like sixty percent," Gator said, nodding.

"And you know that how?"

He shrugged. "Did my research."

"Is that right?"

"Yeah. And I've also worked with one of the top logistics security services companies analyzing cargo theft trends. You're preaching to the choir."

He went on a bit about global and regional trends, the new technology in place to help mitigate risk, and something something something. I tuned out after the second batch of numbers and concentrated on the insides of my eyelids.

When Gator finally cued in to the inattentiveness of his audience he stopped talking. I opened my eyes. "As I said, shit happens."

"Yes. Well, in this case, the shit happening on your route is this: Pharmco isn't reporting the thefts because they're afraid of the press. They said the thieves have stolen nothing more than harmless saline, some empty vials and storage racks, but if word got out, competitors would be all over it and they can't afford to lose face."

"Or money, when the stock drops," I said. "What about the drivers?"

"One's still missing, two others have been found, none the worse for wear. One admitted he'd accepted a bribe to walk away from his idling truck for ten minutes and the other claims he was brainwashed by a beautiful woman."

I smiled. The power of a beautiful woman, the gullibility of a mortal man.

"So, he'll be explaining that to the judge next week," Gator said. "The trucks and trailers were recouped. Of course they were empty and authorities weren't able to get any leads. These are professionals. The one driver still missing is leased to DST. He goes by the handle 'The Baconator.'"

"Shit."

"What?"

"That's the driver we were brought in to help. We took his load to San Marcos, picked it up at a truck stop. It was *his* trailer that broke and caused my crash."

There was something else, something nibbling at my brain. Before I could nail it down, Gator said, "You're sure it was the trailer, not something—?"

"What are you saying?" I asked.

He shrugged.

"Nice. Blame the driver. Listen," I said, heating up. "It's people like you who give trucking a bad name. People like you who make assumptions and form opinions based on— oh, never mind."

I tried to collect myself, doing the count-to-five breathing thing I'd learned from Boone.

Gator touched my arm when I exhaled my third deep breath. I held up a finger and he leaned back. Two more breaths before I looked at him.

"I'm sorry," he said. "I didn't mean to insinuate that all drivers are criminals."

"Just some of us, right?"

"Come on, you know the facts. Most of the time the driver's culpable in a cargo theft, whether he or she actually profits or not."

"We're trying to change that," I said.

"I know," he said. "We've worked with the people at CTIP, the Cargo Theft Interdiction Program. They'll continue to encourage installing GPS systems on trucks and trailers, even in the load itself. You must have seen the new warnings about high crime truck stops. Even routing drivers away from them, forbidding them to park or gas up there."

"Sure. I know about that. Shit like that makes it harder for drivers. We can't stop for the first two hundred miles after pick up on some of these loads, and now we're being told *where* we can stop. It's something the old timers are rebelling against, and another regulation the newbies have to get used to. I know that stolen cargo costs everyone in the end—but I'm not so sure I'd risk my life to stop a thief."

"You're saying you wouldn't fight back?" he asked.

I shrugged and stared at the bridge of his nose, unable to meet his eyes.

A minute later I said, "You know what they say? With a padlock key and a decent pair of pliers anyone could steal an idling eighteen-wheeler from a truck stop in thirty seconds or less."

"You could do that?" Gator asked.

"I can do anything."

"You're pretty sure of yourself, aren't you?"

"If not me, then who?"

Gator pushed himself out of the chair, slowly stretched, then leaned in, bracing himself on the rails of my bed. "I have a confession," he said, lowering his voice. "I was like you once."

"What?" I said, grinning. "Female?"

"No. I used to drive."

"You?"

He nodded. "Yeah. Still got my license, kept up all most of my clearances."

I waited for him to shuffle his stack of business cards again and produce one with a CB handle and photo of a big rig. He didn't.

Instead he said, "Maybe that's why this situation bothers me so much. I know it can be a closed community. There are places a leased driver can get into that I can't—right now." He shrugged and sunk back into the chair.

We looked at each other until he broke the silence answering my unasked question. "I gave up the road—for personal reasons, decided to choose a different life."

"Just like that," I said.

"Just like that." Gator rolled his head on his shoulders. "Don't take this the wrong way, but you appear to be a beautiful, intelligent woman who says she can do anything she wants. So, why drive a truck?"

Why. It was a familiar question. My father, Manny Boudreaux, asked me the same thing when I got my CDL. I tried to explain it wasn't my love for Boone that turned me onto trucking or the idea of being with my man twenty-four-seven. It was another way of proving myself to the world. Josephine Boudreaux never took the easy path anywhere.

"Imagine this, Père," I'd told him. "You have a chance to travel the country and see things no one else has ever seen. You work for yourself and while there are still rules to follow and sometimes a particular job might suck, ultimately, it's you in the driver's seat."

"Literally," he said, smirking. "And don't say suck, Shâ. It's not ladylike."

I wasn't sure if he meant the word or the job.

"Just because women truckers don't show up for work every morning wearing a suit and heels doesn't mean we make any less of a salary or have any less power than those who do," I said. "You shouldn't judge, Père. You know what they say about walking in someone else's shoes."

Manny Boudreaux grinned. "That it'll give you athlete's foot?"

"Funny. Real funny."

I hated to admit it, it kind of was. I shared the joke with Gator, willing to forget for the moment about all the not so funny shit that was happening—cargo thefts, missing drivers, dead fiancés, wrecked trucks, dangerous jobs, jacked-up legs and cramped hospital beds.

When the nurse came in with a tray of meds Gator stood to leave, said he'd call me if he had any more questions. He paused in the doorway. "Hey, don't worry about anything, okay?"

I nodded, pretending it was that simple and then I took the pills, drank the water and succumbed to the poking and prodding of Nurse Caryn, the whole time thinking about what Gator had said, how he needed information, but there were some places only a driver could go.

"Where are my things?" I asked Caryn, as the blood pressure cuff squeezed my arm.

"In the closet over there. What's left, anyway." She glanced at me as she removed the cuff and hung the stethoscope around her neck. "Do you want—"

"Yes."

Nurse Caryn brought me a clear bag tied shut. Inside was

my torn shirt, ripped, bloody jeans, Boone's jean jacket, none the worse for wear, one scratched, dead phone and in a small baggie, the diamond ring—band sawed in half.

"They had to cut it off before surgery," she explained.

I squeezed the pieces together, held the diamond up to the light. I'd almost forgotten the ring. Fucking Boone. How could he do that to me? Leave me with forever unanswered questions.

"It's beautiful," Caryn said. "So, were you…"

"I don't know," I said, dropping the ring parts in the baggie. "He never got a chance to ask."

Caryn turned away but not before I saw the look on her face, the look that said she was young enough, naive enough, to believe in the possibility of happy endings.

"You know what Boone would have wanted me to do?" I asked, watching Caryn at the computer, entering details, clicking boxes.

"What's that?" she asked without turning around.

"Get the hell out of here. Can you call my doctor again, see if I can get released?"

She typed something else, then logged off and dimmed the monitor. "I'll see what I can do. But you'll have to impress them at PT today."

PT. Physical therapy. Also known as personal torture.

Five hours later, I figured I must have impressed them. Either that or my insurance had run out. They were releasing me. Freshly showered and wearing real clothes—if an over-sized T-shirt and gym shorts from the gift shop counted as clothes—I waited with my folder of appointments, therapy exercises and prescriptions for antibiotics and painkillers while Père and his girlfriend Pilar rounded up crutches and a wheelchair.

I slept the whole ride home, waking as the car door opened, letting in a slap of warm Louisiana air and the sound of a baying coonhound.

Before Boone, I would have said that I got my life experiences by dating a variety of men. It was a give and take thing. I gave them sex, and I took their experiences, learning something new from each one, sort of like building up a life résumé. As a result, I knew certain things, like the moves of the Krav Maga knife defense and how to clip the wings of a Scarlet Macaw. What I didn't know was how to be this new Jojo, this broken girl stumbling around Bunkie. Who was I supposed to learn from now?

Gator called me every day, kept me posted on the search for the Hummer, the anonymous white van and the missing trucker. They were short phone calls.

I still got headaches, but the itching in my new skin had stopped and I had bigger arm muscles than ever, or maybe they were just more defined. My clothes hung from me, though I rarely wanted to dress in more than sweats and T-shirts. It was perfect for my busy social calendar.

When Père came into my room, I was counting down the last of two hundred sit-ups. I'd already pounded through a cruel series of pushups, dips and squats.

"We have to talk," he said. "There are certain decisions–"

"No."

"What do you mean, no? Jojo, stop that nonsense and look at me."

I rolled out of the sit-up and propped myself on my elbows. "That's my decision. No."

"About what?" he asked.

"About everything. No, I don't want the fucking truck anymore. No, I don't care that people want to see me. No, I don't want to go out. No, I'm not ready to move on. No, I don't see the higher purpose in Boone's death. And no. *Hell* to the No, do I need to talk to some fucking shrink! Okay?"

My father's fists curled and uncurled at his sides. Had I been a son he might have popped me. He made a move in my direction, but I waved him off and went back to doing crunches, hands over my ears, closing out the memories. No truck. No fire. No broken glass. No twisted metal. No shadow man. No mystery vehicles. No dead boyfriend. No broken ring. No weak Jojo. No sad story. No. No. No. I squeezed myself again and again into a fetal position, relishing the pain.

The door shut a minute later, the gentle click more hurtful than a slam.

They left less than a week later. Pilar explained how the Brazil trip had been planned for ages, but of course they could cancel it.

"No," I told her. "You go. Both of you. I'll be fine."

Père put up a bit more of a fight, but in the end, he was the first one out the door. I have this amazing talent for alienation.

I waved from the porch as they pulled away. Elvis, Père's coonhound woke up, stretched and yawned then padded his way to me, rubbing his muzzle on my thigh.

"Sorry, pal, guess you're stuck with me." *There could be worse things. Right?*

If Elvis could talk, he might have agreed. Especially when he followed me to the barn where I used an electric Dremel and a hand saw to cut off my leg cast. Something about the combination of boredom, stubbornness and Jim Beam.

I was sitting on the porch at dinnertime, ignoring my ringing phone, sipping a beer, scraped up leg braced on a cooler when the truck came down our dirt road.

Elvis rolled over and opened one eye. He wasn't much of a guard dog.

"What do you think, boy? Is it another lady from the church or more feel-better food?"

He thumped his tail at the word *food,* then farted. I shaded my eyes with one hand and waved the air with the other, partly from Elvis and partly from the dust the truck stirred up on its approach.

The man who stepped out of the truck wasn't carrying a pie plate or fruit basket. He raised a hand and called, "Hey."

"Hey," I answered, being civil and everything. I didn't see a weapon or a Bible, so for the moment he was welcome.

"I heard Manny was away," he said. "Wanted to stop in and see if you needed anything."

"Well, if it isn't Ivory Joe Wayne," I said, recognizing my old neighbor. "Haven't seen you since what, high school?"

He stepped closer, and I saw for the most part the years had been kind to him. He shifted his weight, favoring one side like you do with a bad knee or painful back. I ran a hand through my hair, wishing I'd combed it.

"You said you'd stay in touch," he said. "But I guess you had better things to do. Least from what Manny tells me."

He came even closer and hit me with his smile. Now I wished I'd also taken the time to brush my teeth or put on a bra.

"No. No it wasn't like that," I said, not knowing what it was like and wondering if I'd always been an asshole. I crossed my arms over my chest and reached for the ball cap on the table beside my beer.

"You want one?" I said, raising the blue can as I tugged on the hat.

"Sure, thanks."

I pulled a beer out of the cooler, popped the tab and handed it to him.

"May I?" he asked, tipping his head toward the empty rocker.

He had always been a boy with good manners. My mother liked that in him, and I suppose I should have, but with fifteen-year-old girls, manners weren't as important as whether the guy had his own car or was a starter on the football team.

Ivory Joe sank into the chair favoring his right leg, trying to hide a grimace as he stretched it. He drank his beer in peace, scratched Elvis behind the ears and generally made good company, until he started talking. Why the hell do people have to go and ruin a nice day with words?

Sure he tried to dance around the accident, around Boone and me, what we'd been, around anything that had to do with God. But he was a good man and his heart wasn't far from the surface. I could see right through his big brown eyes.

"Could we not have this conversation right now, Ivory Joe?" I asked.

He smiled. "No problem. Be happy to just sit here and drink your beer, Jojo."

A second later he said, "One last thing?"

I raised my brow.

"Can we at least have some music?"

I nodded. "Sure. Stereo's in the front room." I hooked my thumb in that direction, over my shoulder. "You need help?"

"Nope."

He was slow rising, little hitch in his step as he went into the house, but a few minutes later the happy sounds of Buckwheat Zydeco streamed from the front windows.

Ivory Joe returned, handing me a glass of clear liquid, then scooting his rocker closer to my chair. "Found Manny's stash," he said. "Didn't think he'd mind."

We clinked glasses, then downed the liquor, wincing at the potency of the locally distilled rum.

"Ah, that's good," he said with a sigh. "Haven't tasted that since, well, it's been a while."

"Why's that?"

He glanced at me, then looked away, not fast enough for me to miss the flicker of fear in his eyes. His hand went to his leg, massaging a phantom ache.

"What happened, Ivory Joe?"

"Manny never told you?"

I shook my head.

He chuckled, drained the last drop from his glass and reached for a refill. "Yeah, why would he?"

I waited him out.

"I had cancer," he said.

"Wait. What? You can't just say it like that. 'I had cancer.' What does fuck does that mean?"

He told me about the cancer. Like the way people tell you about a bad clutch in an old Chevy, how you got to fix it and that's all are there is to it and sometimes the first mechanic misses something and at least once you'll end up back in the shop with unexpected complications. That's how he put it. Complications. But he was better now. Cancer free. Out of the zone. Stronger than ever. All due to some magic drugs, stuff he didn't want to think about, how one set of drugs went inside him killing everything, followed by another batch that build up the good stuff, warded off the bad shit. It all sounded like something from a science fiction movie, something far from my real life.

I looked at him closer, saw the lines on his face, the stubble on his chin, the gray temples. He was still Ivory Joe, maybe even a better version of my friend.

He raised his glass, clinked mine. "To remission."

"To remission," I said.

At some point, the sun went down and Elvis wandered off. The rum had opened my mouth. I couldn't seem to stop talking. It was as if I was trying to fill a ten-year gap in a single sitting. Ivory Joe had taken off his long-sleeved shirt and sunglasses, and I'd be a liar if I said that I didn't find him attractive in his T-shirt and faded jeans. Not only was I talking nonstop with the help of the liquor, but I'd resorted to my roots, reverting back to the Cajun and Creole slang that I'd tried so hard to leave behind.

I reached for the last beer in the cooler and said, "What time it is? I got *an ahnvee* for some boudin."

Ivory Joe laughed. "Haven't heard you talk like that since you was a *peeshwank.*"

He went off on some long Cajun-infused tirade that I could only follow a bit of. Living with a Texan had taken most of the Louisiana out of me. I tried to hold Ivory Joe in my sights, but my head kept falling back and he seemed just out of reach when I tried to touch his chest. He caught my hand in his and I leaned in, thinking we were on the same page, thinking maybe I was looking as good to him as he was to me, thinking it would be nice, real nice to have someone hold me tonight, keep away the ghost of Boone.

But he pulled back and shook his head, said he was sorry, something about having to go. When he got up and put his shirt back on the porch started to spin and I had that too late feeling: *I should have known better.*

Ivory Joe started toward his truck, then turned back, asking, "You going to be okay, Jojo?"

"Yeah, sure," I mumbled. "It don't matter."

I waited until he drove off, then I wiped my eyes and made my way into the house, making it as far as the couch before I passed out.

Chapter 3

My phone must have died sometime during Ivory Joe's visit and by the time I found my charger and drank my morning coffee, I'd logged in eight missed calls from Gator. Guy was almost as persistent as me. That was worth something. I rang him back, hit speaker and leaned over the phone on the kitchen counter.

Gator sounded much less hung over than me when he picked up on the first ring. "Why the fuck aren't you answering my calls?"

Less hungover maybe, but way more rude. "Hey," I said. "I am. And stop yelling. Please." I steepled my head between my hands and massaged my temples. "What do you want?"

He exhaled loudly, like an exasperated parent. "I got nothing on the Hummer. Thought I'd take a look at the white van angle, maybe get lucky."

"I don't know," I said. "There's got to be more fucking anonymous white vans in Texas than soccer mom mini-vans—all those plumbers, painters, carpool riders. You heard that joke, right? What kind of shoe does a pedophile wear? White vans."

I couldn't tell if it was an amused or derisive snort on the other end of the line. I said, "Just let it go. Take your client's money and close the case. Walk away."

His voice was low enough that I had to ask him to repeat himself. "There is no money."

"What? I thought you were working for Pharmco."

"Was. Not anymore. And I don't need the money."

"Really? Must be nice," I said, thinking of rich assholes in private jets lounging poolside in Dubai. "Listen. This whole thing—I mean, what the fuck's the point?"

"The point?" Gator said. "Jesus. What's wrong with you? The point is—need I remind you—people's lives may be at stake, cargo and trucks are being stolen and you—just you, Jojo—you could have information or access to information that could be very helpful."

I could almost see him pressing his mouth against the phone when he yelled, "Is that good enough to bother you?" before he hung up.

"Shit." I clicked off on my end and sunk to the floor, my bad leg throbbing in tune to my booze-addled brain.

A few days later when the first hunters of the season drove down the private road to the plantation and parked on the front lawn as if they owned it, I had half a mind to come out shotgun barrel first.

Instead, I figured I'd try to be a bit more civil. After all, it was two of them and just one of me. Though I did have Elvis. I stepped over his sleeping body and opened the screen door.

They heard it slam and looked my way. One had the good manners to take off his hunting cap. The other spit in the dirt.

"Morning, ma'am."

"Morning."

They sounded like they were from Alabama or worse, Kentucky.

"Can I help you, fellas?"

"This ain't marked land," the bright one said.

I said. "I'll have to get on that, now, won't I?"

"You saying this is private property?"

"Thought you would have figured that out when you turned off the main road and followed the Historical Landmark sign. If you missed that, the chain across the road might have been a good clue. Or maybe not."

"Didn't see no chain," the spitter said.

The polite one tapped the idiot's shoulder. "All right, now. Leave it be." He opened his truck door, said, "We'll be going now."

The guy looked so disappointed, I said, "You looking for dove?"

"Yes, ma'am."

"Try the Hadden's field. You can pay him twenty bucks for the whole day. Guaranteed to fill your bag."

"That right?"

"Yep. Take a left out of here and go about five miles until you see a white cross. Turn right after that and follow the road. Honk your horn twice. Somebody will hear you."

"Thank you, kindly," he said as he put on his hat. "And we're sorry for the intrusion."

"No problem."

I raised a hand as they left and when I caught the spitter's cold eyes in the side view mirror, I shivered, though it was at least seventy degrees in the shade. Something about him was off. It reminded me of the whistling guy at the truck stop.

I limped inside, found my phone and called The Bunkie General Store.

"Do you have any 'No Trespassing' signs?" I asked.

"Sure," the girl said. "How many do you need?"

"A lot," I said, reaching for my cane and keys.

I knew posting "No Trespassing" signs wouldn't really help, just like the extra chain across the road, because when men wanted to kill there was little you could do to dissuade them. But it gave me something to do, and an excuse to go into town.

I was leaving the Piggly Wiggly, cane in one hand, bag of groceries in the other when I ran into Ivory Joe. Literally. The bag didn't survive. The girl he was with stopped my can of creamed corn from rolling into the street by pinning it under her high-heeled sandal.

"Sorry, Jojo," Ivory Joe said as he knelt down with some effort to help pick up the spilled groceries.

"I got this," I said, brushing Ivory Joe off, staring at his stiff leg, then glancing toward the girl. Ivory Joe's barely imperceptible headshake, and warning look said it all. He handed me the bag and stood.

"Should be using a canvas tote," the girl said, reversing her hold on the can and sending it spinning then rolling over to me. "Better for the environment."

"Yeah," I said catching the can. "Because no canvas trees were harmed in the making of those bags." I scooped up the rest of the groceries and adjusted the sheaf of signs from The General Store that I'd *tucked* in my armpit.

Ivory Joe started to laugh, stopping short when the girl smacked his shoulder.

She gave him one of those looks usually reserved for husbands who fall asleep in church and start to snore, which made me wonder how deep in the shit my friend had fallen with Missy White Sandals.

"Where are your manners, Joseph?" she said, flipping her processed hair. "Aren't you going to introduce me to your friend?"

Joseph? I was pretty sure I hated her.

"Why, yes," I said, using my honey-do voice. "Ivory Joe Wayne, please do. No, wait. Allow me."

Ivory Joe may have muttered a prayer to baby Jesus.

I extended one definitely dirty hand and said, "I'm Josephine Marie Boudreaux. My friends call me Jojo. You can call me Ms. Boudreaux."

This time Ivory Joe did laugh, a deep belly chortle.

I had a hard time keeping my bitch on.

"Well, I never," she said pulling her hand back and wiping it on her skirt like I had just told her I didn't believe in toilet paper.

"Maybe that's your problem," I muttered, as Ivory Joe handed me the grocery bag.

"Now, ladies," he said, regaining his composure. "Let's try this again. Jojo, this is Shannon. She's new to Bunkie. I've been showing her around. Shannon, this is Jojo. Her father owns the plantation on the Bayou Boeuf."

I could have sworn I heard hamsters on a wheel between her ears, her lips moving as she processed the information.

"Everything okay out there?" Ivory Joe asked, pointing to the "No Trespassing" signs.

"Nothing these won't fix," I said. "Can't blame them. We've got the best fields in two parishes. Wait until waterfowl season opens."

"Yeah, I remember the hunting out there. Had some good times, didn't we?"

"Yep, whenever we could sneak out on Père."

We laughed.

Shannon cleared her throat. I'd forgotten she was still there.

"Anyway," I said, "I sent some dove hunters to the Hadden's. You know they won't mind making a buck off some rednecks."

Shannon picked at her nails and sighed.

"Season for teal, rails and gallinules coming up, right?" Ivory Joe asked.

I nodded.

He said, "How do you think Manny would feel about us making some of that Hadden money?"

"What do you mean?"

"No one knows that area better than you, Jojo. We can do a guide service on Manny's land. I'll provide the dogs and give you a hand during the week. It'd be nice to—well, be nice, is all."

Shannon brightened. "Money would be nice," she said. "You sure aren't selling any houses."

Ivory Joe's cheeks flushed.

"Not sure I'd be the best person for the job," I said, unwilling to admit that I was enjoying my hermitage.

"Sure you are, sweetie," Shannon said. "Why, look at you."

"What does that mean?" I raised a brow.

"It means, look at *you* and look at *me*. Which one of us belongs in corn fields and mud bogs?"

"You know what, Ivory Joe?" I said, using my cane for emphasis. "I changed my mind. Why don't you come out to the plantation tomorrow and bring your dogs." I started to walk away, then turned back, "Oh and, Shannon, don't wait on him. We're going to be *real* busy." I flipped my hair and about wrenched my neck. I tried not to wince until I was out of their sight.

That night I slept better than I had since the accident. I didn't dream at all.

I was staple-gunning posted signs to trees when Gator called.

"You were right about the white van. Fucking needle in a haystack. Still running down the leads on the Bacon guy. Truck stop manager checks out, not sure what's going on with the cashier. She hasn't shown up for work in a few days."

He paused, like he was taking a sip of coffee, or a drag on a cigarette. More likely, he was taking a breather between pushups.

He said, "I even went by the salvage yard to go through your rig. See if anything—hell, I don't know." He sighed. "Damn, I'm usually pretty good at this."

"I'm sure you are," I said, slapping another sign up and jabbing at it with the stapler.

"Talked to Charlene at DeSalena Transport."

"Oh, yeah? How'd that go?"

"She's something, isn't she?"

"You could say that."

"She might be able to get me a meeting with the bigwigs at DST and Pharmco. Haven't been able to get past their gatekeepers."

"Is that right?" I said, holding back a yawn, wondering why the hell this guy wasn't cruising on his yacht or playing golf with politicians, surely he had a Super Republican card in that stack in his pocket.

"That's right," Gator said. "By the way, Charlene needs you to come in and sign some papers."

"Yeah, I'll put that on my To Do list," I said. I hobbled to another tree, ran my hand over my aching leg, adjusted the straps of the knee brace.

A few seconds later Gator said, "You still there?"

"Uh-huh."

"How's the leg?" he asked.

"Fantastic," I lied. "Getting stronger every day."

"Good to hear." He cleared his throat. I thought he was going to say goodbye, instead he asked me to tell him about the delivery to Pharmco.

I leaned against a tree and closed my eyes, running

through the day in my mind at triple speed. I'd had a lot of time to replay the days, break down the minutes. Too much time.

Gator was saying, "Maybe something will jog your memory. Right now, this is tough going—"

Tough. I didn't want to go there, instead, I decided to humor him.

"Gator, it's probably nothing, but that day, the girl at the truck stop register was worried about The Baconator being in trouble, seemed scared of his woman, maybe she knew him a little better than she was letting on. And there was a guy—a mean-looking dude hanging around the store when we picked up the trailer. He was whistling the song "Highwayman." Boone knew it, and later at Pharmco, Boone said a guy in the bathroom was whistling it, too."

"Huh," Gator said.

"That's not all." I sat on the quad runner and told Gator about the two security trucks racing past us at Pharmco the day Boone and I delivered The Baconator's sealed trailer. I ran down the set-up at the San Marcos warehouse, the security cameras, satellite dishes, unmarked black cars, the white-haired warehouse manager catching me with my phone camera, yelling at me.

"Damn," Gator said. "The place sounds more military operation than pharmaceutical warehouse. What the hell do they have in there anyway?"

"Good question. A better question is how is any of this connected to me or Boone?"

Gator exhaled loudly, then said, "I wasn't going to tell you this, but another trucker went missing yesterday. His last delivery was near San Marcos, close to the same route you ran."

"Pharmco?"

"No. But, he's been there before."

45

"You think it's related?"

"Yes." He paused, like he was deciding whether or not to say something. "There's something else. That thing with Boone, it's been bothering me."

"What thing?"

"His pockets," Gator said.

"Pockets?"

"Yeah," Gator said. "The night of the accident—if it was an accident—the front pockets of his jeans were pulled inside out, like someone was looking for something specific. So, I keep asking myself, what do guys have in their front pockets, what might Boone have been carrying?"

Stuck on his words *If it was an accident,* I was slow in answering. "Gum, I guess, maybe the extra key to the cab. Sometimes, he'd have mints." *Who'd want to steal mints? And what did Boone's pockets have to do with stolen goods and missing drivers?*

"A cell phone, maybe?" Gator asked.

I shook my head. "Not in his front pocket and definitely not that night. He'd been sleeping on the bunk. His phone was probably destroyed in the truck with everything else."

I squeezed my eyes shut against the scene in my head: sound of breaking glass, snapping metal, acrid scent of burning fluids and fuel, fiery flakes of paper floating into the sky as I leaned over Boone, my ear to his lips as he whispered, "Highwayman."

"What if it was the same guy," I said, snapping my eyes open. "In the Hummer—the guy who was standing over Boone that night. What if he was the creepy whistler at the truck stop, *and* the guy Boone heard whistling in the Pharmco restroom?"

"I'll admit, the whistling is weird. Do you think you could ID him?"

"Maybe. There must be some security footage from cameras at the warehouse or in the lot, right?"

"I've got some contacts at the area monitoring stations," Gator said. "Let me see what I can do. In the meantime—"

"I'm coming to Houston."

Chapter 4

I called Ivory Joe, told him I needed a rain check on our hunting guide meeting, then asked him to watch Elvis for a few days. I fielded his questions like a dirty politician, left him with a vague promise to be in touch, then shot off an email to my father and Pilar in Brazil, assuring them everything was fine and dandy. I left off the part about possibly turning the plantation into a hunting resort, and how my leg felt like a pounded slab of beef. I definitely omitted the fact that I was borrowing Manny's 1967 Fastback Mustang to go chasing bad guys in Texas with a guy named Gator.

Sometimes, it's the little lies in life that keep us going.

Mothers in minivans quickly rolled their windows against the loud rumble of the Mustang's 390 cast-iron big block as I made my way into Eunice, then down to Crowley. *Mercy* had a mind of her own. (The beastly Mustang had earned her name each time Père fired up the engine, and my mother covered her ears yelling, "Mercy!")

I had to hold back three hundred and twenty of those horses, using just my toes on the accelerator. I could feel what Mercy held beneath the surface, what was dying to get out—she was like a hungry man anticipating a platter of fried chicken, a drunk waiting for five o'clock. I connected with that. Power and control. It was a fine line.

At the sign for I-10, I took the ramp going west, then reached for the radio knob and turned it down, preferring the sounds from the engine compartment. Mercy purred like a cat who knew a bowl of milk was in her future.

I downshifted and entered the highway without touching the brakes, rolled down the windows, let my hair fly. Since the accident, I'd only been driving an old pickup truck down slow winding back roads or the quad runner in the fields. It felt strange and oddly absolutely right to be on a smoothly paved multi-lane road with no one in front of me for miles. I hesitated for a second, checked my mirrors, then gunned it. Mercy responded as I knew she would, willingly, like a bitch in heat.

I howled and stomped on the gas, watching the needle rise. My heart pounded in my chest, palms grew sweaty. Just before I could bury the accelerator, I remembered this particular stretch of highway—the stand of trees, the slight dip in the road beyond—the shady spot where asshole cops liked to indulge in coffee, donuts and naps.

Shit.

Easing off the gas, I tapped the brakes and came back to earth, then turned up the radio and drove within ten miles of the speed limit for the rest of the trip. I hadn't lost my nerve, I told myself, I just couldn't afford to be stopped right now.

My cell phone rang as I dropped my bag on the hotel bed, door clicked shut behind me.

It was Gator. "Good timing," I said. "I just got in. What's up?"

Music filtered through the handset, a woman laughed, glass clinked. Bar sounds.

Gator said, "Got somebody I'd like you to meet. My new friend told me some very interesting information about a men's room camera."

"Is that right?"

"Oh yeah. Better yet, she's got video." Gator said.

"Where are you?"

* * *

I arrived at Dan's Place in fifteen minutes, thanks to a cabbie who apparently didn't know the difference between red and green lights. He did however, notice the difference between a ten and five dollar tip.

Gator was sitting at the end of the bar with a busty blonde. He tipped his cowboy hat in my direction. We were in Texas after all. The girl followed his gaze, calculating, as girls do, whether I was threat or potential salvation—the difference between getting your man stolen, and pawning a creep off on someone else.

I slid onto the stool beside Gator, counted the empty shot glasses in front of the girl, then motioned to the bartender to bring us tequila and a round of beers.

Gator introduced me to Taffy or Tammy—one of those interchangeable chick names.

She half-smiled and held out a limp hand. If I was a bitch, I would have pointed out that her money might have been better spent on dental work and mole removal, than bleach jobs and acrylic nails. But I wasn't that kind of girl.

I did have a tendency to lie though. It was the one thing that kept me from being perfect. "Nice to meet you," I said, followed by, "I like your shirt."

She giggled, adjusting the floral, flouncy, low cut number. "Thanks," she said, slurring. "I like yours, too."

I downed the tequila, leaned back and propped my sore, bandaged leg up on the brass rail, trying to ignore Gator staring at my ragged Blondie T-shirt, or the way he continued his gaze, taking in my thigh hugging jeans and floppy combat boots.

Tammy or Taffy also noticed. She leaned in, pressing her breasts against his arm as she stole a cherry from the bartender's stash. There was more giggling and an erotic display with the cherry that Gator seemed to appreciate. There was only one thing to do. I ordered us two shots, each, then excused myself to the bathroom. When I got back, Miss Flouncy Top was whispering in Gator's ear, clinging to him like a life raft.

A cab pulled up out front and honked.

"There's my ride. Oh, here." She pulled a DVD out of her tote bag and handed it to me. "I'm sorry for your loss," she said, as if my cat had just died and she was the one assigned to toss him in the dumpster, then turned her attention and tits to Gator.

"Toodles," she said, slipping off the barstool and stumbling out the door, waggling her fingers and blowing kisses.

I shook my head and scoffed, "Texas Girls," as I watched her trip off the curb. "You know how a Louisiana girl holds her liquor?" I asked, raising my beer for a toast.

Gator clinked my glass. "How?"

"By the ears."

We laughed and signaled the bartender for another round.

Gator tapped the case of the DVD and leaned in, lowering his voice, "We watched it in her minivan. The footage is pretty bad, but you can see two men who seem pretty interested in Boone."

"Is that right?" I asked, trying to not think about Gator and Flouncy in the back seat of a minivan.

"It feels like they followed him in. I mean, how often do two guys go to the restroom at the same time, and it's obvious they're together.

"Do they...*do* something to him?" I ask, thinking all the worst things of strangers in restrooms.

"No, no, it's not like that. Don't worry. There is this weird thing at the end, though. When the bag falls off the counter."

"What bag?"

"A fast food bag. Boone sets it by the sink when he first comes in, and after he washes his hands, he knocks it onto the floor and when he goes to pick it up, something falls out."

I can see Boone, sun glinting off his sunglasses, him reaching for the crumpled bag, telling me how picked up the trash in Baconator's messy rig.

"What was it?" I asked.

"It looked like an SD card."

"Like you store pictures on?"

"Pictures, documents, music. Thing is, when it fell, these guys were suddenly very interested."

"Really? What did Boone do?"

"He picked up the rest of the trash, threw it out and left the room holding the SD card."

"Huh."

"Do you know what happened to it?"

"First I'm hearing of it."

I took a sip of beer wondering what Boone would have done with someone else's SD card, and why he never mentioned any of this to me.

"Who are these guys? Can you see their faces?"

"Not that well, they weren't exactly posing and the camera focus isn't great."

"What do you think's on that SD card, Gator?"

He sighed. "I won't know until I find it. But it's got to be the key."

Halfway through the next pint, Gator asked me to go over it again—where we went after the Pharmco drop, how we got the next assignment, who we spoke to or saw.

I told him how I'd handled the gig myself and about the pickup at the warehouse, how they'd been as busy as Pharmco, but not half as organized. No guards at the gate, no uniforms. Just shaggy, tattooed workers, blaring heavy metal music. It was like being in a rock concert mosh pit on Halloween, except with more forklifts.

Cardboard was heavier than I figured. When I read cardboard on the paperwork, I'd imagined colorful cereal and shoe boxes, perfectly stacked squares and rectangles waiting to be filled, not massive bound pallets of ugly shredded, compacted, recycled corrugated paper.

I made sure to stay out of the way of the forklifts, not wanting to become a fatality like the driver who was crushed between two pallets of lettuce, then loaded onto her truck and shipped—dead—all the way to California with her loser boyfriend at the wheel. The guy told the cops he'd looked for her, but thought she was pissed off at him again and finally kept her promise about leaving. He figured she'd caught a bus back to Orlando.

I told Gator about the road conditions, about Boone sacking out, about it being just another night on the road.

Gator spun his coaster, caught it and spun it again. "So, it was just you and the orange semi, until the Hummer came up?"

"And the white van. I thought it was an ambulance, way it was marked."

He nodded. "Anything else unusual?"

"No, I don't think so. I might have been a little off my game, after I found the ring."

"What ring?"

"A diamond ring, in the ashtray. Boone must have...I don't know. Listen, I gotta go," I said, tipping my glass and draining my beer.

I grabbed my bag and stepped outside before he could ask me anything else. I jogged to the corner and caught a cab, gave him the hotel address and tried to shut down my brain—tried to drown out the memory of the last conversation I had with Boone.

* * *

Unlike me, Boone preferred to sleep with the curtain open between the cab and the sleeper. He said the lights and sounds of the road lulled him to sleep. I told him that didn't make me feel so secure as his passenger.

He said, "No, not when I'm sitting up. I meant when—"

"I know," I said, laughing. "Get some rest, Boone."

I waited until the rustling stopped then clicked on my Bluetooth headset and pressed speed dial one. It was answered on the second ring.

"Well hey, gorgeous. Perfect time for you to call. I just got some time alone."

I said, "Must be hard stuck in such cramped quarters with *her* all day and all night."

"Oh, it's hard all right."

"Wish I could be there right now."

"And if you were? What would you be doing?"

I clicked off the headset and yelled, "Boone! That's almost as bad as saying, 'What are you wearing?'"

The light from Boone's phone dimmed, his face shadowed. I could barely see his white-toothed grin in the rear view mirror when he said, "Hey, I told you I don't need any talking. I just need you."

"The talking is for me, okay?" I said. "Think of me like a crockpot slowly simmering as you add ingredients and spices, then turn up the heat."

Boone yawned. "Well, baby? Hate to tell you. I'm a microwave."

Apparently not when it came to marriage proposals, I thought. In that case, Tyler Boone was a cheap-ass wood-stove stocked with damp tinder.

"Fuck you, Boone!" I double flipped him off, raising two ring-less hands to the hotel room ceiling.

Standing in front of the mini-bar a few minutes later with enough anger and disappointment coursing through me to displace years of love and tenderness, I reached for the first tiny bottle.

I was certain there wasn't enough miniature vodka in the world to make me feel like I was a better person. But I was going to try. I downed the first one thinking that somewhere Boone was watching and was as frustrated with me as he'd been on earth.

"Shut up," I said, grabbing another plastic bottle, downing it. "It ain't your fight no more." Somehow, the booze had turned me into a country bumpkin. My daddy would be so proud.

Two bottles later, I was ready to watch the video from the Pharmco restroom. It was simple enough to insert the DVD. Harder to actually press the play arrow.

The camera must have operated on a motion sensor, as the filming began at the first activity, the opening door. There was no audio and I could see what Gator meant about the poor quality. Captured in black and white, there was a definite graininess and it looked like the lens itself might be smeared with something. I watched the whole thing once, my heart leaping into my throat when Boone walked through the door. He'd turned his ball cap around so that the bill covered the back of his neck, but I recognized that hat, that body, that walk, as he glanced around, then headed to the urinals on the left of the screen, even the way he washed and dried his hands. The men who entered after him were the two guys from the white van in the parking lot. The ones I'd seen propping open that back door. What the fuck?

I played it again, looking at it frame by frame, studying the two men. The sunglass-wearing guy could be the creepy whistler at the truck stop, but the camera never gave me a full on face shot, so I couldn't be positive. The littler guy did a lot of shuffling and shrugging during their muted conversation in front of the sinks until Sunglasses pursed his lips, inflating his cheeks and poked him in the arm, hard, pointing to the floor. They must have heard the SD card fall on the tile. Or maybe Boone said something. I could imagine him mumbling, *What the hell is that?*

I played it again, viewing Boone in stop motion, seeing how he glanced toward the sinks at one point, as if something had drawn his attention. There, the sunglasses guy, whistling.

Back to eyes on Boone after washing his hands, after drying them, then reaching for the bag, knocking it down, the skittering card, every movement became a message. I felt like I was trying to learn the secret of a great illusionist. The way he crushed the bag and set it on top of the full trashcan, how he held the SD card aside at one moment, and then, what? Where did it go? He rubbed his face, he opened the door, no sign of the tiny plastic rectangle. I went over and over the end of the tape, but Boone's sleight of hand was too good, or the angle of the camera was too shitty. Or my eyes were too tired.

"Fuck!"

The frame was frozen on Boone's back, the last thing I'd ever see of him. His favorite jean jacket. One that I had hanging in my closet at the plantation—the jacket I'd been wearing the night of the accident.

My stomach churned as an image squeezed behind my eyelids—Old Blue crushed, burning, Boone laying on the highway, bloody and broken, a barrel-chested man hunched over him.

I ran to the bathroom and puked up the day's liquid diet.

* * *

That night, Boone came to me in my dreams, smiling, happy, healthy and whole. He told me what to do, said everything would be okay. And when he walked away whistling, I knew all the words to his song.

In the morning, I was sure of one thing: I had some serious shopping to do.

I scrolled through my laptop emails and found the one I needed, skimmed the attached photographs, typed up a reply, then sat back and waited.

Twenty minutes later, I had a deal with one of my favorite truckers. All I needed was a tank of gas and directions to Lufkin, Texas.

I pulled up to the big white ranch house, parked the Mustang and got out stretching my arms. The front door swung open and a bear of a man came lumbering across the yard. "Jojo!"

Dusty Matthews greeted me in a rib-crushing hug, releasing me just enough so I could walk.

"You find the place okay?" he asked, nestling my head in his ribcage.

"Yeah," I said. "I asked in town. Guess you're hard to miss." I squinted up at his face a foot and a half above me.

He smiled. "It really is good to see you again," he said. "I didn't think you remembered me when I came to the hospital after the wreck."

"You came to the hospital?"

"Sure. A lot of drivers did. We were pulling for you, Jojo. You know that, right?"

I nodded. Of course I did. That was one thing I never thought twice about. Truckers protect their own. They're the first ones to pass a hat for a person in need. People have no idea how many charities truckers have established, how much they give back to a society that scorns them.

Dusty squeezed me closer, giving me a full body mammogram. "See that? Charlene was right."

"What do you mean?"

"She told me to email you. Said you'd come around." He led the way to the house.

"Is that right?" I said, shaking my head. "Maybe she's smarter than she looks."

Dusty laughed, a big booming sound. "One word of advice," he said, holding the door for me, "don't let her hear you say that."

It didn't take long to fill out the paperwork. I told Dusty that I planned on driving back to Houston right away. He tried to change my mind, but gave up after the first round of me saying "No." I suspected he and Boone had shared a few discussions in the past about my temper, my stubborn attitude, though I preferred to call it my *determined* attitude.

"Come on," he said. "She's parked around back. And don't worry, she's as perfect as you remember."

When the doors to the garage rolled apart, I swore I heard angels sing.

There she was: my new job, home and life. Big, black, shiny Kenworth T800, gleaming metal and chrome, standing nearly fourteen feet high, boasting a two hundred and ninety-five-inch wheelbase. More important than her shiny exterior and technological advances, was her horsepower. This baby could pull through anything.

"You going to change her name?"

I looked at Dusty, practically wringing his hands beside me. I shook my head. "No. How could I? She'll always be *Sabrina* to me."

"Thank you," he said, handing me the keys.

"There's one more thing."

Dusty smiled. "Anything. You name it."

"I need to get my father's Mustang to Houston."

It didn't take long to secure the car's front wheels to Dusty's old tow dolly. I double-checked the tie downs as Dusty said goodbye to his truck, planting a kiss on her grille, cooing, "I'll miss you, Sabrina."

"Hey, what about me?"

I minimized the rib-crushing goodbye by leaping up and hugging Dusty first. It was like hanging from a redwood.

I climbed up the back and entered the rear door of the sleeper, taking a moment to admire Sabrina's interior—sleek wood floors, marble counters, custom cabinetry an oversized bathroom, deep storage, flat screen TV and multi-speaker surround sound system. She was a luxury hotel on wheels.

Buckling into the driver's seat, I felt like a sweet-deprived kid with a buck in his pocket at the penny candy store. There were more dials, gauges, switches and knobs set into the wood dashboard than I'd seen on some airplanes. Dusty had raved about the integrated harmonic balancing of the Paccar MX-13 engine, but right now, I was really glad Sabrina had an automatic transmission. That was going to make what I had to do so much easier.

I blew the custom air horn as I pulled away. Dusty waved, one big tanned bear paw wiping his eyes.

It came back easily. In that way you slide into a pool on the first day of summer and your legs and arms are in sync, even though you haven't asked them to perform for nine months. I was less a gliding, floating, perfectly coordinated swimmer, and more a bumping, roaring asphalt-eating truck driver, and still? It was a powerful feeling, a true and honest high.

* * *

There's a distinct difference between driving a forty-thousand-pound semi and a three-thousand-pound car, especially if you're mostly in one or the other all the time.

I remember coming home to Bunkie one weekend after a hundred days on the road in the Peterbilt. I'd racked up as many hours as Boone and by the time I slipped behind the wheel of my father's pickup truck, the thing felt like a toy beneath me. I imagined the floorboards dropping open as I waved bye-bye then pushed my way to town with my feet.

In reverse, it was much more difficult. The transition from four-wheeled vehicle to ten-wheeled custom sleeper semi-truck was no joke. Blind spots, braking distances, speeds and obstacles all became four times as important to master. For every person who thinks it would be very cool to drive a big rig for an hour, there are five people on the road too scared to even pass one.

I took pride in knowing that I could do things others couldn't. I'd always felt the need to prove myself, grew up wanting to be the best at everything, to never stop trying, which might be the one thing that kept me from being perfect. Today, that was enough to get me behind the wheel and back on the highway.

It seemed like there wasn't anything Sabrina couldn't do with her state of the art technology. Not only did she tell me where Gator Natoli, PI lived, but talked me through the navigation to his front door after discussing the current weather and traffic conditions.

Gator's Houston street was lined with mansions, as I'd imagined. They were Texas large, with land, and land between the land, but they weren't unapproachable or made of marble. Not a single one I passed had courtyards of naked Italian statues or vineyards or helicopter pads—that I could see. Maybe this was just a regular kind of rich. Nothing out of the ordinary in this neck of the woods.

That said, I caused a bit of a stir driving Sabrina through the neighborhood. More so, hitting the train air horn at the gate at Gator's place.

He buzzed me through then came running, buttoning himself into his shirt. "What the hell?"

"He-ey," I said.

He finished with his shirt, shielded his eyes against the sun, stared at the rig, with what I took as awe, perhaps intrigue. "Where you headed?"

I said, "You might want to rephrase that."

"Okay. What are you doing here?"

"Try again."

Gator stepped back, shook his head. "What's this about?"

"You're the one who keeps on saying there are places a driver can go that you can't. Well, you got yourself a driver."

"Whose is that?" he asked, jerking a thumb toward the Mustang on the tow dolly.

"My father's."

"Who's your father? Steve McQueen?"

I laughed. "Not quite. Back door's open if you want the tour."

Gator hesitated, but there was a twinkle in his eye when he came up the back steps and opened the sleeper's door. His grin broadened as he scanned the space. "They sure don't build them like they used to."

"Thank God for that," I said, laughing.

He finished his tour and came up to the cab shaking his head. "Wow. That's all I got. Wow."

"It gets better," I said, punching the go pedal, teasing him with the roar and rumble of the mighty Paccar.

"Okay, Jojo. So, where are *we* headed?"

"Wherever we need to go to get some answers. You want to find out who's behind the cargo thefts and the missing drivers, and I need to find out why Boone had to die, and who the fuck was behind it."

"Hell, now you're talking," he said. "This all looks great." He gave the interior of Sabrina another appraising glance. "But, I think you're missing something."

"Nope. I don't think so," I said, shaking my head.

"Hang on. I'll be right back." He went out the back door, hopped down and jogged toward the big white house.

I was removing the straps to free the Mustang from the tow dolly when Gator returned, a little winded and carrying a brown paper bag. "Here."

I reached inside, felt a cold, heavy piece of metal.

Boone's chrome pig hood ornament.

"How did you…"

"The salvage yard," Gator said. "I thought you might want something…you know."

I did. I held the chrome pig near my heart and willed myself to keep it together. We walked to the front of the truck, unscrewed Sabrina's wings and replaced them with the pig. It was pretty scraped up and I could see where Gator had tried to fix it, but the pig screwed onto the hood just fine, seeming happy to peek out over the road again.

I wiped a tear from my cheek, but not before Gator caught it.

"Shit. I'm sorry. I shouldn't have—"

"No. It's fine really. I'm glad you did. I'm losing him, you know. I can hardly remember his face. Every day, a little more slips away. Without something like this," I pointed to the chrome pig. "He might never have existed."

Gator shook his head. "You can't mean that. You loved

him. You were going to get married. Spend the rest of your life together."

"Were we? Did I? Even if he'd proposed, I'm not sure what I would have said, or how it would have shaken out in the end. I don't know anything for certain anymore. Except a good man died because of what happened on that highway with me behind the wheel and I won't rest until I get to the bottom if it."

We stood there a moment, chrome pig shining down on us, unspoken words in the air.

"What happens now?" Gator asked.

"You go pack a bag," I said. "But first, tell me where I can park the Mustang."

Chapter 5

Gator directed me around back to his four-car garage. He tapped a series of buttons on his cell phone keypad, and the door to the last bay opened. I drove Mercy in, took a second to appreciate the echo of her engine in the big garage, then cut it and stepped out.

I glanced at the shapes of the other cars in the building: a Bentley that might have once carried royalty and a Cadillac that would have made Elvis proud. I wanted to run over, swing open the doors and slide across the polished leather. I wanted to back each of them out and drive across Texas, keep going until I reached the ocean. I mock yawned, as if this was no big deal, then wiped my sweaty palms on my jeans.

"We really ought to hit the road," I said, walking over to the car in the next bay, a fire engine red Jaguar XKE. "Nice. Sixty-eight?"

"Sixty-seven. Fully restored, original parts." Gator said.

"Is that right?" I leaned in. The interior was pristine— white leather, chrome and wood.

"Is this what you really do? Sell old cars?" I asked.

"It's just a hobby," he said, dismissing hundreds of thousands of dollars of vehicular beauty with a wave of his arm.

My eyes must have bored a hole in the back of his head. He turned, the answer on his lips before I'd formed the question.

"Family money. Oil. It's embarrassing how much. And

yes, I'm the *only* one left to spend it. Okay?"

I nodded slowly. *What was I supposed to say? Lucky duck?*

We stepped outside and he used his phone again, setting an alarm whose resounding chirps let me know the cars were safe.

We made a plan to get the trailer in Bunkie and pick up a few things I'd left behind. I gave Gator the quickie driver review after he claimed he might be a little rusty. Guy was a fast learner. I liked that. I let him drive the first hour, just to break his cherry, then I took over.

My favorite part of the trip was a bit of a detour, but it was habit by now. Going home just wouldn't be the same without driving through the towns of Eunice and Mamou. I'd save Gator the headache of having to make out the hand-lettered signs in pigeon English and French. I remembered every stretch of those poorly paved roads, all the way past Chicot State Park and Acadiana.

But I'd forgotten it was Saturday. People were lined up down both sides of the narrow street itching to get inside the Savoy Music Center in downtown Eunice for the Cajun morning jam session—a local tradition since 1966. The place was known for two things. Food and music, and not necessarily in that order.

Long, loud, black and shiny, Sabrina was the center of attention for camera-toting tourists as I inched my way through town, passing lace-curtained corner cafes where people inside might be dining on hot beignets, sliced boudin and strong coffee. An old black man in a red tuxedo with a monkey on his shoulder played the accordion beside a colorful cart on the sidewalk. As I turned the corner, I glanced in the side mirror to see the monkey pull a miniature accordion from the man's beard and join in the music making. We weren't in Texas anymore.

A few blocks north, I lost the sound of Zydeco as I drove down litter-scattered empty streets, passed boarded-up brick buildings. The landscape grew rural; trees, fences, the occasional rotting barn, weathered mailboxes that announced a house somewhere nearby. I turned down one dusty road after another until we arrived at the plantation in Bunkie.

"You awake back there?" I called to Gator.

"Yeah. I was just resting my eyes."

Typical male. Why can't they admit to sleeping like the rest of us mortals?

I backed the truck up to the outbuilding where Boone and I had left our trailer all those months ago, set the brakes, turned off the truck and climbed down.

"Nice place," Gator said, staring at the historical plantation home and grounds. "A bit small though. However do you manage?"

"That's what the slaves are for," I said, walking toward the house.

"What?"

I looked over my shoulder. Gator was still standing by the truck staring at me.

"I'm kidding," I said. "Come on."

I waited for him to catch up. "Gator, nobody has slaves any more. We have servants."

My father had been hiding the house key in the same place for thirty years. I made Gator turn around so I could tap out the loose brick beside the flowerpot and retrieve the key.

When I opened the screen door, a funky mildew-meets-pond scum kind of smell wafted out of the dark interior. I opened the door wider, stopping short in the doorway, pawing the wall to find the light switch, when a quick furry thing dashed through my legs making me jump, brushing the ankle of Gator causing him to scream like a girl.

That made me laugh. It was the one thing that kept me from being perfect, giggling in the face of danger.

I flicked the switch, turned to razz Gator about being such a wuss, when we both got a look at the room.

"Your father isn't one of those hoarders is he?" Gator whispered.

I shook my head.

He drew his gun, put me behind him, then flicked off the lights. We stood in the silence for a few seconds, eyes adjusting to the dim, me crouched behind him, fingers on the phone in my pocket feeling out 9-1-1.

"Hold on a second," Gator said, lowering his gun and turning the lights back on.

I blinked at him. "Why? What are you doing? Obviously, my father's been robbed and vandalized," I said, pointing to the ripped couch cushions, the hole in the wall, the shredded carpet.

"Has he?"

"I don't know where you're standing pal, but from where I am, it fucking looks like it."

"Vandalized? Maybe. Not robbed." Gator pointed to the big screen TV, the stereo and the computer on the desk. He used his shirttail as a glove, closed the front door and guided me by the elbow around the mess in the living room into the kitchen.

A pane of glass in the back door was broken out. The door was ajar, a muddy trail of small paw prints leading away.

Gator said the unnecessary, "That's how they got in— them and that creature that ran out the front door."

Creature. I stifled a laugh. City boys.

The kitchen was trashed. The floor was covered in broken glass. Canisters of flour, sugar, rice, coffee beans and pecans had been dumped. The contents of the freezer were laying in a pile in front of it—most of the boxes torn open and chewed.

Gator looked at me. "They were looking for something specific. Something small enough you'd hide it in a canister of coffee beans."

"Probably just some kids," I said, "looking for money or drugs."

Gator raised a brow.

"Not that my father has either. I mean, sure he has money. And maybe he has some drugs—prescription ones—for his blood pressure. But nothing that anyone would rob him for. Besides, we're in Bunkie."

"This isn't the work of your typical vandal," he said, like he was educating me on the finer points of vandalism.

It took a second, but my sluggish brain finally clicked in. I wasn't used to thinking like a criminal.

"Shit," I said. "Hang on."

I ran out of the kitchen, hurdling over capsized chairs and piles of magazines, made my way to my old bedroom. It had been tossed like the living room. The mattress drooped off the side of the bed, pillows slit open. I flung open the closet doors. Most of the stuff was still hanging—winter coats, sweaters and flannel shirts. I went through the rack twice, then checked the items on the floor.

"What are you looking for?" Gator asked pushing his way into the room, stepping over a dresser drawer.

"A jacket."

"Are you cold?"

I rolled my eyes. "It's eighty degrees outside, Gator. I'm not cold."

He stood there in that annoying way people do when you're supposed to know what they're thinking and how to fill in the blanks. I wanted to slap him. Instead, I sighed then said very slowly, "I'm. Looking. For. Boone's. Jean. Jacket."

I gave him a second to connect.

"The one he was wearing in the video," he said, and began pawing through the closet.

I backed up, sat on the edge of disheveled bed.

"It's not here."

"Damn. They took it."

"But why would they take it, if they just wanted what was in the pocket? They didn't need the jacket, Gator. They needed the SD card."

"I don't know."

Gator followed me to the disheveled living room. "Do you want to call the cops about this?"

I shook my head. "No. We can handle it."

I thought about what might have happened if Pilar or my father had been home instead of camping in Brazil. I put the chairs and the couch back together, rearranged the lights and gathered up the magazines. Gator must have found the vacuum in the mudroom. I heard him running it in the kitchen. He was smart to not waste his breath, not challenge me on this one.

I had my head under the sink in the guest bathroom, gathering up cotton balls and Band-Aids that had been dumped from a first aid kit, when I heard shouts and a crash. I grabbed the first thing I could find and ran to the living room. Gator was pinned against the wall by a dark-suited man. I raised my weapon and attacked, yelling. The guy dropped Gator and spun around. I knocked him off his feet with a leg sweep, rolled him, got in two kidney punches and was about to slam my fist into his Adam's apple when I recognized his eyes.

I let him go and sat back, breathing hard. "Shit. Ivory Joe.

What are you doing here? I almost killed you."

"No, you didn't," he said, wincing as he pushed himself upright. "But you sure would have scared the shit out of my toilet." He pointed to the weapon in my hand—a plastic toilet brush.

"Literally." Gator laughed.

I threw the brush at him. "Shut up." I looked at him harder, focusing on his leg, the way his hand went there automatically. "You're okay, right, Ivory Joe? I mean, I didn't..."

"I'm fine," he said, waving me off, standing taller as he looked around. The living room was as put together as it could be, but there was no hiding the split-open couch.

"Want to tell me what's going on," Ivory Joe asked, "Or do I have to play twenty questions?"

"You're going to need more than twenty," I mumbled. "Nice tie, by the way."

Ivory Joe pulled at the pink paisley tie as if it was choking him.

Gator extended a hand, helping Ivory Joe to his feet. "Gator Natoli, I'm Jojo's new team driver, pleased to meet you."

Ivory Joe brushed off his suit, returned the pleasantries and the two men sized each other up. I was wondering if they were going to circle each other, beating their chests or just drop their pants and compare genetic blessings.

"I could use a tall glass of cold, sweet, tea. How about you boys?" I said. I really wanted a beer with a bourbon back, but I had to drive and that was one line I wouldn't cross.

We sat on the back stoop with our tea, watching the birds flit from tree to tree. No one spoke for a few minutes. The silence was nice, but wrong, and we all knew it, like the way you knew you were in trouble well before the blue light of the cop car began spinning.

Ivory Joe leaned into me the way he used to when we were kids and about to pass a secret. He said, "You may not live here anymore, Jojo, but I do. Is there something I need to know?"

I resented that he thought I'd sell out Bunkie. That he'd even think for a second I didn't care about the place, or the people in it.

"It's complicated," I said.

Gator chuckled, then hid his face behind his tea when I zeroed in on him with my evil eye.

I turned to Ivory Joe. "Listen, we've got this under control. There's just a small disagreement about the location of a certain item, that's all."

"What, are you hiding treasure? This ain't no pirate ship, Jojo. Talk plain to me."

I looked at Gator who shrugged—a man of few words.

"It's not your fight, Ivory Joe. *We* don't even know what this is really about."

"Come on, Jojo."

"I swear. I wish I did."

"Well, what do you think?

"All I can tell you right now is that I think this may have something to do with my accident, with Boone's death."

"Well, that's enough, right?"

"Yeah."

I'll give Ivory Joe credit. He didn't go all crazy on me, he didn't say anything stupid. He did what I hoped he'd do. He offered to help, first off by sending his people over to clean up and re-stage the house.

"That would be good. Thanks. And my father—"

"Don't worry. He can stay with me when they get back."

"I'm not sure that's such a good idea," Gator said. "If

somebody already found this place, it won't be long before they find anyone associated with it. Might be best to move your father and his girlfriend, just for a little while."

I looked at Ivory Joe. It was our turn to chuckle. There was no way we'd ever get Manny Boudreaux to leave town if he knew trouble was riding the next bus in.

"Better yet," I said, "Ivory Joe, call up the Haddens, Burkes and the Fishers. Tell them we've got some outlaw quadrupeds that need taking out and they have our permission to come hunt the grounds."

I turned to Gator and softened my voice, letting the girl out. "Do you think twelve armed backwoods hicks itching to shoot will be enough protection on a plantation in little old Bunkie?"

"Maybe. They'll need to be briefed," Gator said.

"*To pale kreyol?*" Ivory Joe asked.

Gator's expression was enough of an answer. Ivory Joe grinned. "These are good old boys from the swamps. Creoles and Cajuns. People that live off the land, have their own rules and ways. Man like you? You'll never get through to them."

Gator's chest swelled. Ivory Joe stood a little taller. I could feel the testosterone level in the room rise.

"He's right," I told Gator, touching his arm. "Let Ivory Joe handle things here. We've got to get on the road." I tucked in my shirt and brushed off my jeans, saying. "I need to call Charlene," but not going anywhere.

Gator handed me the toilet brush. "Don't forget your weapon."

Ivory Joe was still staring at me. Gator must have felt it too.

"I'll be in the kitchen," Gator said. "Pretending to vacuum."

We watched him leave then I turned to Ivory Joe and met his eyes.

"Damn it, Jojo. You be careful out there," Ivory Joe said, pulling me into a hug. He smelled like a girl. Not like he was bathing in perfume or anything, but like he'd been real close to one. I pulled back thinking of that viper Shannon.

"You okay?" he asked.

"I'm fine," I said, patting his arm, disengaging his hands from me, and wondering where my buddy had gone. Old Ivory Joe never would have been caught dead wearing a pink tie. And what was up with his hair? He looked like an altar boy—in the sixties.

I put two hands on the toilet brush so I wouldn't be tempted to muss up his hair, returning him to the mop-headed Ivory Joe I knew—and once, loved.

"Well, I better make that call," I said. "And you—"

"I'm on it," he said. "We'll get this place back together and bring in the hunters." He smiled. "Ain't nobody who doesn't like a good hog hunt."

In the bedroom I cleared a space, then sat on the bed and called Charlene. She answered on the first ring.

When I explained what Gator and I needed, she chuckled. "Honey, you know what they call me?"

I certainly did, but I needed my job too much to tell her.

"The Miracle Worker," she said.

"Oh. Right."

Charlene got a little teary-voiced. "Honey, I'm glad you're back in the saddle. You know, some things were meant to be."

Before I could jump all over her shit and show my true pessimistic nature—the one thing that kept me from being perfect—she said, "Don't worry, darlin'. Charlene's going to take care of everything."

The idea of that did worry me, more than a little, but I chose at that moment to focus on something I could fix. I started making a list for the hardware store, the gun shop and the local technology shack. After all, a girl needs her toys.

Maybe it was that whole return to the scene of the crime thing? I don't know, all I knew we had to go back to Texas where everything started. That was where the trucks were being taken, where Baconator had gone missing. I knew Pharmco had something to do with it, I just wasn't sure what. The way I saw it, the bad guys had Boone's coat and the mysterious SD card. What else did they need and why?

Gator looked pretty damn fine in the driver's seat. He returned to the role of trucker as if he'd never left. It was easy to see how that kind of guy is attractive to women—the devil may care attitude, the tough guy persona, even the sensitive poetry reading adventurer who knew how to break loose a frozen air brake at midnight in Montana during a blizzard. Sure, the rich part didn't hurt, either.

I was a firm believer that a man's driving skills are the predictor to his prowess in the sack, or so I've read in quite a few men's magazines. The same should never be said of women, as we tend to use our driving time as another multi-tasking opportunity, unless we happen to be driving a race car, then it's all left turns, chapstick and advertising.

The third time I corrected Gator's lane changing, he slipped on a pair of sunglasses and turned up the volume on the radio. It was no coincidence that the Cee Lo Green song playing was about someone driving, well sort of.

I looked in the side view mirror at every mile marker, even

though I wasn't sure what I was looking for. A car emblazoned with the words *Bad Guys*?

When the Qualcomm went off I beat Gator to the machine. It was a load out of a San Marcos pharmaceutical warehouse to the docks at Corpus Christi. Charlene had done it.

I looked at Gator. "Pharmco. We're in."

I unbuckled and squeezed myself out of the cab, heading to the laptop in the kitchenette. I turned back, touched Gator's shoulder. "You okay up here alone?" I was betting his thoughts would distract him. He was probably worried about not only the driving, but now, potential danger. He might be thinking about exit scenarios, weaponry, legal ramifications.

Gator said, "Yeah. I was just thinking that if Wonder Woman and Batman hooked up, would her bracelets bother his sonar? And what if they had a baby, would it have really big ears, or really big tits?"

I turned my gentle shoulder touch into a Spock pinch that left him groaning. Men.

We arrived in the vicinity of the warehouse hours before our scheduled pick up. Time enough to fuel up, a chance to stretch our legs.

I gave Gator directions to the nearest truck stop telling him as we pulled in, "This is the same place Boone and I picked up that abandoned trailer."

"Yeah. I've been here," he said. "Had to ask around about the missing Baconator."

"Learn anything?"

"Not really. I must still smell like a cop to these people."

I wondered if that meant he smelled like accusations and jail time or donuts and coffee.

We paid at the pump, didn't even bother going inside and were back on the road in short order.

I checked my map and smiled. "Pull in there," I said, pointing to the lot of Roane Community Park. "I want to show you something."

Gator raised his brows. "Are you sure? We hardly know each other."

"Oh puh-lease. Get over yourself, would you? It's something in the trailer."

He found a nice pull through spot, and left the engine idling as we climbed out and went around back to the trailer.

I explained how Boone and I had run into some less than honest dockworkers in Miami, when we were doing a lot of harbor to inland runs. Sometimes it was pallets marked as *garments*, sometimes they were marked *electronics*. But always, we had a problem with the before and after count, and always, they managed to have one of their guys in the trailer helping with the unloading—until we caught a worker tossing boxes off the truck to his buddy in the parking lot. Documented on the video camera we'd installed.

"Wish Baconator had something like this in his trailer. Might have helped."

"How's that?"

"There was some discrepancy with the load, or something. I don't know."

"Shouldn't you?"

"Wasn't our deal, we just completed the delivery, never signed for it, never opened it, never touched the seals. If something was off, it wasn't us."

"Think everyone would see it that way?"

I crossed my arms, took a stance, narrowed my eyes into dagger throwing slits. "What are you saying?"

"Nothing. Just thinking out loud," Gator said, waving me off.

I gave him a second, but he didn't bite, so I said, "There's the camera," showing him the wide-angle lens Boone had hidden up in the corner of the trailer. "I need to set up the new wireless controller, monitor and DVR in Sabrina. I should be able to do it in thirty minutes or less."

"It's not pizza delivery, you know," Gator said.

"I know. It's okay," I said patting his arm. "I got this. Don't you worry your pretty little head." I pointed to the sign for the nature path. "Why don't you go for a walk or something."

"Yeah," he said, fists at his side. "I just might do that."

Fifteen minutes later, propped up under the dashboard, wires in my hands and a mini-flashlight in my mouth, I heard gunfire. I dropped everything, rolled out, ran to the oven and grabbed one of the guns I kept stashed there. I jumped from the cab, slammed the door, clicking the remote locks as I ran into the woods.

"Gator?"

No answer.

I moved deeper into the woods, pistol up, safety off, eyes and ears alert. A squirrel rustled the tree branches above my head. I didn't bother looking up. I knew what it was, where it was and what it wasn't. I stepped off the path, walked in deeper, calling again, "Gator, location!"

I heard retching, then Gator called, "Here. Ten yards west of the trailhead."

Gator was bent over, braced against a tree, looking pale. He spit, then wiped his mouth and raised a hand as I approached.

"You okay?" I asked, looking for blood.

"Yeah. I shot a snake. Hate those fuckers. Then I found him." He strapped a gun that I hadn't known he was carrying into an ankle holster, pointed to a lump of red-checked flannel by a fallen tree.

I walked in the direction he pointed, smelled it before I saw it. The wind shifted, taking away some of the scent, blowing the leaves off a maggoty skull in a John Deere hat.

"Shit," I said, backing off fast while pulling my shirt up to my nose in a makeshift mask. "Shouldn't we call someone?"

"Like who?" he asked. "Nice piece by the way. Springfield XD 40, isn't it? Where were you hiding that?"

I'd forgotten I was still holding my gun. "Wouldn't you like to know?" I said, glancing at the chunky black subcompact then stuffing it in the back of my jeans.

"Actually, I would. If we're going to be working together, I'd rather not have any surprises. Don't tell me you're one of these drivers who locks their weapon in the sidebox or leaves it in three parts around the rig—for *safety* reasons." He raised his hands and made finger quotes at the word "safety."

I poked my face out of my T-shirt mask. "For your information, I keep all my guns loaded, and in the oven. Okay? Just don't go baking any fucking casseroles and we'll be fine. Jesus."

We stared at each other and for a second I didn't think both of us having loaded weapons was such a good idea.

I said, "Can we get back to the dead body, please?"

"Sure," he said, standing up, running a hand through his hair, going PI on me. "There's your missing driver."

"The Baconator?"

Gator nodded. "I didn't check for ID, but the clothes and approximate body size fits the description I was given."

"Well, we are near the truck stop where he was last seen alive." I squinted in the direction of the body, scanning it for missing pieces. "How do you think he died?"

"I'm no forensics expert," Gator said, "but there's gunpowder stains and a bullet hole in the back of the dude's hat...I'd say it was murder. Good old homicide."

"Really, Gator? Good old homicide?"

He shrugged. "Don't tell me the thought never crossed your mind."

"Of course it did. I just chose to not dwell on it."

Gator stepped away from the tree and the remains of his breakfast. "Doesn't change the outcome, does it?" he said, tipping his chin toward The Baconator's grinning skull.

What was I going to say to that?

Gator pushed through the brush and started walking back to the path.

"Hey!" I called.

"What?"

"This isn't like someone breaking into my father's house and slitting a few cushions. Don't we have to report this?"

Gator said, "Nope," and kept walking.

I took two steps toward the corpse before the wind picked up again, blowing the smell of dead Baconator my way. I gagged, then turned and jogged after Gator.

He'd returned to his natural color by the time I caught up to him on the path. I hoped he'd regained his strength after puking in the bushes, because I'd only gotten started on my righteous indignation kick. I grabbed his arm, twisting him around. "Tell me you aren't serious."

"As serious as dick cancer."

"Jesus. That's pretty serious."

"Beats a heart attack."

We started walking. I said, "I knew a guy once, got up in the morning, caught a heart attack and still went to work."

Gator nodded. "True dat. If you don't have your health, you don't have anything."

"But that, back there," I said, jerking a thumb over my shoulder. "That isn't a guy who was suffering from a health problem. Nothing natural about that shit."

Gator stopped walking. I could feel the slump of his shoulders in his voice. "I know. Listen, Jojo. We can't call the cops yet. You understand that we can't afford to blow our cover before we even start."

"We're talking about a missing trucker with family and friends. A dead man, alone in the woods."

"And he'll be just as dead tomorrow, or next week, or next month," Gator said.

"What about evidence? What if it rains?"

"Come on. You saw him. He's a condo for maggots, a vacation stop for passing beetles. It's probably the most ecological thing The Baconator ever did. He's not going anywhere and we're not saying anything to anyone until I say so, got it?"

I opened my mouth to object, but he put a finger on my lips. Not a wise thing to do to a woman with sharp teeth.

He said, "We can both get the answers we need, if we play this my way. Can you do that for me? Please?"

He was the king of walking away. He walked away better than anyone I knew. He must have stolen my job when I wasn't looking.

I watched his back disappear in the shadows of the trees. I tried taking five deep breaths, then took five more.

When I got back to the truck, Gator had finished up the install and was ready to test the camera system. I swallowed my pride and a bitter nugget of anger, then climbed into the trailer and danced a little hokey pokey for the live feed. I put my left foot in. I put my left foot out. I shook some stuff about. After the successful playback, I hit delete, 'cause that's what it's all about.

Chapter 6

Gator glanced at the pages I was flipping through on the clipboard held six inches from his face.

"What's all that?" he asked.

I scanned the paper, admiring my neat printing. Trying to remember if the same man who'd taught me to balance my letters like art was the same one with the fancy moves on the dance floor. It might have been. I knew the words were formed from the voices of my Louisiana cousins—boys who had taught me more about killing and surviving than any man. "It's the seven Ps. You must know them. With that cop/military background and all?"

"Who said I had a military background?"

"Don't you?"

He shrugged and gave me one of those I-could-tell-you-but-then-I'd-have-to-kill-you grins.

I said, "This is hardly the time to be coy. As you can see, the first three Ps are Proper Prior Planning."

He shook his head and continued driving. "Technically, you've only got six. Piss-poor is one word."

I tapped the words I'd written down, counting them: Proper Prior Planning Prevents Piss-Poor Performance. I'd always known them as the seven Ps, and seven was my lucky number. I wasn't going to let Gator take that from me. I added a comma after performance and wrote the word *pal*.

"Whatever," I said. "It's the idea behind the words that's important. What's our plan, again?"

He held up three fingers and waggled them, saying, "We go in. We get the load. We deliver the load."

"That's it?"

"That's it. I like to call it the rule of three."

"I like to call it bullshit. I say, we go in, we plant a camera or a mic, I talk up some drivers while you find that restroom, and then—"

"And then we end up like The Baconator," he said. "Trust me. I may have slightly more experience in this area than you do."

"Why do you have to do that?"

"What?"

"Talk down to me like that? Be so condescending," I said.

"Am I?" he asked.

I gave him my *well, yeah* look, complete with head nod and lip curl.

He smiled. "I was simply stating a fact. Of course, you'll be more *prepared* than me, with all those proper plans and preventions. I'd rather work intuitively. Sort of feel my way around. You know, make decisions as the situations deem."

"What the fuck does that mean?"

He smiled. "You'll see."

I stowed the clipboard in the side pocket of the passenger door, mumbled, "God, I hope not," then sunk down in the seat pulling my hat over my eyes.

It wasn't *all* arguments and plan-slashing with Gator and me. When you drove as a team, you worked as a team, even if in our situation that meant he moved the truck forward safely and I did all the other stuff, like tell him where to move the truck.

The GPS chirped awake as we neared the exit in San Marcos that would take us to the warehouse. I'd installed a suave Australian man's voice to direct us, and was still slightly confused by the accent, not sure whether to strip to my undies and put another shrimp on the barbie or be on the lookout for crocodiles.

Of course when Gator said, "I don't know why you picked that voice. The British woman was fine." I told him I preferred the Aussie and since it was both my truck and my GPS system, he should just deal with it. Although I'm pretty sure I didn't say it half as polite.

Driving toward Pharmco, I was struck with a combination of adrenaline rush and déjà vu.

I said, "Adrena-vu."

"What's that?' Gator asked, slowing the truck as the guardhouse came into sight.

"Nothing," I said. "Just thinking out loud. So, you're ready, right?'

He reached up, turned his cap around backward, pushed up his sleeves and winked at me. "Operation Redneck Trucker, engaged, ma'am."

I scoffed. "Nice accent, can hardly tell you're from New Jersey. Here." I handed him a stick of gum. "Why don't you let me do the talking."

Gator lowered his voice, hung his head and put on a new accent, "Yes'm, boss."

I sighed. He was quite the comedian.

I did a quick check of my phone's battery life before I switched on the camera in the trailer, then sat back, glancing in the side mirror. This time there were no speeding security trucks, no sign of tire marks on the shoulder from pulled over vehicles, not even a squirrel to cross our path. The lack of anything was a little spooky.

Even with my adrena-vu super powers, the guard at the booth didn't look familiar, as in the I've-seen-you-here-before way, though he did look a little like a guy who used to cut my hair in Florida, but I thought asking him about a prior profession might void that whole don't-ask-don't-tell thing, so I didn't.

I might have looked familiar to him though, the way he kept his gaze on me even when he was talking to Gator. I was about to ask if I had something in my teeth or had suddenly sprouted a hairy mole on my cheek, but he moved off the stare, asked to see our credentials and clearances, then told us to remove our hats, look into the camera mounted in his window and wait.

Finally, the guard handed back our papers and waved us through, opening the Pharmco gates.

"You're cool, right?" Gator said, rolling forward.

"Cool as a cucumber."

"I never really understood that."

"I know," I said, thinking about it. "They're only cool if you put them in the refrigerator, right? It should be *cool as ice*, or *cool as an Eskimo in autumn* or *cool as Elvis*."

"Elvis sure was cool. Nobody would disagree with that."

I nodded. "Except maybe Priscilla."

Gator laughed.

He had a nice laugh, and real nice smile. If a girl could get past his know-it-all-stubborn-ass-look-at-me-demeanor, he might have a chance out there in the dating world with his strong jaw and bright blue eyes, plus the guy had all his hair, which was a total bonus. He'd let it grow since we first met. It was nice and thick, the kind of hair a girl could grab onto and tug. I squirmed a bit in my seat, imagining a few hair tugging moments in my past.

Gator had embraced his new role as truck driver. There was little left of the clean-shaven white button-down wearing rich boy playing investigator I'd met in the hospital. Of course he still had a broad chest and muscular arms and I'd admit to admiring his physique if you held my hand to fire, but I sure as hell wouldn't tell him that. No one needed to puff that head up any more than it already was. He probably had to have his cowboy hats specially stretched.

We passed through the second gate without stopping, guard on a radio waving us through, no sign of the canine partner. As we passed the first parking lot, I pointed out the same bevy of black cars.

"You're right," Gator said. "Those look like government-issue sedans. Check it out, the security cameras on those poles are not the garden variety commercial install. I suspect someone somewhere is counting my nose hairs right now."

"No shit?"

"And reading your lips."

I snapped a hand to my mouth, then pretended to be wiping sweat off my upper lip.

Gator shot me a sideways glance, then smiled saying, "Cucumber."

The guard had given us a dock number on the opposite side of the building from my previous visit. Gator began to back us in next to a newer Volvo with a weird paint job. It was red and purple, but only if you moved your head side to side, like some sort of visual trick. I was thinking about how much paint some guy had sniffed before he'd come up with that idea and what other places you could use a color changing paint to mess with people's eyes, when Gator slowed the truck to a crawl.

"You're not getting any strange ideas, are you?"

"Nope," I said. "Just observing."

"Good," he said, then hit the brakes as the light near the dock went red. "What the hell?"

"They probably want to load us dock high. You okay to bump the dock?"

Before Gator could answer, a leathery white-haired man in a green jumpsuit—the same one who'd reprimanded me for the cell phone camera—stepped in front of the truck and motioned for us to open our trailer doors.

I looked at Gator. "I got this," I said reaching for the paperwork. Our hands met on the clipboard. I unsnapped my seatbelt and started to pull my hand back, but Gator clamped down harder.

"No need to go playing hero, Jojo."

I looked into his eyes and didn't say anything for a second. It was nice in those eyes, sort of calm and quiet, with a bit of a twinkle behind them, like a joke was brewing, or music being played that made you want to get up and dance. If we'd been anywhere else, at any other time, I might have leaned in to see how far those eyes would take me. I'd never be the one to blink first and with this guy, I had the feeling we'd be stuck in a staring contest for a long time. He slid his gaze from my eyes to my lips, then slowly back up and I saw something new there. I pulled harder on the clipboard until he let go.

I said, "Don't worry. I'm not playing hero. I'm just doing my job."

"All right then."

I used the rubber band on my wrist to gather my hair into a ponytail, slipped on my sunglasses and exited from the passenger door, chasing the white haired man around to the driver's side. He was pointing at his watch and yelling up to Gator to get out of the truck and open the trailer doors when he noticed me.

"I'd be happy to," I said, giving the guy my prettiest smile while tucking the sarcasm under my tongue.

"That's all right, darlin'," White Hair said with a wink. "Why don't you climb back up there and let your man do his job."

There were many ways I wanted to answer the guy. Not many of those ways included words, but I restrained myself and took a deep breath, exhaling my mantra: *cucumber.*

Then I chuckled a little and punched White Hair not so lightly in the bicep, in a good old boy way and said, "Aw, we don't want to bother him. Last time he tried to unlock my trailer he broke a nail. C'mon now."

I jingled my keys and headed toward the trailer, glancing over my shoulder to see him pulling at his neck, smoothing his prickly hair.

I unlocked the padlocks and swung open the doors. White Hair held out his hand for the paperwork, scanned the pages, head down concentrating, as I checked for the light on the trailer's video camera, then pushed my sunglasses up on my head, the cue to Gator that it was *all good.*

I climbed the dock steps to watch as the green light clicked on signaling Gator to back in the rest of the way. I was impressed with his handling of my rig—made me feel all warm inside. I turned to point this out to White Hair, but he'd disappeared.

Like last time, the Pharmco warehouse was fully armed with security devices, from cameras and motion sensors to futuristic buttons and switches whose purpose I could only guess. The place appeared to be operating at peak efficiency—forklifts running back and forth, green jump-suited men everywhere.

Our load was waiting, two plastic-wrapped thermal containers stamped fragile. They appeared small enough to be hand carried, but a forklift driver swooped in and scooped them up, depositing both in the back right corner of the trailer.

I waited for the forklift driver to back out then installed the trailer dividers, designed to keep a small load from shifting, or separate two loads being hauled together. Boone and I had made our dividers from lightweight metal and old trailer walls, even created a wall attachment for easy, clank-free storage. I liked things neat.

White Hair spoke into his radio, then stomped into the trailer to admire my handiwork, or give me some more shit. I wasn't sure.

"Looks good," he said, peering in at the load, nodding to himself. "Get her there before she heats up, right? No stops."

"Right," I said, feeling like I should salute or bow or something. I hadn't had this much oversight since the day we'd hauled a single human heart from one side of Philadelphia to the other.

White Hair finally gave the okay, and we stepped off the trailer onto the dock, waiting beside the forklift driver as the light flashed telling Gator to pull forward.

I took the stairs down to the ground but White Hair jumped. Together we closed and latched the trailer doors, me watching as he installed the security seals, him double-checking the numbers with the paperwork.

I looked past him into the warehouse. The place seemed too clean, too organized. It felt like my father's closet, arranged the way his daddy the major had taught him.

I reached for my phone to text Gator my impressions when White Hair said, "I wouldn't try that if I were you."

"What do you mean?" I said, going for the super innocent little girl voice and coming out with a guilty squeaky one. Sweat from under my arms trickled down my sides.

He grinned, showing his teeth, adolescent bright. "No service around here," he said. "We call it the black hole."

Before I could ask him to clarify, he motioned for me to stand in front of his locked handiwork, and snapped a photograph with an impossibly small camera.

"Hey!" I called to the forklift driver watching us. "You got the same problem?" I held up my phone and shook it.

He glanced at a spot over my left shoulder when he said, "It's a black hole all right." His face was pale and haggard, like a cancerous coal miner freshly washed. He might have said something else, but was cut off by a loud alarm chirping from the interior of the warehouse. Bright red lights flashed over the bay door as it began to lower. The forklift guy turned and zipped away as White Hair pushed the clipboard of papers at me, then vaulted himself onto the dock rolling under the dropping bay door, like he was Indiana Jones or something.

I stood there for a second thinking it was all too surreal, until Gator blew the air horn. I jogged around to the passenger side, climbed up, about to ask him *what the hell*...when I saw the heavy artillery coming in.

"What did you do back there?" he asked.

"Nothing."

"Jojo!"

"I swear, I didn't do anything. Jesus, Are they fucking serious?"

Six black trucks raced toward the warehouse.

I poked at Gator. "Come on, time to switch seats."

"I'm fine to keep driving."

"Maybe so, but there are rules for a reason."

He was near enough to his maximum hours behind the wheel that we wouldn't make the delivery without having to stop and make a driver switch and stopping was one thing we weren't allowed to do with this load. Some truckers could trade seats while running. I wasn't sure we were there yet.

I flapped my hands in a hurry up sign, as the first of the black cars pulled up. Gator grumbled, but he got up. I slipped into the seat and put the truck in gear. As we drove away from the warehouse, I buckled up, clicked on the GPS, checked the side mirrors. None of the other trucks had moved from the warehouse. Whatever was going on, it wasn't about us.

"Your fancy technology appears to be taking a while, isn't it?" Gator said, motioning to the navigation system I had bragged about across two states and back.

"It's never done that before," I said, as the monitor went black then flashed the message: *unable to connect, searching for satellites.*

"Wouldn't think that'd be a problem, with all those," Gator said tipping his chin toward a grove of trees on his side of the road. Beyond the trees, loomed a line of house-sized satellite dishes.

"How did we miss that?" I asked.

"More importantly, how is your NAV system missing it?"

"Good question."

I slowed as we approached the guard shack. The entrance side was shut down and the guard seemed eager to pass me through. That was enough to make me roll down my window and initiate some small talk.

"Lots of noise back there at Warehouse Five," I said, using the right amount of wink, head angle and boobage. "What's the alarm for?"

The guard steeled his jaw. "Appears we have a faulty sensor in the temperature controlled storage, Sector 65B. Protocol is to close down all the bay doors and enter system lockdown mode. Nothing for you to be concerned about." He attempted a smile. It looked like he'd just shit himself.

He glanced at the trailer. "Did you get your load?"

"Yeah. We're good."

The guard nodded, tapped his earpiece, then spoke into his wrist and the gate opened.

Gator leaned over and yelled, "Git 'er done!" as I hit the go pedal.

It would probably be hours before things returned to normal at Pharmco. Thinking like a trucker on a schedule, I felt the agony of someone else's fuck-up.

Gator looked at me with something like concern as I wriggled in the seat, trying to find a cool spot on the leather, trying to not think about the ass that had warmed it. He said, "You okay?"

"Yeah, sure. But something was odd back there. They were like robots. No small talk, no joking. The guys didn't even make a pass at me."

Gator scoffed. "Well that settles it, there's definitely something going on back there. Either that, or they've gone blind."

I smiled. The man sure had a way with sweet talk.

"Did you get anything on the trailer cam?" I asked.

"Got it all. Nice install."

"Cool. You know, when I was back there, I was going to text you. Not that I could have. Guy said there's no service. Called it a black hole," I said, patting my pockets and finding my phone. "Course, you don't need service to use the camera."

I checked the empty access road ahead, then braced the phone on top of the steering wheel and scanned through the pictures I'd taken. "Sweet baby Jesus!"

"Amen, sister," Gator chimed in, raising a hand to heaven and bobbing his head.

I tried not to laugh. "No, I'm serious. Remember the skinny guy on the Pharmco restroom video? Well, here he is again, in the warehouse, behind the forklift." I angled the phone to Gator, jabbed at the picture with my thumb.

He took the phone from me and zoomed in on the picture.

"We should be able to get an ID on him. What do you think?" He held up the phone's image—a ferret-faced guy with thin lips and a knit brow.

I scoffed. "He's not going to win any beauty contests, that's for sure." I said.

Gator scanned through the camera roll on my phone. "So you do this a lot?" he asked.

I almost snapped my neck, wondering what picture he was

looking at, until I remembered it was my replacement phone—with hardly any photos—not the one that had chronicled my last two years with Boone. There were some things I was not prepared to share, yet.

"Yeah, I like to take pictures on the road. Got a bunch on my old phone. Mostly personal stuff."

"I'd like to see them," he said, placing the phone in the holder on the dash.

"Why?" I asked.

"You may have missed something."

"Like what?"

"Won't know until I see the pictures," he said. "Where are they?"

I raised a brow, and a single digit.

Gator shrugged. "I'm just saying, sometimes four eyes are better than two. When's the last time you looked at them?"

"Before the accident. My old phone got jacked up. I don't think it even works."

"But, you're not sure."

I shook my head.

Gator asked, "Where is it?"

"In the safest place on earth," I said.

"Which is?"

"My underwear drawer."

Gator grinned. I could almost read his thoughts. They weren't pretty. He glanced over his shoulder at the small sleeping quarters.

"Uh-uh. Don't go there. Besides, the underwear drawer in question is back at the plantation."

Before he could ask again, I said, "I can see if Ivory Joe can help. How's that?"

Gator scrunched up his face, weighing the options. I wasn't sure which part bothered him more, asking for help or Ivory Joe pawing through my panties.

He said, "Let's hold off on that. In the meantime, what do we have?"

He ticked down his fingers as he spoke. "One. The driver called The Baconator goes missing, is later found dead by the truck stop where his loaded trailer was left untouched. Two. You and Boone are called in to deliver his load. There's an encounter of sorts with a truck stop worker and a whistling guy. Three. The odd drop at Pharmco with their military-esque setup, another encounter with a whistler—"

"They've got to be the same guy, right?"

Gator hesitated. "Maybe." He started again. "Four. Whistler and a skinny guy are captured on the Pharmco restroom video."

"Seemingly very interested in Boone and a strange SD card."

"Right. Five. Boone, possibly, ends up with said SD card."

Gator started on his other hand, curling his thumb over as he said, "Six. Your next assignment is given to you as a favor by DST dispatcher. A drop that you said yourself was quick, easy money—"

"Except we had to run the most dangerous highway in Texas—and haul The Baconator's shitty ass trailer."

"Seven. A dark Hummer, a white van and an orange semi—none of which have been identified—are the only vehicles near you prior to your accident—"

"Which they fucking caused!"

He nodded and continued. "Eight. Boone's pockets are turned inside out by the large man we think is called Highwayman driving the Hummer, a guy who might also be the whistler. Nine. Your father's house is ransacked, jacket missing and now, ten, the same restroom video skinny guy is caught on film inside a Pharmco warehouse, seconds before an alarm sounds and security comes barreling in." Gator shakes his head and drops his fisted hands into his lap

"Wait a minute." I grabbed my phone, clicked on the photo of the warehouse interior and hit the auto enhance button. The shadows lightened around the skinny guy and the shape of a white van materialized behind the forklift. I smiled. "I think you're going to need more fingers there, detective."

Chapter 7

Gator had given me a lot to think about, and I hoped he was mulling over the whole deal too. Maybe his tough thinking only looked like sleeping. Maybe to truly get to the bones of the matter it was necessary for him to snore lightly and drool. I don't know. I'm not a PI. I'm just a little old trucker girl.

About fifteen miles later, as I aimed Sabrina's hood into the bright South Texas sun, heading toward the gulf, Gator yawned then said, "I've been thinking."

"Is that what that was? I thought I smelled something burning." I looked over, half expecting to see Boone grinning back at me, one fake punch ready to land gently on my shoulder. Instead, there was a Jersey cowboy yawning, stretching and probably holding back a fart.

Gator reached for the water bottle in the cup holder, took a long drink then wiped his mouth with the back of his hand and asked, "What was he doing with that ball, anyway?"

"What ball? And who?"

"At Pharmco. The white-haired guy who handled the load. It looked like one of those automated toys they sell at the mall at Christmas—those bobbling, rolling fur balls with a tail, only this wasn't furry. Guy rolled it under the trailer and truck, back to front, then picked it up and stuck it in his pocket."

"I was with White Hair almost the whole time. I didn't see any ball."

"Huh." Gator finished off the bottle of water, burped into his hand. "Maybe it wasn't a ball. Can I use your phone?"

He made the call at the dinette. My eavesdropping skills were awesome, but the noise of the road and engine were a bit distracting. I had yet to master the over-the-shoulder-while-driving-a semi-lip-reading skill. It was the one thing that kept me from being perfect.

A few minutes later, Gator returned to the cab. "Looks like we might have been *lo-jacked.*"

"Lo-jacked?"

"Not the technical term, but the easiest way to say that basically Mr. White Hair is now able to track us by piggy-backing on your GPS system."

"And why would he want to do that?"

Gator reached over and clicked on the camera in the trailer. Even in the low light, I could clearly make out the two square packages we'd just picked up.

"I don't know," Gator said. "But our answer might be inside those thermo units." He looked at me and grinned.

I snorted. "What? The very same thermo units secured in a divided section of a locked and sealed trailer going fifty-eight miles per hour down a crowded highway at noon, pulled by a driver who's not supposed to stop for another hundred and fifty miles or so. Those units?"

"Yep."

I shook my head. "Try again."

Gator got out of his seat and stretched. I tried to not look as his shirt raised revealing a tanned, flat abdomen and just a hint of white skin at the waistband of his jeans. I wasn't very successful.

"I can't think sitting down," he said, heading into the sleeper.

"Why? Are you squashing your brains?" I called out but he didn't answer.

It takes some people a while to get my jokes. I turned on the radio and found an alternative music channel. First time I'd tuned it in with Boone in the rig, he'd said that with a name like that, he thought we should be hearing anything *other* than music. What did you expect, I'd asked him, a channel of silence?

Back in the living space, Gator paced and mumbled to himself as I changed lanes and double-checked the directions to the drop. We were headed to the port at Corpus Christi. It was a straight shot, and with the current traffic we'd arrive in a little over three hours. If we were going to do anything, we had to decide what and soon.

My phone rang and Gator spun around, hurrying to the front.

"Easy, pal. It's just Charlene." I clicked on the speakerphone and said, "Hey, there. Shouldn't you be sleeping? Don't tell me they have you working a double."

"Oh you know, always on the clock. I was just thinking about you, Jojo, and thought I'd call. I'm not interrupting anything am I?"

"Not at all. What's there to interrupt?"

There was a pause on her end, long enough for me to check and see if the call had been dropped.

Her voice was higher than normal when she asked, "You get out of San Marcos okay? No, um...traffic or anything?"

"No more traffic than usual, Char."

"Yeah, you Louisiana people, not used to the Texas way. Anyhow, have a good run to Austin."

What was she talking about? "Austin? We're on the way to the docks, at Corpus Christi, remember?"

On her end, a doorbell rang too loud, as if a special effects button had been pushed.

Charlene said in a rush, "Sorry, hon. I gotta go, there's someone at the door. Bye."

I clicked off the speakerphone and shrugged. "That was weird."

"What's that?" Gator asked.

"That was just *so* not Charlene. She doesn't forget and she doesn't do small talk."

"That wasn't even good small talk. You'd think a woman whose job it was to chat for a living would be better at it."

I shook my head. "Dispatchers don't just talk. Without a good dispatcher, half of these truckers would be lost, or broken down, or out of work."

Gator scanned the interior of Sabrina. "Really? With all this fancy equipment, you hardly need them."

"You're looking at the rig of a *particular* owner-operator. Most company drivers won't put any of their own money into a truck they don't own."

"What about Dorsey, The Baconator?"

"Hell, no. He was old school, and a hot seat driver on top of that. Bet the guy still used his CB for traffic conditions. When Boone had to move it so we could take the trailer, he said the truck was a mess inside, he'd even taken out the guy's trash, remember?"

"Yeah. The fast food bag with the SD card. Wait. Hot seat? You mean he shared his rig?"

I nodded.

"So, a guy like that, driving alone? The only person who'd know his destination besides his dispatcher would be—"

"The hot seat driver."

We looked at each other.

I shrugged. "Or his woman. The shit-beating one."

"What if his woman *is* the hot seat driver?" Gator asked.

I smelled the burning nose hairs leading to Gator's working brain. Before I could ask if he had hamsters or squirrels running the wheel between his ears, the guy threw me a curve ball.

"I'm going to see what's in those thermo units."

Gator had a plan. It sucked, but I liked that he had taken the time to think it through—at least a little. Though to me, climbing onto a hot metal trailer zipping down a busy high-way and squeezing yourself through a hole in the roof wasn't exactly a brilliant idea.

When we were simply *what-iffing* the situation, I'd told him about the soft spot on the front edge of the trailer roof. It had been a rookie mistake on my part, driving under that low bridge and assuming we'd fit. Apparently assumptions only go so far in the trucking world. The repair of the rolled back aluminum had cost Boone and me a week's pay and a day off the road, but the load hadn't been damaged in the least, and if you didn't walk around on the roof, you'd never notice.

Gator thought he'd be able to pop the rivets and slip himself under the aluminum, then drop inside onto the pallets. He had answers for all my objections, and when he said, "I'll fix it later. For now, don't worry. I can make it look like nothing happened." He held up a swatch of cardboard, some craft paint he'd found in the junk drawer and a roll of clear shipping tape.

"You're kidding, right?" I asked.

"Nope. I'm a man of many talents."

I snorted. "Oh, yes. You can craft. How lucky am I?"

He must not have heard me, because he went back to the dinette and sat down with a paper napkin paintbrush and his cardboard.

I scrolled forward on the digital map and saw what we needed, an incline in the road that meant I could drop my speed without it being obvious. Gator had the idea of a secondary distraction—loud music and skin. He said that if people's attention were drawn to the driver, they'd be less likely to be scanning the roof of the trailer she was pulling.

I'd been happy to oblige his plan, undoing a few buttons on my shirt to reveal the hot pink bra underneath.

"Think this will this work?" I asked.

He went into full redneck mode, combining an exaggerated accent with a series of immature gestures and appreciative sounds. "Hooo, Daddy! Call the fire department. Someone is smokin' hot in here! I said *smokin'*!"

I knew he was playing, trying to make light a very heavy moment. But I also saw underneath the teasing, a sincere appreciation for the finer things in life: boobs and easy women.

Not that I was easy. Hell, no.

I shooed Gator away and went back to driving. I checked the road, the traffic ahead and the weather on the NAV system. There was no rain in sight for days, no reported accidents—yet—and the roads had cleared to relatively light traffic. This crazy idea just might work. But damned if I'd tell Gator that.

A few minutes later, I heard the hair dryer running and glanced over my shoulder to see Gator drying his fake ceiling patch. I had to admit from here, squinting my eyes, it looked pretty good.

"Hope you don't mind that I used your computer. I needed a better look at the interior of the trailer," he said.

"Not a problem. Wait, how did you get in? I have a password."

"No, you don't." He laughed. "A real password is a combination of letters and numbers that are difficult to figure out. *Password* is not a password."

"But it's easy to remember," I mumbled, then added, louder, "Hey, you have six minutes until we hit the incline. You'd better get ready, and make sure your headset's on."

"Got it."

I clicked mine on too and dialed Gator's number. In a few seconds I was greeted with the sound of heavy breathing accompanied by the clanking of metal as he went through the toolbox.

"This should work," he said, holding up a small cordless drill, metal punch and mini crowbar-hammer combo. He threw them with the cardboard artwork into a knapsack that he hung over his neck. He did a few deep knee bends at the counter, then windmilled his arms and did some neck rolls.

"Two minutes," I said, moving into the right hand lane.

He nodded, pulled on a pair of gloves. Standing at the back door of the trailer, one hand on the knob, wind whistling on the other side, I don't think Gator knew that I could hear the quiet prayer he offered up to a very busy God. I echoed his words as he opened the door and stepped outside.

The transmission whined before Sabrina's gears fully engaged and we began to climb the hill. I unbuttoned my shirt some more and let equal parts of flesh and pink bra show, cranked up the country station, lowered my window and hung my arm out.

The headset crackled as Gator said over the traffic noise, "I'm going up."

"Roger that."

I looked behind me and saw his ass, then his legs and feet as he pulled himself onto the trailer roof, with the help of a few metal rungs. I closed my eyes for a second telling myself *it's going to be okay.*

I slowed down even more and watched for bumps in the road as I heard the drill start up.

"Shit!" Gator's voice came through the headset.

"What's the matter?" I yelled, thinking cops and black security trucks.

"The drill slipped, scratched my leg."

"That's all? Well, hurry up!"

There was more noise from the drill, then the dull thud of metal against metal, followed by a grunt and curses.

I'd slowed enough to attract the attention of two college boys in a beat-up sedan two lanes over. They crossed the highway and pulled in front of me in a total jackass move. I gave them the finger and was rewarded by a full moon from the passenger side. It wasn't anything to howl about.

I tapped my Bluetooth earpiece. "How you doing back there?"

Gator cursed in my ear. "Fucking thing seemed easier on paper. Must be about a hundred degrees out here."

I checked the thermostat. "Ninety-five, actually, but I bet with the wind—"

"Jojo!"

"What?"

"Shut the fuck up. And I mean that in the nicest way possible."

We were nearing the top of the incline. I could see all the way down the road now, and I saw something I hadn't figured on.

"Um, Gator. You really need to get in that trailer—now."

"Yeah, I'm working on it."

"No, you don't understand. Look behind you."

I imagined him up there on the roof, facing the back of the trailer, prying up a sheet of aluminum, baking in the hot sun, balancing against the cross winds...then slowly craning his neck around to see the low bridge coming up.

"Holy fucking shit."

"You could say that. What do you want me to do?" I took my foot off the accelerator. The warning button on the NAV system flashed, letting me and anyone who was watching know that I had reduced my speed below the run settings.

"Don't slow down!" Gator yelled. "I got this!" He grunted and I heard a thunderous ripple of metal sheeting then silence.

"Gator! Gator! Goddamnit. Where are you?"

I winced as Sabrina rolled under the low bridge with merely inches to spare. I imagined my co-driver hanging off the side of the trailer, dangling like some stunt double for James Bond.

I was straining to see in both of the side view mirrors when I heard, "Aw, were you worried about me?"

I let out the breath I hadn't realized I was holding then said, "Don't flatter yourself. I didn't want to run you over and get blood on my tires."

I reached over and clicked on the trailer cam. In a small shaft of sunlight, Gator, squatting on top of the metal divider, smiled back at me, wiggled his fingers.

As I watched, he slipped into the area I'd cordoned off and dismantled the divider, laying one wall to the side, small flashlight in his mouth, giving him a beamed area to work in.

He pulled a small knife out of his pocket and scoured the thermo units with the light. I could see his torn pant leg where the drill had met fabric.

He cleared his throat, sighing. "I was hoping there would be an easy access point," he said, running his gloved hands over the plastic wrapped exterior.

"Try the back," I said.

He moved around the thermo unit stack. I lost sight of him as he passed under the angle of the camera.

"Talk to me, Gator. I gotta watch the road here."

"Not much to say right now. Unless you want me to talk dirty to you."

I stifled a laugh. I was glad he couldn't see my face turning pink.

"Ah, *Ma petite chou. Vous avez les lèvres d'une reine—*"

"Shut the front door! You speak French?"

Gator chuckled. "Only bedroom talk."

"And how did you—crap—hang on," I said. "Got a grandma in my lane."

I moved to pass the old lady in the puttering Buick, gave her some space, then slid back in to the right hand lane.

Before I could ask Gator to conjugate some verbs for me, he came online asking if I could see him. I looked in the trailer cam monitor. He was taking pictures with his phone.

"Found a weak spot here." He motioned vaguely at the top thermo unit. "Pretty sure I can slip the top off and replace it with being noticeable from the outside."

I saw a glint from his knife before I turned my gaze back to the road.

We had agreed beforehand that this was a twenty-minute shot. He'd have ten minutes inside, giving him enough time to climb out, return the roof to as good condition as possible and be back inside the truck before we hit the weigh station just outside Corpus Christi.

"Whatever you're going to do, you'd better make it fast," I said. "And clean. And don't forget to give yourself time to—"

"Jojo, please."

I sighed into the headset, loud enough to give no doubt how I felt. I was usually the one in the action position. I was used to being in control, used to getting things done—not standing around watching, and hoping. Worse than that, I had to trust someone to do things the right way—my way.

I concentrated on the road and pressed the accelerator.

In the trailer, Gator said nothing. I heard the twang of plastic, scratch of metal on something, a squeal like something was stuck, then a whoosh of air, followed by the clicking of a camera phone shutter and underneath it all, the hot breath of a virile man. A sound that continued to remind me how long it had been since that sort of breath was directly in my ear, and how small this space was that I shared with Gator Natoli, PI

A minute later the man in question reassembled the divider, climbed on top of it and put his face in the camera saying, "Got it. I'm coming back. Is the coast clear?"

"Wait. Got what? What is it? Are we in trouble? Is it bad?"

"I'll tell you all about it in a minute, okay, Jojo? Just let me get the hell out of here."

"All right. All right. Hold onto your panties."

I checked the road. It was even more empty than before, except for me, the grandma, a few minivans and two eighteen wheelers riding side by side about a quarter mile ahead.

"You're good to go. Be careful."

Gator grabbed his knapsack and blew me a kiss, before he pushed the roof back letting in the sun.

I waited until his feet passed the lens, then clicked off the monitor and counted the seconds of wind and traffic sounds coming from his headset.

There was a loud thud as Gator leapt to the walkway outside the back door, then a rush of heat accompanied by the scent of sweat when he opened the door and stepped inside, pausing to look back at the trailer roof and inspect his handiwork.

I let my shoulders drop, reached up and pulled the headset off my ear, breaking the connection.

"Well?" I called over my shoulder. "What's the deal?"

"Oh, you're going to love this," Gator said, tugging off his gloves and turning on the water at the sink to wash his hands.

How the fuck could the guy be so calm? How could he care if his hands were clean?

He turned toward me as he wet a wad of paper towels,

then dabbed at his bloody leg. It was much worse than he'd let on. I gasped, and swiveled my head back to the road.

"Shit."

"It's just a scratch," he said, wincing as he pressed the wound.

"Bullshit. You need to get out of those pants and clean it and dress it."

"So, finally," he said, limping toward me. "You're getting me out of my pants."

"No," I said, feeling him close in. "I mean—"

Gator squeezed in beside my seat and leaned in until his face was next to mine. He held my chin in his hand, his clean, cool hand and said, "Shut the hell up, Jojo, and kiss me."

I did. With one eye on the road the whole time.

Chapter 8

As much as I wanted to pull over at the nearest rest area and return Gator's kiss properly, and as much as I could tell he wanted me to do just that, we had other priorities—more pressing matters at hand, like what exactly was in the mysterious thermo units from Pharmco.

"Maybe I should start with what it isn't," Gator said, retrieving my laptop from the dinette. "It's not ice cream or lobster or computer chips."

"Well shit, I wouldn't think so," I said, checking my mirrors, watching my speed. "It's drugs, some kind of medicine, right? I mean, we did pick up at a pharmaceutical warehouse—and it is being shipped temperature controlled. Wait. You didn't keep it open too long, right?" I asked.

He shook his head, buckling back into the passenger seat, opening the laptop, typing rapidly as he spoke. "No, the package is fine, well within the temperature limits they requested. It's just that—"

"What?"

Gator raised a brow. "How well did you inspect the thermo units?"

I shrugged. "Didn't really get a chance. They lifted them in. I signed the paperwork. Looked fine to me. Why? How bad is it?" I changed lanes, found the most empty one, so I could concentrate on what he was saying.

"Stamped on the side of the units, down at the bottom, it says we're hauling human NPH insulin, which is consistent with the paperwork, but inside those weren't the only vials..." His voice trailed off, as he pecked at the keyboard. "Some of them were marked like this."

He enlarged a page on the screen, turned it toward me, saying, "NewGen."

"NewGen? Never heard of it."

He turned the screen back to him, scanned the page. "Says here it's a miracle drug for cancer patients."

"Well, that's good, right?"

Gator was quiet, reading, then staring out the windshield.

"What?" I said, unconsciously slowing the rig. "Gator, what is it?"

"NewGen was pulled from the market four months ago. The FDA revoked approval due to some risks: kidney failure, something called embryolethality. All production and distribution should have been halted. Disposal requirements were issued by the regulatory authorities—"

"So how does Pharmco still have it? This doesn't make sense. Wouldn't they have had to destroy their stock?"

"According to this, yes," Gator said. "But there's still a demand. Lots of folks swear by the results they got with NewGen, think the FDA was wrong, jumped to conclusions. There's a guy in Michigan who claims the only reason he's alive is because of NewGen. He's started a petition to get it reinstated. Has a pretty good following too."

"Not all drugs work the same for all people," I said, remembering my aunt who everyone had called a hypochondriac, until the day she died. When the insurance company insisted on an autopsy, and the results came back showing her body riddled with cancer, the doctors had not been soft in telling the family how much the woman must have suffered. For years.

"That can work in the favor of these crooks," Gator said. "Who's to know what's really in that syringe or that pill? Do you think they test everything? Listen to this."

He read from the screen. "One vial of NewGen costs a patient seventy-six hundred dollars, with most common treatment schedule requiring ten vials per person."

"Seventy-six grand? That's more than most people make in a year."

"Well, there is insurance," he said, earning him an eye roll. He knew exactly how I felt about healthcare plans.

"Anyway," he continued, "the odd thing is, according to this guy, the drug isn't that expensive or difficult to make. The main cost is in advertising and marketing, and there is, of course additional markup tacked on by doctors and hospitals, like with all these drugs. In some cases it could be one hundred to six hundred percent."

"That's a nice margin."

"Sure is, but when you're talking the difference between life and death?"

"Yeah, what's six hundred percent? Assholes."

Gator pulled up more pages, spent the next few minutes educating me on the finer points of pharmaceutical drug theft. From kids in India replicating a popular prescription cough syrup and mocking up labels at the Kinkos, or whatever they had in India, then turning that shit loose in America, to a group in Miami that busted through a pharmaceutical distributor's warehouse roof, dropped in on ropes, sledgehammered the alarm panel and made off with millions of dollars of chemotherapy drugs. Two guys in a pickup.

They stored the drugs in shoeboxes in a closet in their apartment, then sold them to the highest bidder on the wholesale market. By the time they were administered to patients at five grand a pop, they were as worthless as the shoebox they'd been stored it.

The fake drug scene was a ninety billion dollar business. Definitely worth some jail time.

"These other guys," Gator said, "They at least knew how to store their product. But they made fake labels, changed the strength on some, sold saline as a cancer drug called Atibane. Over three hundred vials at a cost of four grand per vial to the end user."

"Shit. Where are people getting this money?"

"Savings? Fundraisers? Mortgage the house? Who knows. You're talking about access to a drug that is your only hope. What would you do to get some?"

He was right. Where there was a need, supply followed. I glanced at him, head bowed, brow furrowed, lips pursed as he scrolled though thefts and trickery, scams of modern hustlers. I knew what he was thinking. We thought the same way. People are mostly good until they aren't. The pieces were coming together, missing truckers, greed, hijacked loads, counterfeit drugs. All the nasty floating to the surface. It took everything in me to fight the urge to pull over, drop the trailer and run.

"Do you think the vials of insulin back there are going to be re-labeled and sold as NewGen?" I asked, sorting the puzzle pieces in my head.

"That's my guess," Gator said. "There's certainly enough sales to be made. According to these stats, over one-point-six-million people will be diagnosed this year. Those are just new cancer cases, that doesn't count the existing cases. Did you know one in four deaths in America is from cancer?" He cursed under his breath, a long string of seriously bad words in a very creative combination.

"How is that even possible?" I asked, partly curious about his string of words, but mostly wondering if we were simply smarter now and better able to correctly diagnose cancer, or if we were slowly killing off our population, one mutated cell at a time.

"Bad shit's always possible. It's the good shit we rarely see."

"Nice one, Einstein."

Gator mock bowed, looking so cute that for a second or two I forgot about a whole bunch of bad shit. I let myself think about the potentially good stuff that was right here in my cab. Until I remembered what was in the trailer, and the kind of people that needed it verses the people who we were handing it over to, then I kind of wanted to find a bathroom—fast.

I knew we were close to the water, the way clouds dispersed, how things started to feel open and empty, the salt in the air. I cracked the window and tried to imagine a view of sandy beaches and palm trees instead of asphalt and dead dried up snakes.

As we passed the sign for the Port of Corpus Christi, Gator closed the computer, rapping his fingers on the lid. "Hey, you okay?"

I nodded, gave him a half smile. "Yeah. I was just thinking about the thermo units. You sure they won't know we, uh, tampered with them?"

"I think we're okay," he said, reaching for his phone and clicking on the pictures he'd taken in the trailer, enlarging them, then looking at me. "We might want a back-up plan."

I pushed a little harder on the accelerator. I wanted to get rid of this load as fast as possible.

The gate guard directed us to Port Terminal Two, said he'd call ahead so they knew we were coming. We drove past signs for public storage and gaming ships, for cold storage, and a road that led to the old naval station, Ingleside. Gator was still messing with his phone and the laptop.

"You all right there?" I asked.

"Yeah. I'm trying to pull everything off my phone."

"Good idea." I looked at the computer he had braced on his knees. "Hang on. You're not putting all of that on *my* hard drive, are you?"

"Don't worry. I'm just using it to transfer everything to an encrypted email account. There won't be any traces." He glanced up as I pulled into the terminal area. "Give me two minutes, can you?"

"No problem."

"Oh," he said. "You might want to fix that." He tipped his chin toward my chest.

I looked down to see my shirt was still unbuttoned, with equal amounts of skin and pink fabric dampened by the Texas heat. "Shit. Sorry."

Gator smiled. "Don't be. I'm not."

Five minutes later, we were backed into the loading dock of a long metal warehouse, number seventeen, our electronics stowed, and Plan F in action. The plan in which we would: 1. Distract; 2. Confuse; 3. Cover Gator's tracks where he'd broken into the sealed thermo unit; and 4. Slip away like a fat rainbow trout in the grasp of a small-handed man standing waist deep in a rushing stream.

Gator jumped down to meet the receiver, then walked around back for the paperwork and breaking of the bolt seals. He told me to wait inside until he signaled, then make my entrance. I watched the camera monitor, admiring Gator's ease. He made a pretty believable dumbass. But I knew better.

As the forklift driver backed out of the trailer with the thermo units, Gator wind-milled his arms. Quite the signal. I shut off the monitor, climbed down from the passenger side and yelled over the noise of four idling semis, "Where are you? You piece of shit!"

I ran the length of the trailer, invoking my best banshee shrill, conjuring up the cuss words of my youth and a few I'd recently invented.

Gator must have sold the whole I'm-a-battered-man-thing to the receiving clerk, because the look on the guy's face as I appeared with a plumber's wrench in one hand and a printed copy of a stolen Facebook conversation complete with pornographic pictures in the other, was worth a thousand bucks.

The speed with which the forklift driver assessed the situation and potential for fall-out was priceless. As he backed out of the truck onto the dock to zip away, Gator slid the ramp back, then slammed and latched the rear doors, the whole time calling me baby and telling me I must have misunderstood. I threw the papers at the clerk, then chased Gator up onto the dock and around a bunch of stacked pallets. He dashed in and out, backing us toward the approaching forklift of thermo units.

"Fuck you! You fucking fucker!" I screamed before flinging the wrench in his direction. Gator ducked. The metal tool connected with the plastic wrapped side of the top thermo unit, making a splitting sound like tape pried from plastic. The forklift driver turned his head to yell at us and ran his machine into the edge of the shelving system that stored precariously balanced cardboard boxes labeled "Alleron Allergy Relief."

We'd attracted the attention of a handful of warehouse workers, and now security guards.

Gator stood up and opened his arms. "You know I love you, baby. You're the only one for me. Now and forever, right?" He took two steps forward, flicking his eyes toward the blue uniformed men heading in our direction.

I ran into his arms and kissed him. It might not have been the kiss I'd wanted to give him earlier in the truck. But it was damn close.

The warehouse workers whistled and shouted encouraging words that I was pretty sure Gator didn't need.

I opened one eye long enough to see the guards slow from a jog to a walk.

"All right, you two," the receiving clerk said, approaching and stuffing the porn pages in his pocket. "You better get out of here before you cost me my job."

We hurried back to the truck, checking over our shoulders as the security guards split up. One spoke to the forklift driver inspecting the damage to the thermo unit, while the other talked to the clerk, apparently asking to see our paperwork and signatures.

As we pulled away, we watched the scene unfold in reverse through the side view mirrors. Figures hustled around on the dock. A guard wiped at something on the back of the thermo unit.

Gator looked at me, mouthing the word, *shit,* while rubbing his wounded leg. A few seconds later, there was a good deal of shouting and pointing in our direction.

"Uh oh," Gator said.

"Uh oh, is right," I said, as I sped up to clear the gate.

Two colorful eighteen-wheelers passed us on their way in. They waved and one blew a train whistle that rattled our windows. Following them was a minivan with a banner taped to its side telling everyone about "The Melons for Guatemala" project. Two TV vans and a small parade of vehicles followed that—apparently melon enthusiasts.

A deep blue Charger came up fast on our tail, the light-bar on its roof circulating in that pulsing rhythm hated by criminals everywhere.

I looked at Gator. "What do you want to do?"

"I want to get as far away from here as possible, with as little company as possible. Maybe go to the plantation and find out what's on that phone of yours. What do you want to do?"

"I'd love to order a deep dish cheese pizza with extra cheese, and plop down in front of a cute little rom-com flick. But I have to admit, I'm feeling a bit distracted." I smiled, then tipped my chin in the direction of the speeding sports car in the side view, saying, "You know, Gator, I can't outrun them."

"I don't think we're going to have to," he said, as the Charger pulled off the road onto the shoulder and a few seconds later made a U-turn, kicking up a cloud of dirt.

"Was it something we said?" I wondered out loud as I cut over two lanes and set my sights for Louisiana.

Gator was still staring out the window, tapping his chin and mumbling. I let him work it out while I declined the incoming pickup load requests on the Qualcomm, checked my phone, then called my father back on speakerphone.

Père answered on the first ring. "We home, Shâ. How you be? Everything okay?"

I answered too quickly. "Yes. Fine. It's all good. How was Brazil?"

"Uh-huh. Something smells like week-old possum to me. Come on, tell me what's going on. You don't call in a houseful of hunters offering a free-for-all-hog hunt if everything is fine. Especially not the Fisher Boys. No, you don't. I sent them away, you know. Bad enough to come home from vacation to all this new furniture. What you do that for, Shâ?"

"Wait. They're gone? Shit. Listen, we're on our way. I'll explain everything when I see you. Right now I need you to—who's that?" I heard a man's voice in the background.

"It's just Ivory Joe. He came by for supper. Oh yeah. I met

a guy in town, today, says you have a common friend. Nice guy. Even though he's from Texas."

"Texas?" I looked at Gator.

Père's voice filled the cabin. "Yeah. He be driving one of those big Hummers."

Shit!

I clicked the phone back to my headset.

"Père, please. I need you to do one thing for me, okay? Don't let anyone in. I don't care who they say they are. Now let me talk to Ivory Joe."

There was a rustling sound as the phone switched hands. "Hey, Jojo. You okay?"

Why was everyone asking me that? It was beginning to piss me off.

"We're coming to the plantation," I said.

"We?" Ivory Joe asked.

"Yeah," I said, lowering my voice. "Me and Gator."

There was an uncomfortable silence that I refused to break.

"Don't know why I'm surprised," he said. "You never were one to—"

"To what?"

"Never mind. Listen, you want to tell me what's going on? Maybe I can help."

"It's okay," I said, "I don't want you to get involved."

"That's real kind of you, Jojo Boudreaux," he said.

"I didn't mean it like that, Ivory Joe. I know you enough to worry about. I just—"

"You just what—shit. Forget it. You are just *you*, Jojo."

We batted around the *I'm sorry* ball until the cover about split open, then eventually murmured something and were back in each other's good graces as if nothing had ever happened. Like we were still in grade school sharing PBJs because Ivory Joe's mama had been too hungover to make his lunch again. And me thinking all along how did you get the cancer Ivory Joe. You were the better man. You've always been the better man. It should have been me.

"Please take Manny and Pilar somewhere safe, okay? I'll explain when I get there."

I hit the end call button, looked at Gator. "Why would he come to Bunkie now? They've known about me from the beginning."

"But you weren't a threat then."

I snorted. "And I am now? How?"

He said, "You're back on the road. You're hauling for Pharmco. Maybe they think you know more than you do. Maybe they still need something."

"But they got the SD card when they took Boone's jacket."

"Did they? We still don't know that for sure."

"So why didn't they do something at Pharmco, or back there at the dock?" I asked. "And that lame chase attempt? Why did they stop?"

Gator shook his head, then whispered, "Of course."

He pointed to the navigation system. "There's no need to follow someone when you know exactly where they're going."

I reached out to turn it off, but he grabbed my hand. "Too late. Besides, that may come in handy later."

Chapter 9

I sped down the road, pushing Sabrina to her max, wishing the whole time I was racing to Bunkie in the Mustang.

Gator must have read my mind when he said, "All those fast cars in my garage and we're stuck in *this*?"

I threw him one of my best dagger looks then leaned over the wheel and pushed a little harder on the gas. Bunkie was less than thirty miles away.

I had to slow down over the dirt roads, under the overhanging trees. I wished we'd had time to drop the trailer along the way, but I had a lot of wishes and the list kept getting longer and longer.

The plantation house was dark. Not even a porch light.

"I thought they were expecting us," Gator said.

"I told Ivory Joe to take them somewhere safe, didn't I?" I said, shutting down the rig.

Gator had loaded us up as I drove. We came out of the truck with flashlights and guns, packing phones and wearing Bluetooth headsets. I felt like a modern warrior.

The night was quiet and with the help of the moonlight, it took less than a minute to determine we were alone.

I looked around for Gator, found him squatting in the mud, looking feral. I imagined him clad in nothing but a loincloth, making fire with twigs and flint. The recent rain had softened the ground enough so even the son of an oil baron could read the tire marks and footprints. He ran his hand over the deep gouges then held up two fingers, which either meant *two vehicles* or *peace, man.*

I shook my head and headed toward the house. "C'mon, kemosabe."

The door was unlocked, the house undisturbed. We went in, guns first. I noticed he'd switched from his Glock, but my Kimber Custom Crimson Carry II outclassed his Colt Python .357. I made sure to wave it around a bit and show off. Gator twirled a finger, which either meant whoop-de-doo or please spin in circles and make a cyclone, Superhero Storm. I took it to mean the first option, and motioned back for him to fuck off, but first, please check the left side of the house while I took the right.

We met back in my bedroom, where I'd put away the gun to paw through my underwear drawer. He stood in the doorway wiggling his brows like a lewd Groucho Marx.

"Down, boy. There's nothing here you haven't seen before," I said, pushing aside black lace-edged boyshorts, and pulling out what we'd come for—my old phone, scratched and cracked and dead. But hopefully, there was a working memory card of old photographs.

I dangled the phone in one hand and a red thong with a half-bitten apple embroidered on the small triangle of fabric in the other. Gator's eyes bounced back and forth like a Wimbledon spectator.

He swiped his right hand at the phone and snagged the panties in his left, capturing me in the middle. He pulled me close and brought his face right up to mine, our lips almost touching, drew back then closed in again, whispering, "The things I want to do to you."

I angled my head, tilted my chin, readying myself for a kiss that never came.

When I opened my eyes, Gator was backing away, opening a compartment on the side of the phone. A bit of red string peeked from his front pocket.

"Hello?" I said, popping a hip, striking a pose.

"You got your phone on you?" He asked, not looking up.

I cleared my throat, almost flipped my hair. Still no reaction from Gator. I held out the phone, sighed and flopped on the bed.

There was a bit of a tug of war with the phone, which in all other circumstances would have ended up in a naked wrestling match, perhaps with pudding, but this time, it was just me, giving up.

I could appreciate his playing hard to get, even the amping up of anticipation, but seriously? Enough was enough.

I was about to tell him exactly how I felt when he gave an excited little yip, then ran out of the room.

I yelled after him, "What? What is it?" When he didn't answer, I chased him to the truck.

The guy could move fast for someone so muscular. I was almost out of breath when I burst through Sabrina's backdoor.

Gator sat at the dinette table, my phone attached to the laptop. Photos were loading and filling the screen—a tilted sky, Boone giving his cheesiest grin, a cat sleeping on a pallet of dog food, the ass crack of an obese man at a urinal, a T-shirt with a pole dancing stripper that said "Support Single Mothers," a forklift driven off a ramp dangling from the edge, a busted-up fence and a tangle of rusty barbed wire, a white van inside a warehouse, a skinny guy in a ball cap—

"There. Stop!" I pointed to the last few images loading. "That was the grocery drop Boone and I had before our blown tire in Sulfur. We thought we'd been porched when no one showed up. Finally some guy in a beat-up pickup truck let us in."

I remembered the disagreement Boone and I had about directions and delivery time.

* * *

When Boone was driving, I took my navigator role seriously. Tired of all the negative comments about women and map reading, I'd taken a course in orienteering. Getting from point A to point B on a clear road in daylight was usually simple—if the address the dispatcher had given us was right. And that was a big *if.*

"Take the next left and it should be on the right," I said.

We drove through an industrial area, pulled up to a chain link fence with a padlocked rolling entry gate.

I could see the warehouse across the empty parking lot, a typical non-descript gray building.

"Did they know we were delayed?" Boone asked.

"Yep. Charlene told them we'd be here at eight o'clock."

Boone looked out his window. "Well it's five minutes before eight and nobody's here."

"I'm on it," I said, cell phone to my ear. After a few rings, I put the call on speakerphone. It kept ringing.

"I guess we wait," Boone said.

I watched the vein throb on his temple as I hung up the phone and slipped it into my jacket pocket.

He said, "You're sure this is the right address? Remember last time, they said road and it was avenue?

"Look around, Boone."

"Don't get pissy, Jojo. I'm just sayin'—"

"And *I'm* just saying. This is the place. Trust me."

Ten minutes later a yellow pickup came speeding down the road, stopping short at the fence, brakes squealing.

A lanky guy wearing a hooded jacket tugged over a ball cap got out of the truck, worked the lock on the gate then rolled it open. He drove in, motioning for us to follow.

"See?" I said.

"You couldn't resist, could you?"

Boone knew I loved being right. Loved even more throwing it back. It was the one thing that kept me from being perfect.

I was about to bring up another recent moment in which I had also been correct, but was distracted by the twanging country music coming from the warehouse.

"Do you hear that?" I asked.

"Sounds like someone's doing a little boot-scootin'," Boone said.

"Boot-scootin'?" I laughed. "Did you really just say boot-scootin'?"

"It's a good word. Fun to say. Try it again."

And I would have, if the pickup driver hadn't started waving at us to back up to the loading bay. Boone made a nice, wide turn and began positioning the semi.

On the end of the building, bumping up to the woods, the music wasn't as loud, but I still had the idea that when the dock door rose I'd see a barn dance going on.

I watched in the side view mirror as Mr. Pickup entered a door near the docking bay. A few seconds late, the wide dock door began to rise. I had a bad feeling—one of those moments when your Spidy-senses are tingling. I was tired, maybe a bit off my game—with the tire blowout and all, but still, something wasn't right. I looked back to where we'd pulled through the chain link fence. Nothing. Nobody. That was unusual for a Thursday. Unusual for any day.

"Hey, Boone?"

"Yeah?"

"What are we unloading here?"

"That pallet we picked up in Houston."

"What is it?"

"I don't know. You signed the invoice."

I picked up the clipboard, scanned the paperwork. It just says 'Grocery.' Does this look like a grocery to you?"

"Maybe it's the temporary grocery warehouse," Boone said, inching back until the green light turned red. "Maybe they're separating the shipment here. Maybe I don't care, because we're doing what we get paid to do, Jojo. Let it be." The brakes hissed as Boone parked the rig. He waved to Mr. Pickup then unbuckled himself and reached for the clipboard.

"Stay here," he said climbing down. "I got this."

"Boone—"

Before the door slammed shut, he pointed a finger in my direction and shook his head then grabbed the pair of gloves he kept tucked under the seat. I hated how he did that dog trainer thing with me, hated worse that it almost worked. I stayed in my seat for five seconds, then moved over to his, to take advantage of the extra mirror he had attached to the side view. Boone handed the clipboard to Mr. Pickup, showed him where to sign. I felt the shudder as heavy metal doors opened and flattened out against the side of the trailer. I rolled down the window to try to hear them over the sound of the idling engine, then remembered the trailer camera.

The six-inch monitor's picture was black and white, and surprisingly sharp for as dark as it was back there. I zoomed in as much as I could and focused on Mr. Pickup. I may not be the best judge of character, trying to see good things in bad people, but I could tell a great deal about someone from their body language, and Mr. Pickup was either a nervous liar or a tweaking addict. The guy had more twitches than a horse's tail in fly country.

I watched as they unloaded the pallet, laid a ramp to connect dock and trailer, allowing Mr. Pickup to maneuver a small forklift in and out. It was an easy job, had paid us well, and kept us headed in the right direction. So, why did I have a problem with it? I glanced at the monitor again, tried to see past the retreating forklift, past Mr. Pickup into the dark warehouse. All I could see was Boone sliding the ramp back onto the dock then reaching for the trailer door. Before he closed one side, I saw daylight in the warehouse, like someone had opened another door.

I leaned out of the window, pretended like I was trying to get better reception on my cell phone, and snapped a few pictures of the warehouse, dock, and Mr. Pickup. It might be nothing, like Boone said, but hell, it might be *something,* and that was good enough for nosy little me. I heard the clanging shut of metal doors, imagined Boone securing the trailer, then doing a final check for the all clear. When he opened his door a few minutes later and climbed in, I was back in my seat, tapping my feet to the country tune.

He looked at me funny. "What's that about?" he asked.

"Just boot-scootin'," I said.

"What's he doing?" Gator asked, pointing to the photo of the forklift halfway between our trailer and a white van.

"Looks like he's cross-docking." I filled Gator in on the odd "grocery" drop, the blaring music, the feeling that something had been off about the whole thing.

Gator bobbed his head as the last images uploaded: part of someone's leg beside a tire, an open rollup warehouse door, the front of a van in shadows, a pale man's arm and a slice of pavement.

He clicked and imported them all, then opened each in a larger window and scrolled through them slower.

I squeezed in beside him. Before I could tell him how to get to the photo editing software, he was there, tweaking contrast, exposure, definition and sharpness. It was like one of those TV crime shows where in seconds they rebuild a fuzzy image into a real person with identifying birthmarks and a name-tagged shirt with an arrow pointing to the bad guy. Well, sort of, except we were still looking for the arrow and all the name tags.

"Look at that," Gator said, pointing to the white van. "Looks like the one we saw at Pharmco parked behind the skinny guy." He enlarged the photo.

"What's that say on the van?" I asked. "Medical Squadron, CTCR?"

He went back to the photo, brightened the image, zoomed in to the lettering over the windshield. I squinted, leaning in closer, pressing my chest against his arm. He didn't move away, but leaned in equally close, pointing to the "R." I could feel his breath on my shoulder when he said, "I think that's an A."

He pulled up the image from the trailer cam we'd shot at Pharmco. The vans were identical.

"Nice," I said. "CTCA? What does that stand for?"

"Let's see if we can find out." Gator opened a browser window, typed in the letters. The hits came back immediately leading us to a page for Cancer Treatment Centers of America. Gator scrolled through the list clicking on Medical Squadron, Houston, Texas.

"Huh," I said, as the page loaded with photos of hospital beds, transport vehicles, smiling nurses and bald people in wheelchairs hooked to IVs. "That's not groceries."

"Nope," he said going back to the picture.

"Hey, what's that?" I pointed to a yellow tag on the van's dashboard.

Gator zoomed in, tried to clean up the image. He said, "I've seen that before. Hang on." He tapped more keys, clicked a link and we were looking at the same image announcing an exclusive Houston community, full of amenities and protected by a wall and gates.

Gator hmm-ed. I hate when people hmm.

"Curiouser and curiouser," he said.

I slumped back in the banquette, shook my head.

"I don't get it," I said running my hands over my face. "I'm so tired," I moaned. "And hungry." I crossed my arms on the table and laid my head on them. "When was the last time we ate?"

Gator rubbed my back. "When was the last time we slept?"

"God, we're pathetic," I said, laughing.

"Speak for yourself," Gator said. "I'm a professional."

I turned my head and opened one eye. "That's even worse."

We were laughing when a car drove up. Seconds later, the back door of the rig slammed open. Gator pushed me down on the seat, popped up pulling a gun I hadn't even noticed he was carrying.

Pilar must not have been wearing her contacts, because she barely blinked facing down the Colt's barrel. "Hey, now. Manny and Ivory Joe sent me to pick up gumbo for dinner. You're early."

Gator looked out the window at Pilar's small sedan. "What was Ivory Joe driving?'

Pilar paused. "He had his convertible. That cute little Mini."

Gator and I looked at each other. The deep tracks we'd seen could only come from a large, heavy vehicle.

"Pilar? Where are they now?"

"I think they went down to the barn."

I leaped over the banquette and raced out of the truck, around the back of the house to the lit up barn. I rolled open the door, ran inside.

"Père! Ivory Joe!"

Nothing.

Pilar appeared in the doorway, cheeks flushed. "Jojo? Where are they? Is something wrong?" She hugged her arms around her, snugged her jacket closer.

I looked at her fully for the first time. "Pilar? Where did you get that coat?"

"This? I borrowed it from your closet. Do you—"

I grabbed her, patted the pockets of Boone's favorite jean jacket, pulled out a wad of paper towels peeling them open to reveal a small black SD card. As I held it up for Gator to see, my phone vibrated in my back pocket. I grabbed it, glancing at the display. *Private Number.*

"What the fuck?" I slid my thumb, about to decline the call when Gator said, "You'd better take it."

I hesitated then held the phone to my ear. "Yes?"

"Shâ, it's me—"

"Père? Are you okay? Where—"

"I—listen, you have to give him what he wants. He says he'll let me go. No funny business, right, Shâ? Please. For your sake, not mine."

My father never said please. I could hear the pain in his voice. I wanted to kill the man that had him.

"Père, it's going to be okay. Know that. I—"

There was the sound of a scuffle, someone grunted, then a yell and a gunshot.

"Wait!" I shouted. "What do you—"

More gunfire. Père yelled, "Don't shoot!"

A man with a deep voice came on the phone. "You heard him. Give up the SD card and you can have your father back."

I tucked the card in my pocket. "I don't know what you're talking about."

There was a pause before the man said, "I'll be in touch." The phone went dead.

"Fuck that," I said, shaking my head at Gator. "I don't play like that—not by someone else's rules. Hell no."

Pilar burst into tears, fell into Gator's arms.

"I need to find Ivory Joe," I said, punching digits on my phone.

A second later, somewhere in the barn, a snippet of Zydeco music played—Ivory Joe's ringtone.

I followed the sound to the other side of the barn. Ivory Joe's phone lay in the dirt. There were drops and smears of blood on the ground, and a large boot print. I picked up the phone and turned it off.

Ten minutes later, Gator and I managed to wrangle a distraught Pilar into the truck, load her up with sleeping pills and tuck her into the bunk.

Gator was right, we needed to see what was on that card, and we needed to get to Houston, the place all arrows pointed.

"You think he's holding Père in Houston?" I asked.

"That's what I would do," Gator said inserting the SD memory card in a reader device, then plugging the whole thing into my laptop braced on his knees. "Bring you to my turf."

I nodded. "Oh, I'm bringing it all right."

I slid into the driver's seat and started up Sabrina. The shudder and rumble never felt so empowering. I kept her in check down the plantation's dirt road until I felt pavement under the wheels, then let her fly. It never stopped giving me a thrill—that promise of freedom—of space and air and open highway.

Looking out the windshield, it wasn't freedom and open highway as much as it was dark night, single lane, cracked asphalt, tree-lined road, but still, there was a scent of promise.

"Got it!" Gator said, turning the glowing screen toward me.

I glanced at the image. "That's definitely the same boot-scootin' guy from the grocery drop—and the skinny dude from the Pharmco restroom video."

"Well, whoever took this picture wasn't focusing on him," Gator said, circling the warehouse in the background with his finger on the monitor.

"Not unless they were filming for an acne commercial."

Gator smiled. He cropped out the background, lightened the exposure, added some contrast, then he concentrated on the background, zooming in and defining until I was pretty sure that it was the same Pharmco warehouse building we'd been sent to. I half expected old White Hair/pseudo-Indiana Jones guy to scramble across the screen, but all we could see was a nondescript trailer backed up to the loading dock and a few uniformed men moving boxes on a hand cart.

"What else is on there?"

Gator clicked and scrolled and called out what he was seeing, so I could keep my eyes on the road. It might have been a slideshow of criminal intent: a sealed thermo unit photographed from all angles, a black rack of vials with color coded tops, a blank gray prescription pad, medical labels in various languages—one in English for NewGen, three color ink cartridges, a specific brand of printer paper, three photos of oval shaped pills with engraved numbers, front and back, and the blurry trunk of a blue vehicle parked in front of a building with a red sign.

"There's enough here to make someone want it back," Gator said. "But nothing that couldn't be explained away."

"Maybe we're missing something," I said.

"Or, maybe the people who want the card don't know *exactly* what's on it."

"Like *we* do?" I said.

Gator shrugged. "We'll have to use that to our advantage, won't we?" He ejected the card reader, plucked the tiny SD card from its slot and slipped it into his pocket.

I thought about the trucks leaving Pharmco. *Which loads had counterfeit drugs or recalled drugs or the real deal? Where were they going and who were the drugs going to? Who made that choice? And then there was the end all question, who was making money here? Who was losing it?* Maybe that was what the card was showing us.

"Can you enlarge and print that NewGen label?" I asked Gator.

"Sure," he said. "What do you have in mind?"

"Nothing. Yet."

Chapter 10

We were starting to gel as a team. Gator knew when to be quiet and when to let me grumble and drive too fast. I glanced at him, lost in his thinking/resting mode, and had to admire the sharp line of his jaw, the scruff on his chin, the way he flexed his large thighs.

As if he was reading another part of my mind, the clean one that was on track to get my father back, Gator said, "He'll be figuring on us sitting and waiting for his call at the plantation, so we've got the jump on him."

"And you're sure my father's with him?" I asked.

Gator hesitated—just enough that I could tell an alternate possibility had crossed his mind—then he said, "I'm sure."

Before I could insert any more confusion into the situation, Gator pointed at a car on the shoulder ahead. "Hey, what color is Ivory Joe's Mini?"

"Red," I said, as I braked and moved to the outside lane, bearing down on a bright red Mini Cooper parked crooked on the shoulder of the highway. I slowed to a crawl, deciding whether to stop or not. In the headlights, the car didn't appear wrecked, had all its tires, but the driver's window was down and a dark blotch stained the tan steering wheel.

"Shit. Is that—"

Gator grabbed my arm. "Look!"

He pointed ahead to the grassy shoulder where a doubled-over figure rose and began to jog away. I pulled back onto the road and sped up.

Ivory Joe turned as he heard us approach. His nose was a bloody mess, dripping from his chin to his chest, one eye was swelling up bad. He raised a hand, then sunk to the ground.

Gator was already unbuckling and making his way through the sleeper to the back door as I hit the air brakes and pulled off the road.

I left Sabrina idling, climbed down from the driver's seat and ran around the front of the rig, thinking *cancer, cancer, cancer,* how the word itself sounded cruel, how they could have called it something else, something with a softer sound, with a letter on the end that made your voice rise with hope, an upward inflection, instead of the hard *c,* that finality, the *er.*

"Hey," Ivory Joe said all casual like, as if we were meeting for lunch in the neighborhood cafe.

"Hey, yourself," I said, determined to keep it just as casual. I jerked a thumb toward the truck. "How about we get you inside and clean you up?"

He nodded, tried to stand and fell back. Gator caught him under the arms and together we helped Ivory Joe up the back steps and into the sleeper. I glanced at Pilar still knocked out on the bed over the kitchenette.

"Hold him," I told Gator. I grabbed a portable chair from the closet, popped it open and held it steady for Ivory Joe. Gator looked at me, then directed his eyes to the sink.

"I'll just...get some water and towels," I said, backing away, as Ivory Joe adjusted himself in the chair.

"You want to tell me what happened?" Gator asked.

Ivory Joe swung his head. "I don't know."

"You don't know what happened, or you don't know if you want to tell me?"

"No. I mean..." Ivory Joe ran his hand under his nose, loosening a glob of blood. It fell to the floor with a distinct splat.

"What?" Gator said. "What do you mean?"

"Hang on," I said, approaching them with a handful of wet towels and a baggie of ice. "Here, Ivory Joe, lean your head back."

I gave Gator a towel for the mess on the floor, pinched Ivory Joe's nose, put ice on his swollen eye and began to wipe the blood from his face and neck. I'd never seen him so pale, or weak.

"I'm sorry," he said, when I finally released his nose and he could speak.

He held the ice to his face, looked at Gator and said it again. "I'm sorry. He came to the door. I thought it was you. He pushed his way in, held a knife to my throat, told me to get your father out to the barn, no one would get hurt. He had a picture of Shannon on his phone, said he knew where I lived and he'd..."

I crossed my arms and sighed.

"I know," Ivory Joe said, "I know better than that. What the fuck, right?"

"Yeah," Gator said. "What the fuck?"

Ivory Joe pushed himself out of the chair, faced Gator. "What the hell is really going on? What does Shannon have to do with this and why did they take Manny?"

Gator and I looked at each other.

When neither of us said anything, Ivory Joe grabbed my arm. "Listen, I can help. I heard the guy on the phone, he told someone to meet him at some warehouse. I was following his Hummer until I ran out of gas." He shook his head. "That shit never happens in the movies."

I caught Gator's eye. "Now we know your hunch was right."

"Yep. That's something." He checked his watch.

"Be my guest," I said, tipping my chin toward the driver's seat.

We were headed to his place first, he'd know the best way in.

Ivory Joe looked around, seeing the bed for the first time. "Is that Pilar? Is she okay?"

"Yes," I said. "She's resting."

"Probably best," he said.

Something about Ivory Joe's words, or the way he was saying them didn't fit right with me. Why was he being so proper, so quick to apologize? I'd known that boy since we were both in diapers and I could count on one hand the number of times sorry had crossed his lips and still have fingers left over.

I watched him a little closer. "Are you sure you're all right? Maybe you should change," I said. We probably have a clean shirt around here."

He answered quickly, unable to meet my eyes. "No, I'm fine. It's just blood. Trust me, I've been worse."

He leaned against the door to the bathroom, bracing his legs as Gator accelerated onto the highway. As the rumble of road came up through the floor, Pilar stirred on the bed. I stared at Ivory Joe, tried to see what was different.

"What?" he asked, pulling the bag of ice off his eye.

"Nothing," I said, turning away. Before I took two steps, he grabbed my elbow and turned me around.

"Jojo, it's me. You need to tell me what's really going on. Listen, I'm tougher than I look right now. You make it past cancer, survive that? Nothing scares you. Now let me help. Hey, you can trust me."

Could I? I found Ivory Joe's good eye, saw my friend, the boy I'd grown up with. The healthy laughing boy I'd once loved. I wondered if I'd told him more before we left, if he would have been safer, if Père would be home right now. It was time to trust those instincts that made me such a good hunter. Time to let my guard down and let go of the one thing that kept me from being perfect.

I told him everything.

He didn't blame me or correct me, all he said was, "Tell me what you want me to do."

I loved him all over again for that.

Ivory Joe went to sit up front with Gator while I outfitted myself, then filled two bags with things we might need, the old boy scout in me surfacing. I checked the contents, dropped my knife into one bag, and added a bottle of hot sauce for the hell of it. Hey, it was Texas, after all.

It was quiet in Gator's posh neighborhood. The sun had risen and the last of the sprinkler systems were in play. I stared at manicured yards of multi-million dollar homes, telling myself they weren't more special than me, they just had more bills. As my father always said about famous actors and high profile politicians, "They shit on a toilet just like us, Jojo. Ain't nothing special about that." I smiled to think of my father, Manny Boudreaux, the practical billionaire.

Gator pulled Sabrina around and backed her up beside the four-car garage, then hopped out to initiate the security code sequence.

The doors rolled up and from the look in Ivory Joe's eyes you'd think we'd just walked into a high-class strip club offering free lap dances and complimentary T-bone steaks.

He went straight to the Jag as Gator pointed a remote starter at a 1959 Eldorado Seville.

"Uh-uh, pal," he said, running a hand over the hood of the Caddy. "We're taking her. Like most women, she's hiding something *special* underneath that hard exterior." He winked at me. "And besides, we might need the trunk space." He tossed one of the bags I'd packed into the back seat.

I laughed and headed toward the classic Mustang that I'd parked in the fourth bay. "You boys have fun."

"Whoa," Ivory Joe said. "Where you going, Jojo? Hey, is that Manny's car?"

"Fitting isn't it? Saved by his own Mustang. Sounds like an afterschool special." I waved at Gator. "Toss me the keys."

He walked to a metal box built into the workbench and spun the combination lock. "Was she always this bossy?" he asked Ivory Joe.

He grinned. "Nah. I think that came with age."

"What the fuck does that mean?" I said, approaching the workbench. "I'm younger than both of you."

Gator's fingers slowed on the padlock dial. I could almost feel the weight of the old Mustang key dangling from the rabbit's foot keychain.

Gator raised the lid of the lockbox and reached in. I held out my hand.

"Wait a minute," Ivory Joe said, jogging over, clapping a hand on my shoulder.

"What?" I looked at his serious face, the swollen eye.

"You can't come with us."

"Of course I can. And I am." I reached for the rabbit foot keychain, snatching a pinch of fur before Gator dropped it back into the box and spun the lock.

"What the fuck? Come on, Gator."

He shook his head. "He's right. We need someone here for backup."

Ivory Joe added, "Don't forget Pilar. Manny will try to reach her if he can."

For a second I saw myself as the babysitter sipping cocoa, listening to the light snore of my charge while the parents went out on an exciting date.

"Fuck that. I'm here to get my father and you're not going to stop me—"

Ivory Joe's hand tightened on my shoulder. "Jojo, you know I'm right. Besides, Manny would never forgive me if something happened to you."

"Jesus, Ivory Joe, I've saved your ass a thousand times. Do I need to remind you?"

"This is different. We're not kids anymore. You're staying here."

"That's not up to you to decide. I knew what I was getting into from the start."

"Your father wasn't a part of this back then, Jojo," Gator said. "Things have changed. Listen to Ivory Joe."

I pulled myself away from Ivory Joe's grip, brushed off my shoulder and stepped back, arms crossed over a heavily beating heart. I looked from man to man. Steel eyes to steel eyes and back.

Sure, I saw it. I was being selfish, and stupid. I was letting my emotions get in the way. Thinking of the smallest piece, instead of the whole pie. It was the worst way to go into a situation—any situation. I had my reasons for getting involved in this from the beginning. Gator was right. It had nothing to do with my father. It had to do with righting a wrong, solving a murder, stopping crime and bringing justice for people who couldn't fight back. It had to do with understanding why Boone died—and why I didn't. And it also had to do with Ivory Joe needing to prove something—maybe to himself, maybe to me.

"Shit."

I closed my eyes and rolled my head on my shoulders. "Shit. Shit. Shit. Okay, I'll stay."

They started for the door.

"Ivory Joe? Ask Gator for your phone. It's in the bag."

They were planning on driving to the exclusive subdivision where they hoped to find the white van or the Hummer, or Manny. Or all three.

I told them to be careful and keep their headsets on. At least we'd be connected by voice. Before they left Gator put Pilar up in his house. I told him I'd rather wait in the garage. It had all the things I needed and was full of the smells I loved: grease, gas and rubber.

"I'll be fine," I told them, and almost believed it.

I paced the garage, made two full rounds of all four bays before I activated my headset. It was strange to listen in on Gator and Ivory Joe. I felt like an intruder, even though they knew I was on the other end, and my presence was welcome. I heard the deep rumble of the jacked-up Caddy, a hum that might have been interference from a radio, people shifting their weight on leather seats. Someone cracked their knuckles, the engine switched from rumble to purr and then finally, a voice.

Gator said, "We're coming up on the back gate. See that? Same symbol as the sticker on the van."

I imagined them driving through a neighborhood where people were walking dogs or watering lawns, a neighborhood with kids on bicycles, a mailman delivering mail. There'd be nosy women in sweatsuits staring out their window, phoning friends to ask if they'd seen the strange car in the neighborhood. The same woman who'd be interviewed days later only to tell police that she never would have expected Mr. Kind Neighbor was a ruthless kidnapper. He had always been such a quiet man, a good person. He'd even watched her poodle once when they were on vacation.

"What do you see?" I asked.

Ivory Joe answered first. "Suburbia. Upper middle class. A lot of the houses have for sale signs. Pretty quiet around here."

Gator said, "Most people will be at work."

"Try that road," Ivory Joe said.

The boys went quiet as the sound of the Caddy's engine filled the headsets.

"There!" Ivory Joe said.

"Do you see the van?" I asked.

"Better. The Hummer with plantation mud on its tires," Gator said. "I'm driving past and parking at the end of the street."

The engine shut off, car doors opened, clicked shut. In a few seconds, both men sounded like their breath was labored, as if they were running, or carrying something heavy. I wanted to ask what they were doing. I wanted to say I was pissed they hadn't let me come along. I wanted to tell them to hurry up. But I knew the last thing they needed was me bitching.

Ivory Joe said, "We're going silent, Jojo. Acknowledge."

I knew that tone. This wasn't debatable. "Ten-four."

The sudden silence mocked me. I reached up and turned off the headset, expanding the cursing list George Carlin had once made so popular.

I paced the garage. End to end and back again. My mind flipped through images. My father in a rowboat on the river. Pilar dancing. Smiling. Happy. The determined face of Gator as they drove off in the Caddy. Boone, grinning, then walking away from me toward the Pharmco warehouse. I thought about how one choice—Boone picking up that damned SD card—changed my whole life. Or was it more than that. Was every choice I'd ever made the wrong one? Even being here? Being alive? What if I was supposed to be the one who died in the accident? Maybe I was just some big horrible bad luck charm. My life wasn't interesting and exciting, it was me avoiding death, putting others at risk. Like now, with Père, and Ivory Joe and Gator. Jesus, if something happened to them.

I forced myself to take a deep breath, focus on tangibles. Stop fucking thinking. I sat on the workbench and swung my legs, staring at the shiny, clean cars, perfectly aligned tools, shelves of parts. A strip of paint samples was nailed to the bench, greens, yellows, blues. I spun one with my finger and watched the colors swirl, blues of every hue.

Blue. Something clicked. I stared off trying to focus my memory on images from the SD card. There'd been a poorly cropped photo with a building in the background. I remembered the blurry trunk of a car, an odd curve. At the time, the partial sign meant nothing to me: bright red with a sketch of a low-slung chair beside white letters *Mod Sq*—But there was something about the foreground: two shadows against a yellow quarter panel, the edge of a deeply treaded tire—we figured it was the pickup from the grocery drop, but what was the other car? Who did it belong to?

I ripped the paint sample swatch from the nail and held it up, reading the fine print. I knew that retro blue, what year it had come off the line, and what car it belonged to.

I hopped off the bench, tapped the button on the Bluetooth headset: on, off, on, off, as I paced the empty bay, thinking.

I knew I needed more before I went to Gator with this. Right now, it was simply a hunch. I pulled out my phone and opened up the browser window. Google was my best friend. I typed the letters from the partial sign, adding the stuff spelling lessons had taught me—thank you, Mrs. Garbus.

M.O.D space S.Q. I added a *U*.

The potential hit box gave me four choices. The first one was a coffee shop in a mall called Mod Squidoodle. The second one looked like a winner: Mod Squad, modern furnishings warehouse for the discriminating Houstonian. Open five days a week, by appointment only. Shop our warehouse and save.

"Bingo. I got you, motherfucker."

I tapped the directions link, pleased to hear my phone GPS tell me Mod Squad was just seven point five miles from my present location. All I needed was some transportation. I jiggled the combo lock on the metal box I'd seen Gator open, thinking maybe he hadn't spun the tumblers. No such luck. Scanning the wall of tools, a heavy sledgehammer caught my eye.

"Get real, Jojo," I whispered to myself.

Thinking maybe one of Gator's classic cars had a hidden key, I ran to each and checked under the seats, over the dash and inside the tire wells. I may have hesitated just a few seconds longer inside the gorgeous Jaguar, inhaling the scent of Brits and Beef Wellington.

I didn't bother checking the Mustang.

"Shit!"

There had to be something. I looked outside. Sun glinted off Sabrina's chrome. I smiled.

Locking the garage behind me, I ran to the truck, sending up a little prayer to God or Her angels, or whoever out there might be listening. I needed as much help as I could get.

Some people had teams of advisors, large families, a caring husband. But me? All I had was a feeling.

I hoped that was enough.

Chapter 11

Seven miles can seem like forever when you're driving an eighteen-wheeler down narrow suburban streets behind people who have chosen that moment to catch up on phone calls, apply their make-up or teach their teenager how to drive. It occurred to me that one blast of Sabrina's train horn would remedy all of those situations, but I practiced restraint. And bit the inside of my cheek, a lot, while silently or not so silently screaming, *Get the fuck off the road, you dumb ass.*

I finally caught a break as I turned right and the rest of the traffic went left. The GPS on my phone reminded me that I'd arrive at my destination in one mile, and it was on the right. What did I do before navigation systems? Oh yeah, I read maps, real ones on paper, that I had to learn to fold.

My phone flashed once, then rang. I hit speakerphone. "Do you have him?"

"Negative."

My heart sank as Ivory Joe told me how he and Gator had spotted the Hummer in the driveway, broke in the front door and checked the whole house. There was no sign of my father, or anyone else.

"Where's Gator?" I asked.

"He went around the back of the house, said he thought there might be a shed or—"

The booming sound that emanated from the tiny speaker of my phone was loud enough to make me drop it. Bouncing off the center console, it landed on the floor in front of the passenger seat, well out of my reach.

I yelled in the direction of the dropped phone. "What the fuck? What happened? Ivory Joe, hold on. I dropped the phone. Don't hang up!"

There was no shoulder, no place to pull over. I checked my mirrors. Two cars were bearing down on me.

"Goddamnit!" I pressed the accelerator and surged forward, still yelling toward the dropped phone. "I'm in the truck. Can you hear me?"

I saw the red sign for Mod Squad and quickly signaled, practically standing on the brakes.

The store was at the end of a deserted strip mall with a parking lot that appeared to be empty, except for two large blue metal dumpsters and a rusty bike rack. Most of the stores in the low-slung building bore faded signs that told a tale of urban renewal, or more exacting—urban failure.

There was plenty of parking for the rig. I drove to the rear, then pulled around to the side of the building. If anyone was inside, they wouldn't be able to see the truck unless they stood on the sidewalk or leaned out the front door.

I turned off the engine and unbuckled myself, scrambling for the phone.

"Ivory Joe!"

There was no connection. I must have lost him when the phone dropped. I clicked on recent calls, hit the last one, then ran into the kitchenette. I wedged the phone between my shoulder and ear and used both hands to stash my gun in the back of my pants, a spare clip in my pocket.

"C'mon. C'mon c'mon," I whispered, begging the call to go through.

Five rings. Six.

"Jojo?"

His voice sounded weak, and too far away.

"What happened? Where's Gator?"

"There was an explosion...I can't see—"

"What do you mean, an explosion? Are you hurt?"

"I don't know. Shit. I'm stuck." He grunted, as if he was pushing or tugging on something, then moaned. "The house was rigged. Guy must have been waiting for us, the bastard."

"What are you saying? Wait. Put me on video."

"Hold on."

More grunting. A stifled scream and deep breathing. More cursing.

I waited for the live video streaming. There was a brief delay, then Ivory Joe. His lip was split, blood ran from his mouth. There was a black scorch mark in his blond hair. Smoke filtered around him, as ashes fell. The crackling sound of fire was louder now through the speaker. He propped the phone in front of him, hands on his leg. I tried to look around him, hoping to see Gator, wondering why Ivory Joe wasn't moving away from the house or the fire.

He grunted again, tugging on his leg. As his arm dropped to the ground, I saw why. His leg bloody, pants torn, a chunk of wood impaled his thigh staking him to the ground.

I wanted to yell at him for getting hurt, for their stupid plan. Instead I said, "You're going to be okay. We'll fix this."

On the other end of the phone, Ivory Joe moaned. "I fucked up, Jojo. I'm sorry."

My words came out in a rush. "Cops will be there soon, you need to get out of there. You said Gator's okay, right? He wasn't in the house. You said no one was in the house. I'm going to call him, get him to you. Hold up your phone, so I can see the area."

I sent an urgent text to Gator, added his number to the call, then concentrated on the sight in front of me. The house had been reduced to rubble. Broken glass, busted bricks and twisted iron fencing strewn across a green and black yard. It was like the setting for a Tim Burton movie.

Cars were on the street behind Ivory Joe. His breathing was more labored, more dark smoke filtered past. The picture went out of focus.

"Ivory Joe, sit still. Can you turn phone around?"

He reversed the phone and set it on the ground angled against something.

I saw his hands go for the wood in his leg. *Aw, shit.*

A woman ran past, looked toward him and began screaming. Neighbors ran from their houses at the sounds of collapsing walls, sirens, an injured man's wail.

Gator logged on yelling, said he could barely hear, the fucking explosion had been so loud—worse than third row for Metallica. He had Ivory Joe and they were in the Caddy getting the hell out of there.

"We're coming back to the house. Have you gotten a call yet?"

"No," I said, softly.

"What?"

"No!" I looked out the tiny window over the sink, saw a slash of yellow behind the rusty dumpsters, the tail end of an old pickup truck.

I smiled. "Forget the call. I know where they are."

"Where's that?" Gator said.

"About twenty feet from me." I said reaching for the bag I'd packed.

"Jojo, what are you talking about?'

"Don't be mad. I had a hunch and followed it. You would have done the same. Now don't tell me to wait, because I won't."

I spit out the address for Mod Squad, turned off my phone and slipped it in my boot.

I had two options. Come in the front door like a customer, or around the back like a trucker.

Standing at the rear door, finger over the buzzer, I remembered the label copy I'd shoved in my pocket earlier. I took it out, smoothed it flat and held it up in front of the security camera to cover my face, then pressed the buzzer.

The same ugly skinny guy from the grocery drop and the Pharmco bathroom opened the door like he was pissed off. Worked for me. I shoved the paper at him, raising the gun I'd hidden behind it. That seemed to work for him. The boot scootin' hat-wearing, yellow pick-up driving loser slumped quicker than a dog with a case of the garbage can guilties.

I touched my gun to his chin, raised it. His bloodshot eyes ping-ponged right and left then lost focus. I looked closer. His skin was sickly yellow, a sheen of sweat covered his forehead.

"You know who I am?" I asked, shoving the paper back into my pocket.

He hesitated, confusion took over the bloodshot in his eyes, finally he nodded.

"Then you know why I'm here." I backed him up and let the door close behind me. As my eyes adjusted to the light, I saw a white van parked in the nearest bay. The lettering on the side read *Medical Squadron, CTCA*. Mod Squad. Clever.

I told him to turn around and grabbed one elbow behind his back, chicken-winging him. "Where is he?"

"Where is who?" He slurred, then slumped in my arms, like a sleepy toddler.

I shook him, asked again, slower. "Where. Is. He?"

The guy raised his head slow, wincing, then jerked a thumb in the general direction of the open, better-lit part of the building.

"Who else is here?" I asked, grabbing him by his bony shoulder and turning him around. Beads of sweat rolled off his forehead. His skin feverish under my grip.

He swiveled his head, staring at the back door. His eyes rolled back as he shuddered, a shiver running through him. His leg jerked, foot slapping the floor like a horse taught to count. *What the fuck was wrong with this guy?* I buried my gun in his bony back under the shoulder blade, jabbed hard spouting some nonsense about a main artery to the heart just on the other side.

"Who else is here?"

"No one," he said too fast. His voice changed as he said, "No one's here but us, Mom."

Mom? "Cut the shit. You better not be lying to me. Trust me, no one wants to die like this." I pressed the gun deeper. "Close range gunshot, triggering spinal nerves, the eventual bleeding out. It's *painfully* slow."

He raised his shaking hands. "Okay, okay," he said. "You're right. I don't."

God, the guy was a pussy.

The warehouse was quiet, empty and open. I had no reason not to believe him. Besides, Ivory Joe and Gator would be here soon enough. I pushed the guy forward, trying to not touch his sweaty back, his hot skin. I pulled back, then pushed him again, getting a whiff of him, sick, rotting.

We made baby steps toward the storage area of the building. Sections of the open space were broken into squares and rectangles, decorated like rooms in a house—a very sleek, contemporary home, with clean, geometric lines. No fluff or extras, lots of black, white and gray. It was glass and steel, industrial meets architectural.

The guy stopped about five feet from a black door. It seemed to lead into another squared-off space, but this one had walls. A room in the middle of nowhere, fronted with windows, shades drawn, light within.

"He's in there," he said, tipping his chin, as if there might be some confusion as to where *there* was.

I nudged him with the gun muzzle. He didn't budge, just looked over his shoulder staring unfocused in my general direction. "Wha-at?" he said, in a creepy, there's-nothing-going-on-here-I swear-heh-heh-heh kind of way.

If I was one of those big, flowing dress-wearing aura-reading ladies that you see at fairs and empowerment conferences, I might have picked up on the bad juju sooner. As it was, I just thought the guy was squirrelly, and kind of a wimp ass. I had no explanation for the shaking, the sweating, the scent coming off him like the smell of a refrigerator left unplugged and closed up for too long.

"What's your name?" I asked.

He shifted his weight from foot to foot, squinted at me and said in the voice of a toddler, "Why you wanna know?"

"Didn't your mother ever teach you to not answer a question with a question? What is your name, son?"

The guy shrunk even more into himself. I was about to ask him who'd cut off his balls when he said, "Clayton. My name's Clayton."

Figures. "Well, all right then. Now, Clayton, is there any reason I shouldn't open that door?"

He shrugged.

I leaned in and said, real soft, "Is there any reason *you* shouldn't open that door?"

He shook his head, neck spasming, flicking his sweat onto my cheek. "I don't feel so good," he said.

"Tough shit," I said, pressing into him, my fingers clamping his scrawny neck, urging him forward. We might have looked like two kids who believed in ghosts standing on the porch of a haunted house.

"Père?" I called, as Clayton fidgeted under my grip. "Père,

are you okay? I'm outside the door. We're coming in."

A series of muffled, emphatic grunts came from behind the door.

I remembered the explosion in the neighborhood with Gator and Ivory Joe, figured if Highwayman would do that to his own house, he'd have no problem doing something similar to his buddy's store, especially if it was a two for one deal.

"All right," I yelled. "It's all right. I'm not opening the door."

"I leaned into Clayton's ear and whispered, "Boom."

He squeezed his eyes shut and stiffened.

"Jesus, you're pathetic," I said, pulling him backward, shoving him toward the towering metal shelves of furniture. "Take off your belt."

He fell to the floor, shaking, opened his mouth to object, but when I raised the gun and lined it up with his left eye, he clamped his lips shut, removed his belt, held it out for me.

"Turn around, cross your wrists behind your back."

I tucked my gun in my pants and with a bit of difficulty— the guy was like melting Jell-O—I belted him to the support of the metal shelves, making sure he was facing the office and its black door. Then I felt around in his pockets, finding a phone and a wallet, old, Velcro. It had seen better days, and hopefully more money.

He was a Clayton, confirmed by his Texas driver's license. He was also a loser, confirmed by his frequent video gamer card and a single worn, expired condom, which from the looks of *this* guy, had never seen better days.

He didn't have a password on his ancient flip-style cell phone, thing was so outdated it had a pull-out antennae. The screen was scratched, even the protective cover was crappy plastic. I scrolled through his minimal contacts, unable to understand how someone could sell futuristic decor, but seemingly not give a shit about modern technology. I almost asked him to explain the conundrum when I noticed the name of the recently added contact: BOOM!

Shit. The phone wasn't old and crappy because he didn't appreciate technology. It was old and crappy because it was a throwaway trigger device.

"Well, fuck me."

Clayton shook his head. "You shouldn't say that."

I started to close the phone, saw his eyes go big and stopped. I held the device at a distance, pinched between two fingers. "How does it work?"

His head drooped.

"Clayton?"

He didn't answer.

"Clayton!"

He lifted his head, opened his eyes halfway.

"Look at me."

His face paled as his body convulsed. Sweat ran freely from his hairline. I almost asked if he was okay, then remembered I didn't care.

"I need my medicine. Momma?" He sunk into himself, squeezed his eyes shut. When he opened them, he focused on me, all skeletal and spooky. "H-man was wrong. You ain't smart."

"Excuse me?"

He attempted a laugh that came out more like a sad gurgle. He fought for breath, spitting out choked sentences, "He said you was dangerous. You and your friends ain't shit. When I did your daddy—"

"When you did what?" My clenched fist shuddered.

He tipped his head at the phone-device in my hand. "I learned from the best. You should have seen H-man back in the day." He winced, then groaned. "You don't know nothing. Not even about that paper in your pocket." He grinned, gaining a bit of strength, going smug, then leaned back on the metal pole, eyes deep in their sockets.

What paper? The label? As much as I wanted to fuck this guy up, I backpedaled, trying to figure out how to play it, knowing we still needed him. "Well, hell yeah, we got that. We got *all* that. I was talking about—"

He choked out the words. "You wasn't talking about shit. Fuck you."

He pumped up his sweat-drenched chest and jutted his chin in my direction.

I could see the boyish charm he might have once had. Could even see a sort of appeal, if I strained. Wash the greasy hair, fix the dead front tooth and give him clothes that actually fit, and who knows? He might have a chance to use that condom after all.

Or maybe now that I was seeing Clayton as a mother-fucker he became more attractive. I had a thing for bad boys. I wasn't so sure how I felt about sick, smelly, dying mother-fuckers though.

I backed away from him, glanced down the first ware-house row. One side was stacks of plastic-wrapped chairs and large boxes marked fragile. On the other side were sofas, lamps and a long table with packing materials. Gripping the phone tighter, I jogged to the table, found a box that appeared to be empty except for a deep layer of Styrofoam peanuts. I gently laid the phone inside, buried it under another layer of peanuts and stepped away. If the device was a trigger, I was counting on it taking more than slight pressure to set it off.

What was keeping Gator and Ivory Joe? Pacing, I told myself to focus, to block out the things I couldn't control. I had to make this as simple as an outdoor hunt.

In the field you analyzed the obvious—what you knew, what you saw and what you wanted. Then you broke it down to two things: a target and a task. I'd approached trucking in the same way. The target was the destination and the task was the delivery. To think like that now took out the emotion and helped me focus. What did I know? What did I see? And what did I want?

I knew my father was in that office. I knew I needed answers. Boone deserved answers. I knew people were on their way—good and bad. I might not be able to see inside that room, but I sure could see everything outside of it, and if I got high enough?

I grabbed the huge, steel shelving unit and tried to shake it—nothing moved. Staring over boxes through to the other side, I measured the distance between the rack and the wall of the makeshift office, the height of the ceiling. It just might work.

I loosened the noose on my sling bag and geared up before heading back to Clayton.

He greeted me with a smirk. I flipped him the bird and started climbing up. Over chairs and end tables, around boxes and lamps. At the top of the rack I stood and scoped out the place, counted possible entrances and exits—windows, doors, and loading bays. I estimated the space between the room installations and the storage racks. Wide enough for two forklifts, or one car. I tallied the number of security cameras, air ducts and fluorescent light fixtures. Observation was important. But you had to know what to do with what you saw.

A thick pipe ran the length of the warehouse. If I was five inches taller, I'd be able to reach it. Knotting the rope from my bag, I gave it enough weight to toss over the pipe. Tugging, I tested the strength, satisfied, I tied it around my waist and through my legs in a makeshift harness. It took two tries to catch the pipe, warm in my hands. When I swung my legs up and locked my ankles I hung underneath the pipe, just like monkey bars on the playground.

As I moved out over the open space, I asked myself the last question. *What did I want?*

The answer? I wanted my father—alive.

Chapter 12

I had an inchworm rhythm going—reach right hand, left hand, pull up my knees, adjust the rope and repeat. My shoulders were starting to scream when Clayton yelled, "Hey, don't leave me. You aren't going to leave me here like this, are you?"

I didn't reply. He'd been yelling things for a while. Some made a little sense, some were off the wall crazy. I glanced back to see him straining against the belt that held him, his body shaking, convulsing with dry heaves.

A minute later, he yelled, "Help me! Please? Hey! I know things. H-man told me it wasn't just the SD card he wanted from you. I could tell you."

Oh you'll tell me all right. "What did you say to me earlier, Clayton? Oh yeah. Fuck you. Well, backatcha, pal."

I moved two feet forward, snugged my knees up.

"You got no idea what you're getting into. Highwayman never stops until he gets what he came for."

I couldn't help but linger a few seconds on the name, *Highwayman.* My heart sped up, palms began to sweat. I saw Boone on the ground under the overpass, his broken body bleeding out, his lips moving, speaking his last words, "Highwayman."

"Don't you worry, Clayton. We know exactly what we're getting into."

I wiped my hands one by one on my shirt and readjusted my grip. I was going to fucking kill this guy *and* his pal.

Clayton, sick as he appeared to be, still did not know when to shut up. He said, "Yeah, right. That is bullshit."

I steadied my voice, careful to hold my tone as I said, "Hey, I could tell you, but you know, then I'd have to—"

"What?" he scoffed. "Kill me? Look at me. I'm already dead. You need a better line. That shit's as old as—"

"The condom in your wallet?" I offered, pausing to rest my arms.

Clayton yelled, "Shut up."

It was my turn to laugh. I inched forward. The pipe was warmer under my hands, but still not too hot to hold on. I said, "Big talk for a boy tied to a storage rack."

He gathered himself up and found some pride. "I ain't a *boy* and I don't need no condom, anyway. My girlfriend, she—well never mind."

I laughed. I was almost to the wall of the office. "You got a girlfriend? Well, shut the front door! I bet she's a real catch."

"She is. You don't even know." He babbled on something about his lady, her real good job and how they had plans to go places.

I was only half-listening to him, as I wrenched my neck to see over my shoulder. From this angle the office looked like a small room within a room. It was perfectly square and the walls appeared to be about the width of a 4x4. Pretty sure I could land on that.

I inched up the last few feet, aligning myself over the right side wall of the office. I uncurled my legs, let them dangle, then dropped, hoping the harness would hold if I missed. Blood rushed into my hands and fingers, relief in my screaming shoulders. From here, I could see Clayton perfectly. His shirt was pasted to his chest, wet with sweat. He'd tipped his head back to watch me, and appeared to be having a tough time keeping his eyes open. My feet hung off the sides of the wobbly wall. But that didn't bother me half as much as what I saw inside the room.

My father, blindfolded, gagged and duct-taped to a rolling office chair. A complicated series of wires connected him to the doorknob, a lamp and a filing cabinet drawer, that was half open. I pulled my phone from my pocket, hit the camera button and zoomed in on the file cabinet.

"Fuck me."

Clayton broke out in a sick, cackling laugh, the kind you hear in cheap horror movies just before the crazy guy pulls out his bloody machete.

"Told you..." he sang.

I called down to my father, "Père, don't move your arms or hands, Okay? Trust me. I'm going to get you out of there. But I need you to do exactly as I say. Nod your head if you understand."

He nodded, twice.

"Good."

I searched the rest of the room, shooting photos with my phone and enlarging them to be sure I wasn't missing a booby trap.

I looked at Clayton. His eyes were closed. "Hey! That whole cabinet rigged?" I asked, watching my father tense up in the chair. "It's okay, Père. I got this. Don't move."

My father grunted something and I looked back at Clayton. He rolled his head on his shoulders. His eyes and cheeks were more sunken. "Maybe," he said. "I ain't telling."

I pulled my gun and sighted down the midline, firing once. A hole appeared in the toe of Clayton's cowboy boot, exposing a red sock on his left foot.

"Jesus Fucking Christ! Goddamn it! What did you do that for? You almost shot my foot."

"Notice how you said *almost*. Now answer me. Are all the

drawers rigged?" I readjusted my aim.

He shook his sweaty head. "Just the top one. But that's plenty."

I went back to reconning the room.

It looked like Clayton had kept the modern theme in his office space, except for the wrinkled survey map thumb-tacked to the wall behind his desk and two cheap picture frames on the credenza. One picture showed a beefy grinning NRA shirt-wearing Clayton standing beside his buddies, posing with a dead deer in front of a rustic building. The other photo was a close-up of a woman's face, wind blowing her dark hair, strands caught in her red lipstick, eyes ob-scured behind cat-eye sunglasses, a sort of European feel to the shot, or a cheesy perfume ad.

There was a small cot in the back corner of the office—the kind you'd find in camping stores, or a Boy Scout lodge—definitely nothing you'd expect to find in a modern furniture store in the heart of Texas. At the end of the tiny bed was a stack of used thermo units, seals broken and hanging. They looked like the same kind we'd hauled from Pharmo.

I followed the path of the wires, walking my eyes through the connections—up, down, left, right—like solving a paper maze in the back of a kid's magazine. When I got to the file cabinet, I saw a possibility.

Clayton was mumbling to himself and moaning. He yelled, "Ollie, ollie in come free!" Then giggled maniacally. I glanced in his direction. He was worse, red-faced, spasming.

I looked at the wires again, judged distance and height. I had one shot. One chance.

I called down to my father. "You doing okay? Give me a nod."

He did.

"Good. I'm going to get you out of there, Père, but it's going to be loud. All right?"

Another nod.

I sent up a tiny prayer to the Goddess of Perfect Aim then said, "On the count of three. One, two—"

I shot the handle off the file cabinet. The wire remained intact, but now there was enough slack for me to work with. I was lining up my sights with the doorknob when a speeding black Hummer crashed through the front windows of the store.

"Shit!"

I aimed for the wire leading to the knob, took another shot for good measure, then dropped into the room, slamming the cabinet drawer shut with a roundhouse kick. I ripped the map off the wall and grabbed the framed photos, shoving it all behind my father in the chair as I rolled him to the door. In three seconds, we were clear of the threshold with me running, tugging at Père's gag and blindfold, pushing the chair—directly into the path of the speeding Hummer.

With his head cranked around to look at me, Père yelled, "That was not on *three*, Shâ. That was two!"

He was right, and I would have told him so, but the Hummer was coming fast, looking like an animal interrupted during a meal. A shiny chrome coffee table dangled from its massive grill.

I spun the chair, stood in front of my father, steeled myself and raised the gun, taking aim at the driver side window.

The Hummer braked—hard and sudden. Tires squealed as its back end went out, swerving left, pulling the big vehicle into a spin. Eight thousand six hundred and fourteen pounds of beast on wheels smashed into a tall storage rack of furniture, tipping it. The rest of the racks fell like dominoes, crushing high-end lamps, pony hair chairs and imported leather couches.

Smoke rose from the Hummer's tires and engine compartment. Two empty hands appeared in the passenger window, followed by a face I'd known forever and one I'd grown to love.

"Ivory Joe! Gator!"

I lowered my gun and ran to him as he climbed out of the truck, brushing glass from his lap, bracing himself on the doorframe.

"Where were you? How did you get the Hummer? Where's Highwayman? Wait. Are you okay?" I asked, slowing down, sandwiching his cheeks between my hands, checking him for injuries.

"Shut up and kiss me," Gator said.

Sometimes, I don't mind all that much when people tell me what to do.

Ivory Joe cursed as he pulled himself out of the trashed Hummer dragging his leg behind him. He limped over to help the man we came to rescue, while I reacquainted myself with Gator's lips.

My father had a million questions, beginning with, "What the hell just happened?"

Ivory Joe tried his best to fill him in while Gator and I were occupied.

When the room went silent behind me, I opened my eyes and turned to see Père wriggling and kicking his legs, spreading them just as Ivory Joe fell to the ground between his knees, a long bladed hunting knife in his hand.

"Shâ! Little help, here?"

I raced over with Gator close behind.

Ivory Joe's foot long blade had sliced my father's pant leg, inches from his groin. Père muttered in Cajun under his breath, *Embrasse moi tchew,* something about kissing someone's ass, about slicing off a man's business, about close calls and people paying attention.

I bit my tongue to keep from laughing as I cut him loose from the chair, slicing through the tape on his arms and legs. When Père stood and shook out his limbs, the map and framed pictures I'd stashed behind him fell to the floor.

Père's rant continued in Cajun—how I was going to be the death of him yet, and that if he'd wanted to be kidnapped, he would have stayed in Brazil where the food's better. I listened a little, more interested in the pictures I'd taken from Clayton's office. I pulled them both from their frames, checked over my shoulder, then slipped them in my pocket.

Gator had given up trying to understand Père, instead turned his attention to Ivory Joe who was coming around. "How you doing?"

Ivory Joe sat up, ran a hand over his face. "I ain't no pussy. I can handle this."

Gator said, "No one's calling you a pussy. You lost a lot of blood and—"

All the talk of men being pussies reminded me of Clayton. I ran to the rack where I'd tied him earlier. It looked like a scene from *The Wizard of Oz*, the one where the house falls on the bad witch and only her legs and shoes are sticking out.

"Damn," Gator said, sliding up beside me.

"Meet Clayton," I said. "What's left of him, anyway."

Ivory Joe hobbled over using Père as his crutch. He took one look, shook his head. "Poor bastard."

My father cleared his voice, then said very softly, "This is all too much for me."

I went to him, tried to hug him the way he used to hug me when I was twelve and confused and he had all the answers.

"It was him," he said, his mouth near my ear. "Clayton killed Boone."

"What?" I bucked, tried to pull myself away, determined to kick the shit out of a dead man, but my father's arms were strong and his broad warm chest felt like home.

"Easy, Shâ," he said stroking my hair. "After the big guy hauled me off the plantation in the Hummer, I woke up in the back of a van—Clayton driving. He was all too happy to talk. Not sure if he was bragging or confessing. Something not right about that *cowan*."

I squeezed him tight, smiling at his use of the Cajun curse word for pussy. "I'm sorry I didn't get here sooner."

"Not your fault, Shâ." He held me at arm's length. "But you need to know. It was him, Jojo. On the highway. He said it was easy to jack up the trailer, kept talking about some guy named Edwin who double-crossed them with his crew, something about a BLT? Does that mean anything to you?"

The Baconator? "What else did he say?"

"Not much. Bunch of crap about collateral damage and choices. Said the road is only so wide. He took a call, from a woman. I couldn't hear much, but she had a real strong Texas accent, and he mentioned a port."

I looked at Gator.

Ivory Joe righted an overturned loveseat and sat, elevating his bloody thigh. He said, "Clue me in here, Jojo. You said you recognized the sign from the picture on the SD card, came here alone—"

"I told Gator where I was going, and besides I wasn't really alone. I had Kimber and Springfield." I pulled the Springfield XD 40 from my waistband and lifted my pants leg, exposing the Kimber 1911 Custom Crimson strapped to my calf. I spun the Springfield, one finger in the trigger guard, caught it and blew across the muzzle, in my best Annie Oakley impression. More of me than I wanted to admit wished I had known exactly who the fuck Clayton was when he was alive, and my guns had all their bullets.

I could tell Ivory Joe was trying not to smile.

"So what were you guys doing, while I was *saving* Père?" I asked.

"Oh, not much," Gator said. "Surviving an explosion, getting the gimp out of Dodge, fighting crosstown traffic. You know, the usual."

"Gimp?" Ivory Joe said. "Right. I don't recall me slowing you down. We got here just behind the Hummer. Guy must have been hiding in it when the house blew up. Anyway, if he had a larger bladder, we might be telling a whole different story."

I snorted. "You jumped a guy taking a piss?"

"Nah. We just had a little chat with your whistling pal. Isn't that right, Gator?"

Gator grinned. "Let's just say that parts of him might still be whistling, but it isn't coming from his mouth."

"Nope," Ivory Joe said. "He won't be doing that for a while."

"Where's he now?" I asked.

"Don't worry. There's only one place for trash like him."

Both men laughed, and my father smiled, but it didn't feel funny to me. Maybe because I wasn't in on the joke.

Before I could ask anything more about their informative chat, Gator asked about the photo.

"What photo?"

"The one you shoved in your pocket."

"Oh." I handed it to him. "Found it in the office."

"You think this is Baconator?" Gator pointed to a toothy guy in a John Deere ball cap.

"Could be," I said. "Wearing his lucky hat."

"Or not so lucky, as it turns out."

"There's that."

"So, we've got a positive connection. Here's our pal the Hummer-driving Highwayman, the dead-in-the-woods trucker, Edwin The Baconator Dorsey…"

"And next to him, that's got to be the newly deceased Clayton. Wasn't always such a skinny little fuck, was he?"

"So who's this guy?" Gator asked.

I squinted at the last guy in the picture. He stood behind the others, shaded by a floppy hat. Posed like one of those awkwardly fashionable models selling overpriced clothes or specialty items for the rich and not so famous.

"I don't know. Looks like he'd rather be anywhere else, doesn't he?" I said.

Gator chuckled. "Hard to blame him. With this cast of characters?" He shook his head, slipped the photo in his pocket and straightened up.

"Hey, Gator," I lowered my voice, touched his arm. "Hate to say this. God, do I hate to say this, but don't you think it's time we called in the cops? Ivory Joe needs a hospital, and there are going to be questions."

I stared past Gator to where my father was mumbling, rocking on his heels. Ivory Joe had shut his eyes, appeared to be napping.

Gator tugged an imaginary beard, then nodded. "Let me handle this. I know who to call."

He motioned my father over. "Manny, you okay to handle this? We need someone to stay here and…explain."

Père stared at the trashed warehouse, the rolling office chair that still held vestiges of his kidnapping—sweaty imprint of his back, strips of duct tape, crinkled map. He shook his head. "That's not going to be easy."

"It'll be okay," I said handing him my phone. "But first, call Pilar, she's worried."

We watched him slowly punch numbers into the phone. Gator pulled me close. "You okay?"

"Yeah. I'm fine. What now?"

"We've got to get Highwayman out of here before I make that call. Come on."

"Wait." I snatched the map I'd stolen from the office and jogged after him, rolling it as I went.

Gator reached for my hand to help me over the last bit of mangled wall. We stood in the parking lot under a slice of moon. High in the sky and far from city lights, stars shone bright, sparkly even. It could have been a perfect night—take away the kidnapping, the bombing, the injuries, the file cabinet of explosives, the dead, half-squashed man—

"Damn it!" Gator dropped my hand and ran to the dumpster. The lid was closed, but a small side door hung open.

I didn't need to look inside to figure out Highwayman was gone.

Gator ran a hand through his hair. "Great. Just fucking great."

"He couldn't have gone far. Come on. We'll find him."

Gator shook his head. "Jojo, he took the Caddy.

Chapter 13

Gator was still beating himself up about letting High-wayman escape when we went back inside the demolished store to tell Ivory Joe and Manny what had happened.

My father, being my father, had only kind words of encouragement, and Ivory Joe, being very much unlike the Ivory Joe I knew, gave Gator a ration of shit, calling him everything from a slack-jawed Sherlock to a window-licking, mouth breathing fucktard with questionable parentage. Though, to his credit, he said it all in Cajun and I'm pretty sure it went right over Gator's head. Or at least around the left side where he didn't hear so good.

"Putting him in the dumpster seemed like a smart idea at the time," Gator said.

Ivory Joe scoffed, "Right," as he tightened the tourniquet on his leg.

"It was!" Gator said. "You heard the shots. What was I supposed to do? There were people in here. Our people." He looked at me.

Ivory Joe sighed loudly. "I don't suppose you have GPS on that old junker?" he asked, rubbing at his leg and wincing.

Gator puffed out his chest. "Junker? Excuse me? That pristine automobile happens to be quite rare. Do you know that there are only ten original, 1959 argent silver Cadillac Eldorado Sevilles in the world? Add in the 345bhp, 390-cubic-inch V8 engine, three Rochester two-barrel carbure-tors, a three-speed Hydra-Matic automatic transmission with independent front suspension on coil springs, live axle rear suspension with air-assisted springs, and four-wheel hydraulic drum brakes all on a hundred-and-thirty-inch wheelbase and you've got quite a machine."

"Stop," I moaned. "You're giving me a lady boner."

Ivory Joe smiled. "And he hasn't even mentioned the interior of the ride. Used to be pretty sweet, buffed leather, all kinds of chrome and fancy shiny shit. Of course, currently it's a little bloody."

Gator said, "Hey, you said you'd pay to have it cleaned."

Ivory Joe raised one finger in reply.

Manny groaned. "Now, boys."

Gator and Ivory Joe glared at each other.

I said, "Cut it out you two. This isn't helping. If anybody has an idea how we can find the Caddy—and Highwayman—I'm all ears."

That thing about hearing a pin drop? It was pretty damn close.

With nothing else to do at the warehouse, we called the ambulance and some cops that Gator trusted, gave them the short version. Clayton was dead. Manny was safe. Ivory Joe was hurt. The kidnapper was missing. And those strange looking thermo units in the office? That could very well be the connection to a counterfeit drug ring and might need special handling. Also, there was a dead trucker named Edwin Dorsey in the woods, ten yards off the trailhead at Roane Community Park.

We figured that would give them enough to keep them busy before we got back. Gator thought it would be a good idea if we weren't readily available. I understood that to mean, if we hang around, we're screwed.

"Sabrina's around back," I said. "Let's go."

I blew a kiss to Ivory Joe, then leaned over to hug my father goodbye.

"See you soon, Père," I said releasing him and straightening up.

He nodded, tried a little smile. "Be careful. Both of you."

"We will," I said, tapping my leg with the map, then turning to go.

"What you got there, Shâ?" he asked.

I shrugged, unrolling the map. "It was in the office on the wall. Looked important. I don't know."

Gator and Père looked over my shoulder as I spread the map, holding down the edges.

"That's a topographic survey and site plan," Père said. "Pretty big place, whatever it is."

"Let me see," Gator leaned in, squinting. He tapped on some faded words in the corner. "I know that place. It's the old naval base in Corpus Christi, closed in 2010. They've been trying to sell it ever since. Must be hard to move a hundred million dollar property."

"But it's on the water, with views," I joked.

The room remained silent. Finally I said, "What's our pal Clayton doing with this?"

Gator shrugged.

"Shit. Another piece of the puzzle," I said, rolling it back up.

At the sound of approaching sirens, Père hurried us along, shooing us out. "Go on. Git."

We raced out the back of the warehouse to the truck. Gator slid into the driver's seat as I buckled in. He sped across the lot, turning right onto the street and pulled away as a row of red and blue lights appeared in our side mirrors. They were coming fast. I watched until they turned into the strip mall, pulling up short outside the destroyed Mod Squad. Only then did I exhale.

We drove for a mile, until Gator burst out laughing.

"What? Don't tell me. You finally got my fucking joke?"

He looked at me and shook his head.

"No, a better one. And this time, the joke's on them. Do me a favor and enter Naval Air Station, Corpus Christi in the NAV system."

"But you said it was lo-jacked…"

I was tired. It took me a half a second. "Ah. Good thinking. I'm on it."

A minute later, the turn-by-turn directions were loaded and we were heading south. "We'll stay on the fifty-nine for a while," I said. "I'm going to grab a water, you want anything?"

"Not right now. Thanks."

Back in the sleeper, I drank glass after glass of ice cold water standing at the sink, staring out the window in the dark. It was an image you might see on a TV commercial, but it would be a proud, young mother watching her child playing in the backyard as she washed the dinner dishes. The kid would be sitting quietly in a sandbox, or tinkering with his bike, or maybe, pushing too hard, leaping from a swing set, landing wrong and breaking a leg.

I don't know why I always went to the dark side.

I thought about the map with its tiny print and secret abbreviations, things I didn't understand. I spread the paper open on the dinette, held down the edges with a cup, a book, a pen, my hand.

"Hey, Gator? What did you say about the writing on this map?"

"Nothing really. I just recognized the NAS part."

"Why would he have this map? I don't understand."

"Jojo, maybe he wanted to know where to go."

"What? Why? Why there?"

"I don't know. But that's why people have maps. That's

how we find where we need to go, right?"

"Hey," I said, "Not everyone had maps, and they found shit. Look at Columbus."

"*He* was looking for India," Gator said.

I stared at the map, willing it to speak to me, to leap up and dance, show me the riches of China, the mountains of Nepal, the whores of Babylon, something. Anything?

Nothing.

I pulled out the copy of the NewGen label, read it another five times, then woke up the laptop and opened a browser window typing in the names of the ingredients, the name of the manufacturer, anything I could read. As the search loaded, slowly connecting, I opened a map program and began a search along the Texas coast for Corpus Christi. I highlighted and zoomed in to the area, then clicked the earth view and played eagle, soaring over treetops and buildings.

The other window pinged notifying me the ingredients list had loaded. I swapped windows and slogged my way through medical terms, frustrated that the language was as confusing to me as the Queen's English must be to rap stars.

I lay my head on the table and woke a few minutes later, not much clearer for the nap.

"Here," I said, bumping Gator's shoulder with a cold bottle of water before tapping the NAV monitor to check our reading. We still had a lot of road to cover before we reached Corpus Christi.

"I don't want to push it," he said, nodding at the truck's speedometer. "Last thing we need is to get pulled over."

"I know," I said. "What are we supposed to say? We're just your ordinary truck drivers—between loads—chasing down a kidnapper who's probably associated with a bunch of drug thieves and counterfeiters—"

"Don't forget bomber and car thief," Gator said.

"Oh, yeah. There's that, too. What the hell have we

gotten ourselves into?" I dropped into the passenger seat and stared out the windshield. "Maybe we should just give up."

"That doesn't sound like the Jojo I know."

"Maybe you don't know me very well. Maybe the real me wants to live a nice, quiet life in the country raising chickens."

Gator laughed. "Ri-ight. And the real me wants to wear sequined dresses and sing Cher songs on a small stage in New Orleans."

I laughed. "Actually? I can see that."

"You think? I mean, I know I have the legs for it."

I smacked his arm. "I know what you're doing."

He smiled.

"You're trying to make me feel better, like this is one happy adventure. Well, it isn't. A dude called The Baconator is dead. Ivory Joe's hurt. My father was kidnapped! Seriously, this whole thing is bigger than us, Gator."

"What? You want to give up? Fine by me. I'm going to finish what I started. I want to find this Highwayman and have a little chat, find out where the stolen loads are going, who's stealing from Pharmco and why. I thought you wanted the same thing."

"I do. I'm just tired. I feel like I'm missing something, something obvious." I ran my hands over my face, hoping I didn't look as crappy as I felt.

"So, where did you stash that SD card?" I asked. "Or should I say cards? You made a copy, right?"

Gator checked his mirrors then changed lanes. The highway had narrowed and there were more cars than a half an hour ago. He looked at me, back at the road, then puffed out his cheeks, exhaling a short burst of warm air.

Finally he mumbled, "The cards were in the glove box."

"In the Caddy?" I asked.

He nodded.

"Both of them?"

He nodded, again.

"Damnit!" I slapped the dashboard. "Are we ever going to get a break? Shit. Now, who's going to believe us?"

"Don't worry about that." Gator said. "Besides the other card was just a fake. I uploaded bogus docs and some images from a Google search. Enough to show there was data on the card. I sent a backup of the real card to my email account. All we need to do is get to the port, find the drugs and expose the cargo theft ring."

I laughed. "Yeah, right. You make it sound so easy. What about the rest of this—" I jerked my thumb back at the kitchenette, the open computer, the map and label, back at the empty space in our trailer where we'd hauled the stolen NewGen, even to the road behind us where a bunch of questions were floating around.

Gator used his now, now voice. "One step at a time, Jojo."

I fucking hated those words.

The why probably didn't matter in the end. We were simply trying to right a wrong. But I couldn't help thinking about it.

I popped the tab on my third energy drink, took a long gulp. Gator was still driving us through the big ass state of Texas and the sun had long given up its spot to the moon. The dinette was covered in crumpled papers.

"Keep going. What else you got?"

We'd reduced ourselves to brainstorming, covering every angle from competitive pharmaceutical firms to health care providers seeking new business, to a single rich individual who needed NewGen supplies to live, an option that brought to mind a crazy evil genius type, someone with a secret lair and a bed propped up with bars of gold bullion.

I threw another wad of paper at the back of Gator's head.

Gator had an idea that involved rich American bad guys, even though Corpus Christi was close to Mexico, water, air fields. He thought high profile cancer drugs would fetch enough money in the U.S. when sold to expensive clinics and specialty treatment centers, that there was no reason for white collar crooks to subject themselves to border wars or drug cartels. I had to agree. I couldn't see a bunch of low-level pot and heroin runners wanting to deal with the specifics necessary to properly store and distribute delicate cancer-curing drugs, or even give a fuck about sick Americans.

Gator asked, "With the cargo thefts coming out of ware-houses on the way to other warehouses, like the run we did, isn't it possible they're just stealing from each another?"

"Apparently that happens often enough," I said, citing from one of the pages I'd read. "Wholesaler A might sell to Distributor A who then might sell to Wholesaler B who might then sell to Wholesaler C who would then turn around and resell to public entity X, like the local clinic or even the grocery store in the strip mall down the street. Sometimes, distributors ended up buying from wholesalers the same product that had been stolen from their own warehouse, after thieves changed the lot numbers, or labels"

I wasn't sure it even mattered if we understood exactly what the bad guys were doing. Stealing, then peddling one drug as another? Stealing, then selling drugs that had been FDA revoked, like in the case of NewGen? Selling poorly stored, mislabeled, fake vials of drugs without any medicinal properties disguised as a miraculous cancer cure?

All I knew was that it was wrong and we were in the middle of it.

I was searching the aerial map again, double checking

with the survey map when Gator called over his shoulder, "We're getting close."

"Okay," I said, not looking up from the map. "I hate to ask, but what's your plan when we get to Corpus Christi? And please, don't embarrass yourself by saying we're going to *wing it*."

"I have a plan," Gator said. "But it sort of depends on how you feel about your bumper."

"I don't like the sound of that," I said, sliding the laptop off the map, putting my hand on the warm place it left. I couldn't let go of the feeling that something was eluding me.

I remembered my first week on the job when I got lost driving our rig through rural New Hampshire. Phone service was practically non-existent and the GPS had proven useless. Boone was sleeping and I wouldn't have asked him for help anyway.

Finally, I stopped at a small general store, showed the old man behind the counter my map with the highlighted route and asked for directions.

He'd chewed on the inside of his lip, then shook his head. "Nope. Can't help you."

"What do you mean?" I tapped the blue road on the paper. "It's right here."

"It may be on the map," he said, shaking his head. "But it ain't on the ground."

I pulled the laptop closer, zoomed in on the current aerial view of the abandoned naval base.

"Gator, when did you say they closed NAS Corpus Christi?"

"Early 2010, I think. But the place had been vacant for years. They ran a skeleton crew."

"They update these satellite maps every year, right?"

"Mostly. At least every two years. Why?"

"Because I'm seeing cars, trucks, people and obviously occupied buildings at an abandoned naval base."

I brought the laptop up front, showed the zoomed in screen to Gator. "This is the section of the base north of the airfield, on the same side as the warehouses."

We stared at the map—green trees, landscaped grounds, a rainbow of cars in a full parking lot, doors propped open, figures frozen mid step, a dog raising its leg on a light pole.

Gator put his hands at ten and two, gripped the hard plastic steering wheel, eyes on the road.

I barely recognized his voice when he said, "And they know we're coming."

Chapter 14

We had resigned ourselves to an ambush.

We didn't know how far we were behind Highwayman, who he had on his side, or what was happening at the old navy base in Corpus Christi. All we knew was we'd let them know with clear intent exactly where we were headed and when we'd arrive.

I tried to play it cool with Gator, but if I was honest? I was having some serious flashbacks to the years in grammar school when we made *kick me* signs and taped them to the backs of our pals as we complimented them, told them how nice they looked. Only to have them return the favor with a back pat later that day.

"Is it too late to ask for help?" I said from my slumped position at the dinette.

"You want to ask for help, Jojo, or do you want to turn around and head for the hills?" Gator called back.

I stared out at the flat low land surrounding us, the lanes of traffic and wondered what hills he was dreaming about.

Gator slowed the rig, began to merge into construction traffic. The road had suddenly shrunk from three lanes to one.

"Thing is," I said, "If he'd wanted us dead, there certainly have been opportunities, right? I mean, what if he needs us as much as we think we need him."

"Well, we kinda do."

"But does he know that?" I said, with a grin.

I brought the computer up front, opened up the doc that Gator had mailed himself, the one with the SD card info, the pills and the labels and the vials.

"What if we're not the good guys? How about that?"

"Oh-kay," Gator said, hesitantly.

"Remember what you said about NewGen? Some odd fact about its use?"

"Ummm. Not off the top of my head," he said. "Lucky for you, though, I am filled with odd facts."

"Oh, how lucky for me," I said with a sigh, searching the history bar for the NewGen site.

"Here's one for you. Did you know that Popeye had four nephews? Their names were, Pip-eye, Peep-eye, Pup-eye and Poop-eye."

I snorted. "Get the fuck out."

"Absolutely true," he said. "Here's another interesting fact: Porcupines float in water."

"Is that right? Well, you *are* full of it, and by *it*, I mean a good amount of bullshit."

"Nope, it's all true," he said, filing in behind a slow moving bull hauler. "See? I am so much more interesting than the average bear."

"Isn't the average bear dumb as shit?" I said, raising my voice to be heard over the mooing cattle in the other rig. "You are talking about a hairy, lumbering animal that shits in the woods."

"Yep," Gator said. "And that idea alone was the motivation behind some pretty cute toilet paper commercials."

Before Gator could have a chance to bring up Yogi or Boo Boo or that adorable grizzly, Big Ben, I remembered the NewGen fact.

"Didn't you say anyone with a basic chemistry background could recreate the drug in their basement, if they wanted to, how the cost to make vials of NewGen isn't much at all? The biggest expense for pharmaceuticals is in advertising and marketing, not R&D."

"I do remember that. A bit of the *Breaking Bad* influence, maybe."

"So what would stop people from making these super expensive cancer drugs, even the pills they need and can't afford?"

"The law?"

"Fuck that."

Gator shook his head.

"I'm serious," I said. "If I knew there was a drug out there that could cure me or my loved one and I couldn't get my hands on it because of some crappy insurance plan or the FDA and its red tape or money? Are you kidding me? Of course I'd figure out how to steal it or make it or find some-one who could. Wouldn't you?"

"What are you saying?"

"I don't know. I just know there are a shitload of reasons the wrong people would want what we just hauled. And even more reasons why we can't let them have it."

Gator broke the silence. "Are you thinking what I'm thinking?" he asked.

"Maybe," I said. "What are you thinking?"

"I'm thinking nothing is as it seems on the surface. Maybe we should be looking deeper. What if the real truth is buried under the layers like an—?"

"Onion?" I asked.

He shook his head, then said, "Maybe," mocking my Louisiana accent. "All I know is, something sure stinks."

The road opened up, orange cones directing us to the new lanes. We passed the bull hauler, leaving his mess in our wake just as a large green road sign let us know we were twenty miles from Corpus Christi.

"We're running short on road—and answers," Gator said.

I closed my eyes, thought about what he'd said about looking deeper, about layers. Growing up in Louisiana, there was school learning and there were Père's lessons in the woods. He'd taught me to look past what I saw on the surface. That it wasn't just woods, or a pretty field or a copse of shady trees. Hoofed and furred creatures lived there, hidden in burrows, tucked away in thorny bushes, hunkered down in thickets. There were birds high in the trees, rodents underground, insects on every surface, and beneath all of that, micro-organisms making all the rest possible.

Père taught me to scout and track, all the work you need to do before you pick up your shotgun, load your rifle, sharpen your arrows. We'd spend weeks before a hunt slogging along the bayou, humping through cornfields. We'd watch patterns of birds to see when they fed and where, what spooked them, what drew them in. We'd smell the leaves on broken branches, pluck hair from tree bark, study scat on trails. I remembered him setting out decoys during duck season, how he'd said, "You need to have something already there to encourage the others to fly in."

"Gator?"

"Yeah?" he said cautiously.

"What's one of the largest and best identified buildings on a military base?" I asked, as I woke the page and scanned the aerial image.

"Have to be the—"

"Hospital," I said, turning the screen around and revealing the red cross on the roof of the sprawling building, surrounded by cars, and at least two eighteen wheelers.

"Bingo."

"There's more. Those rectangular structures in the aerial aren't buildings. I think they're shipping containers. I pointed to a shape, reddish, brick colored, enlarged it.

"Hey, can I see that picture from the office?"

Gator leaned forward and pulled the photograph from his back pocket, handing it to me, warm and a little bent.

I looked closer at the building. "I wish I had a magnifying glass, but I'd swear they're standing in from of one of these containers. People make them into houses, you know."

"Or, they ship stuff in them," Gator said. I could almost hear his eyes rolling.

The phone rang as we rolled onto the exit ramp for Corpus Christi. Gator had finally agreed to put it back in the cup holder, after his thigh made two outgoing calls, one to China.

"Technically, it was my hamstring," he said.

"And technically, you'll be getting the bill," I said, reaching for the handset.

"It's Jojo. Talk to me."

"Jojo, it's Dusty."

"Dusty? Is everything okay?"

"Shouldn't I be asking you that?" he said.

"What do you mean?" I shot a *what the hell* look in Gator's direction while trying to maintain my innocent girl act with Dusty.

It didn't last long. "Jojo, Manny told me you might be in over your head, that you could use a hand. Don't worry. You can trust us."

"What are you talking about, Dusty? And who's us? Hang on, I'm putting you on speaker so Gator—my, uh, co-driver can hear."

"Co-driver? Oh. Right," Dusty said, his voice booming through the tiny speaker.

I tried to ignore Gator's grin, concentrating instead on Dusty's words. *Why was my father calling him? How did he always know when I needed him most?*

Before I could ask, Dusty said, "You're headed to the port at Corpus Christi, the old warehouses, right?"

I looked at Gator, who nodded. "Yeah," I said.

"Good. Ronny thought he saw you on the thirty-seven. Knew you'd get caught in that construction, slow you down."

"Ronny? Is that the driver out of Minnesota with the red-winged Volvo?"

"Yep. He's at his drop now and can head your way in twenty. I've also got Gearhead and Bones coming west, and those gals from New Mexico, The Zipper Twins, they've got your north side."

"Wait a minute," Gator said, "I don't think we want to involve anyone else. This could be dangerous."

"Tell that to the families of the truckers who were robbed, the drivers that lost jobs because of these jokers," Dusty said. "I might not know all the details, but I know truckers help truckers."

He was right. I started talking before Gator could stop me, filling in the spaces that Père had left, telling Dusty our plan to return to the same warehouse where we'd delivered the thermo units. I sort of left out the have-a-chat-with-the-bad-guy-kidnapper-and-steal-back-our-original-load,   but sometimes vague is best.

Dusty said, "Word has it you caused a bit of trouble last time you were there. Afraid they've blacklisted you. Unless you have a priority load with all the clearances, you're going to need some help."

"Great," Gator said. "Now what?"

"No worries," Dusty said. "Text me when you're two miles out. I've arranged for a little distraction at the gate. Once you get past the guard shack, head right to the ware-house."

"I didn't know about the blacklisting. We'd planned to

finesse our way in," I said, pawing through a bunch of old paperwork I'd shoved under the seat. "But, there's just one teeny little problem."

"What's that?"

"Our trailer's empty."

"Not an issue," Dusty said. "I've got a disabled driver pal working those warehouses, told me he's got a bad foot but was hired because he still has his clearances from Enahel. Not sure what the hell is rolling through there, but apparently you need some serious background checks to get on staff, and this guy? He's got some swag."

Swag? I mouthed to Gator.

He shrugged.

I said, "How will we know your guy?"

"Big dude, shaved head, tattoo of a lion on his neck. But don't approach him, he knows you're coming and he's got your back. From what I hear, something's been going on there for a while. And it ain't pretty."

Gator looked at me. I could read his expression—part *I told you so* and part *oh shit.*

We rolled past a sign announcing the exit for the docks.

"We're getting close," Gator told Dusty.

"Good," Dusty said. "I'll look for your text. Good luck."

The line went dead.

Chapter 15

"You good with this?" Gator asked.

"Like I got a choice?" I said.

"Everyone has a choice," he said staring out the windshield.

"We're doing the right thing, aren't we?" I asked, my voice going soft.

"Of course," Gator said, in the same way my father used to assure me Santa Claus ate the cookies.

"Two miles," Gator said, slowing the truck.

I sent the text to Dusty, took a deep breath, gathered my hair into a ponytail, then checked for the gun in my boot. Party time.

The motion lights hit us buzzing and flickering as we rolled up to the guard shack. Everything looked different at night.

"Kind of late for a delivery," the gate guard said, checking our credentials, but barely touching the messy documents.

Gator said, "You know what they say, 'Neither rain, nor snow, nor gloom of night, can keep us from our duty.'"

The guard hesitated, pulling back his hand that held our creds. "I thought that was the U.S. Postal Service."

I leaned over and said, "Not anymore. Have you been in a post office lately?"

Before the guard could reply, a sleek white and chrome Mack truck came coasting in behind us, brakes squealing, engine racing. The guard glanced at the driver and the rig, then back at us.

"You said you had—"

The Mack driver pulled his air horn. Not any air horn, but what sounded like a five chime locomotive air horn, loud enough to shake the pavement. The guard tossed our paperwork at us and jumped back into his shack, clapping his hands over his ears. He motioned us forward with his elbow, and when the gate opened, we rolled through.

Gator raised the window and shot me a grin.

"No more stupid quotes, okay?" I said.

"Really? Not even some Rumi?"

"Some what?" I asked.

He stared straight ahead and lowered his voice. "*Dance, when you're broken open. Dance, if you've torn the bandage off. Dance in the middle of the fighting. Dance in your blood. Dance when you're perfectly free.*"

I didn't know whether to kiss him or shake him. I shook my head. "Who the hell are you?"

He grinned as we passed the sign directing us to the old naval base. The arrow flaking off, the name, Ingleside, barely legible. We turned down the road toward Port Terminal Two, driving in silence, as if we were waiting for something bad to happen, or like the faithful, waiting for a sign of something good, which usually took longer.

More outside motion lights came on as we neared the familiar Warehouse Seventeen. None of the bay doors were open and I couldn't see any of the other buildings. As Gator swung around, lining up the rig to back us in, our headlights revealed a vacant lot.

He looked at me before he put the truck in reverse, reassuring me with his eyes and a nod. "Here we go."

We were about twenty feet from the dock, when the door began to rise, revealing a muscular man standing spread-legged in the bay, hands on his hips. Lit from behind, he seemed like a figure from a music video. All that was missing was a fog machine and a handful of scantily clad dancers. And maybe a guitar.

When the guy raised his hand, telling us to stop, it was my cue to get out and ask to use the bathroom, while Gator kept him busy with questions and paperwork.

I tapped my pockets triple checking for phone and knife. Gator had finally agreed that I'd have a better chance than him of getting into the warehouse. Women's troubles can not only get you *out* of high school gym class or a long day of work, but get you *into* employee-only restrooms.

Gator set the brakes, watched me unbuckle my seat belt and reach for the door handle. He started to say something but I leaned over, meeting him halfway, and put my finger on his lips. He smiled. I removed my finger, replaced it with my lips. Pressing into him, I let my mouth say what my mind felt. When I broke the kiss, our eyes met, then I pushed the door open and jumped down without looking back.

"He-ey!" I called to the guy on the loading dock.

I heard Gator's door slam shut on the driver's side of the truck as the guy turned his attention to me.

"Check 'dis out," I said, cranking up the dial on my accent, leading with my chest. I had no problem using my feminine wiles to get what I wanted. It was the one thing that kept me from being perfect.

The guy shaded his eyes, puffed out his own chest, like we were fighting cocks in a dusty ring.

I got close enough so I didn't have to yell over the sound of the idling truck engine. "Co-driver back there says these give you cancer." I held up a super-sized tampon and started to tear the paper cover off. "You ever heard such nonsense? You'd think the guy never had a girlfriend before. He won't even let me use the toilet in the rig."

"Well, that's between you two," he said, backing up, the color draining out of his face.

I climbed the steps next to the dock and stepped in closer, swinging the tampon. "You hear that joke about the dumb Southern girl going to the drugstore for tampons?"

The guy shook his head. I could see his lips moving in a silent prayer for me to shut the fuck up. I pushed in closer, read the name sewn onto his blue uniform and said, "Well, Tom, the clerk asks her if she wants mini or maxi and she says, 'What's the difference?' Clerk says, 'What's your flow like?' and she says, 'It's linoleum.'"

I started laughing, smacking Tom's back, stealing his ID badge. Tom's puffed-up chest was now in his waistband and he looked like he was going to puke. He must have a problem with linoleum.

Gator was walking toward us, pretending to be engrossed with the papers on the clipboard. I looked into the warehouse, saw the white sign for the restroom and said, "I'll be right back, then," as I waved the tampon around.

Gator said, "Is she telling you that sick drink joke?"

"No," Tom said.

I hurried away as Gator one-upped my tampon joke with his own about a vampire bartender serving bloody marys with strings hanging out of them.

There was a radio playing somewhere that sounded like a local call-in show. Across the concrete were two guys in the same blue uniform as Tom. One was big and bald with a black lion neck tat, the other was smaller and gorilla hairy. They were smoking cigarettes under a no smoking sign, passing a can of soda that might not be soda. Lion Tat raised his hand to the back of his head, his elbow making an arrow for me.

I opened the bathroom door, reached in, flipped on the

fan and light, pressed the knob lock, then pulled it closed without ever entering.

I went in the direction of Lion Tat's elbow, making my way along the wall, shoulders skimming the posted signs for safety in the workplace—a crapload of tiny printed codes and regulations that I was sure no one had ever read. I paused in front of the evacuation map, checked the warehouse layout, then quickly moved toward the cold storage rooms.

The cell phone in my pocket vibrated, signaling a text from Gator. I checked the message: *u got 4 min*

Shit.

Sprinting to the rear of the building, I noted the blackened screens on the monitors, how none of the security cameras were rotating. If I wasn't such a pessimist, I'd think someone was watching out for me and had killed the security.

There were two cold rooms active with lighted panels and sealed doors. They looked like big walk-in freezers, the kind you'd find in a restaurant or a morgue. For that specific knowledge I can thank boyfriends number nine and sixteen, respectively.

I sidled up to the first storage room. Mounted beside the door the digital readout blinked as a temperature control gauge showed a needle in the green *safe* zone. Below this was an access control card reader. I ran the ID card I'd pinched from nauseated Tom into the slot and was rewarded with a beep. I pulled the door, stepped inside, being certain it didn't latch behind me, then took a second to still my pounding heart. The light switch on the wall brought two long rows of fluorescent bulbs to life revealing a chilly, not freezing room filled with wall racks, mostly empty, except some food items, regular grocery things, soda and someone's sandwich. Was this a joke?

I followed the racks to the rear. Three large, deep boxes

were on wooden pallets, jammed so close I could hardly pass between them. None of them looked like the thermo units we had hauled, or anything close to pharmaceutical grade packaging.

I opened the flaps on the one nearest to me. Empty. The next, empty. The last one was filled with bags of ice.

I started to pull them out of the box, got half way through when my phone started vibrating in my hand.

I checked the readout: *come NOW.*

What the hell? Gator needed to work on his virtues, beginning with patience. I fished around the rest of the bags, finding nothing, then exited the cold room, stepping backward through the door, almost managing to turn around before two gloved hands grabbed me, pinning my arms behind me.

Chapter 16

We were in a glass-walled break room. Sink, fridge, microwave, the smell of ramen. My head pounded, shoulders sore at the socket like I'd been dragged. I was duct taped to the leg of an industrial table bolted to the floor, probably having proved to be uncooperative or some such bullshit. Gator was across the room bound to a fabric chair, the kind soccer moms pop open on the sidelines of ball fields every Saturday. His hair was mussed, his lip swollen. It would have been sexy if I'd done it to him.

Tom and the other blue uniformed dockworker were interrogating the gorilla guy. No sign of Lion Tat.

Gorilla Guy was holding up pretty well, denying everything, but I thought that if they actually used the Taser gun they were brandishing, he'd cop to something, then give up his Grandma's secret Snickerdoodle recipe.

I was pleased to see I'd gotten in some defensive moves before they'd taken me down. A trickle of blood on Tom's forearm emanated from a perfect set of teeth marks. I'd had a great orthodontist.

Gorilla Guy kept babbling, going on about his wife, his kids, his clean driving record, how he'd smoked but never inhaled. He looked like he was about to cry when the interrogation was interrupted by someone whistling. Not a cat call or warning. It was a familiar song. "Highwayman."

I looked at Gator, then past him, as Highwayman approached limping, favoring his left side. His nose was swollen, cheek grazed and bruised, one eye blackening.

He stared at Gorilla Guy, cocking his head right and left like an owl zoning in on its prey. Finally he said, "Get him out of here."

Gorilla Guy left with the dock worker. Tom handed Highwayman a gun and a phone with an earpiece. They exchanged some hand signals—which could have meant go out there and teach Gorilla Guy the Macarena or slap him around a little, then release the poor SOB.

When Highwayman turned around, the rough, tough road cowboy I'd seen as a shadow bent over Boone that night, the same guy who'd been in line behind me at the truck stop when we picked up the Baconator's rig, and on the tape in the Pharmco restroom was gone. In his place was someone who looked old and tired, like he'd been sold a bad bill of goods. The irony was not lost on me.

Gator caught my eye and tipped his chin at the condition of our nemesis, as if to say, "See? I did that."

I threw him a smile, then turned my attention to Highwayman.

"Is that all you know how to whistle? Jesus Christ. Get a repertoire, try "Mary Had a Little Lamb," "America the Beautiful" or "Baby Got Back." Shit. People going to think you have some kind of Tourettes or something, stuck on Willie Nelson all the damn time, H-man."

The nickname got his attention. He turned slowly, focusing on me with his good eye. "You been talking to somebody, Ms. Boudreaux?"

"Yep, sure have. That Clayton is a chatty little guy. Had a whole lot to say about you and your pals."

"Is that right?"

I pushed the bluff. There was no way he could know that Clayton was dead. "We know about the vials and the labels." His face didn't crack. "The NewGen." I pushed. "And the base hospital."

Finally, a reaction. More maniacal grin than anger.

"You have been busy, Ms. Boudreaux, haven't you?"

"We know what you've been doing. We won't let it happen. You fucked with the wrong group of people." I tipped my head toward the window. "You do know we're not here alone."

"Oh, really?" He made a show of looking around, before he turned his attention back to me. "You mean your trucker buddies? No. Sorry. They've been detained. A certain little birdie may have given their GPS a little re-direction. And there is that thing with the air brakes on the Peterbilt. Shame, really."

I strained at the duct tape, edges digging into my skin. "You piece of shit! You better not have done anything to my friends. I'll kill you—"

He raised his hand, cutting me off. "You're hardly in any position, Ms. Boudreaux. I will deal with Clayton and his...insubordination. And as far as your friends are concerned? Would that be..." He patted his pockets, produced my cell phone, swiping the touch screen bringing up Dusty's profile, turning it around to show me. "Him?"

I bit back rage, released my clenched fists, played it cool.

He smiled and approached, speaking real slow, like I had a mental problem. "Cell phones have many uses in this day and age. You would be surprised what we can learn about you from this single device."

I leaned back, hoping he wouldn't try to pat my head.

"Now here's a text message from one *Ivory Joe*? Oh, you Southerners are so *quaint.* Is that word I'm looking for?" He looked at Gator, got mean-mugged, looked back at the phone and read, "Remember what Paw Paw used to say: *The man that hunts two hares from one bush is unlikely to catch either.*" He stroked his chin. "Well now I don't know what the fuck that's supposed to mean. Do you, Ms. Boudreaux?"

I sent him a telepathic *fuck you*.

"Maybe we should ask your Ivory Joe. What do you think? Or maybe you should simply call him and tell him that you're fine, this was all a misunderstanding. Tell him that you and Mr. Natoli have settled everything, and that he can stand down, just walk away—like your pal Dusty agreed to do. Amazing what the threat to a certain amount of bodily damage can do to a man who cares so much about his body."

I looked at Gator. So much for winging it. So much for bluffing and conning, pretending we had all the answers. So much for the hope that an army of truckers would come and save us.

"You will co-operate, Ms. Boudreaux. You are into something that is no concern of yours and you need to leave things be. What you think you see on the surface is nothing compared to what lies beneath. This is one ditch you do not want to fall into. Seldom do people get out alive. That is not a threat. That is a promise. Now, I'm giving you one last chance. Drop this. I know you don't want Ivory Joe to meet the same end as the precious Boone, do you?"

Before I could reply or spit or tear a chunk out of him, he held out the phone, hit the call button, engaged the speaker.

Ivory Joe answered on the third ring. I could hear the hospital in the background: beeps, whooshes and clicks of machines, crepe soles on a tile floor, a wheeled cart passing by, someone crying. Those sounds might have been louder in my head than anyone else's, stuck there from the time when I existed on the in-between—when I'd been living a half-life under bright lights in a narrow bed.

Ivory Joe said, "Jojo?"

I looked at Gator who nodded.

I took a deep breath then shouted "Hey," toward the phone. "How's the leg?"

"It's okay. They're taking care of me. Should be able to get out of here soon. Oh, I had Gator's cop pals take Manny to Houston to be with Pilar. Figured that was what you'd want."

"Good."

"So, you all right? You get my text?"

"I did." I looked at H-man. "Listen, Ivory Joe, this was all a big mistake. I never should have gotten you involved in the first place. We're fine, Gator and me. And now that you and Père are safe, we're leaving this to the proper authorities. So, there's nothing for you to be concerned about."

My words were met with silence.

"Ivory Joe? I hope you read me?"

"Yeah. Loud and clear." He hung up.

H-man clicked the end button then dropped the phone on the ground, crushing it underfoot.

"That wasn't too hard, was it?" he said.

I really wanted to kill him. But I also wanted real answers. My bluff hadn't exactly made him open up.

There was a buzzing sound. H-man stepped away, touching his earpiece.

"Yeah?" He listened for a moment, jaws clenching, hands fisted. "You're fucking kidding, right? I thought that was handled. You know what—I'll go. No! Find Mickey. Tell him to finish up here."

H-man tapped his ear, then started for the door.

"Aren't you going to say goodbye?" Gator asked.

H-man spun around, drawing a long bladed knife from a belt sheath with lightning speed. The cowboy was back. He bent over Gator, lowered his voice, saying something until Gator swallowed and nodded. It was just like the night on the highway with Boone. My stomach turned inside out.

"Don't!" I yelled. "Please."

Highwayman looked at me grinning, then turned back to Gator, flicked the edge of the blade against his cheek, pricking red.

"Goodbye." He stood, then turned back. "Oh, and thanks for this." He held up the SD card. "You can't imagine the possibilities."

As soon as the door closed behind him and the whistling faded, Gator dumped himself onto the floor, began wrestling with the fabric chair in a comedic attempt to free himself.

I wasn't faring much better across the room squeezing and hunching my shoulders until they burned, trying to wear down the tape binding my hands to the heavy table leg.

"Whoa. Easy there."

I looked up to see a white-haired man enter the room, close and lock the door behind him, then stoop and upright Gator's chair, with Gator in it—not an easy task.

I shook my head, blinking away the sweat dripping into my eyes, recognizing him instantly. The Pharmco warehouse old man who'd lo-jacked us—though looking closer, he wasn't old—his leathery skin was more over-tanned than elderly and his white hair had dark roots.

"Oh, fuck balls. What now?" I slumped back against the table.

The man went to the window of the break room. There was the sound of engines starting, vehicles driving away. The man stood tall and straight. He ran a hand through his hair. Something I'd seen Gator do a hundred times. Suddenly, it didn't seem so innocent.

He waited a minute, then turned to us.

"Now where were we?"

"You were going to cut us loose," I said.

"Was I?" he asked, smiling.

Chapter 17

I rubbed my sore wrists, trying to get circulation back into my fingers. Gator sat beside me on the table, swinging his legs, staring down the white-haired guy pacing in front of us.

"Could you not?" White Hair said, pointing at Gator's legs. "It's distracting."

I touched Gator's thigh. "C'mon, he said he'd explain. So let him explain."

Gator tipped his chin. "He could start with telling us who he is."

White Hair stopped pacing. "Name's Mickey Bonafano. I'm on your side."

"Right. You and those guys?" Gator jerked a thumb toward the warehouse.

Mickey shook his head. "No, they just think I'm one of them. Listen, I know you have questions, and I'll get to those, but first, H-man said you've been talking to Twitch."

Seeing our blank stares, he added, "Clayton? Clayton Woods?"

"Right," I said, remembering the driver's license in the Velcro wallet. "Twitch." I smiled. "Yeah, we had words."

"Last words." Gator said.

Mickey looked at me. "Shit. What did he tell you?"

I found a blank spot on the wall, concentrated on burning a pinhole into it with my eyes.

Mickey said, "Twitch was an asshole. Greedy and stupid, plus he was a junkie. Got himself hooked on the stuff that might have later saved him. The real Clayton died long ago."

When we didn't say anything, he ran a hand over his face and sighed. "We think he was working with somebody else. Did he say anything about that, or give any indication..."

His voice dropped off as he noticed my lack of interest. "Listen," he said. "I'm sorry—for the things he did to you, the people you care about. I know what's it's like to lose someone."

Gator scoffed. "What the fuck? Is this the good cop turn? Because I know how to play that."

Gator started to slide off the table. Mickey had his firearm between Gator's eyes before his heels hit the ground.

"Sit down."

Gator sat, arms raised, chin up.

The gun barrel never wavered. Mickey asked, "What do you know about this?"

He held up the group photograph I'd taken from Clayton's office, the picture H-man's warehouse guys had found on Gator when they searched him.

Gator shrugged.

Mickey tapped my arm with his gun. "You?"

I looked at the gun, then him. "Could you not?"

He put the gun back in his waistband, cocked his head as I leaned back on my elbows, and said, "I know that Highwayman and Clayton—Twitch—were connected. And that picture was taken at the old naval base, pretty much around the corner from here. That's it."

Mickey stared at the picture as if seeing it for the first time. He touched the faces on the photo, giving them names. "Highwayman, H-man, AKA Harry Minot. Edwin Dorsey, you might know him as The Baconator. Twitch, the now deceased Clayton Woods." He paused at the fourth man, face half in shadow, a blurred image. "And that's Doc. He's my in to these guys. I met him when my sister got sick the first time.

"He was her lead physician at the hospital in Chicago. Something happened over the years. He got caught with his hand in the cookie jar or something. Ended up in New Mexico, working at some shysty clinic. But by the time Susan, that's my sister, got sick again, that was the place everyone said she should go.

"He said he had access to cancer meds, treatment centers. We trusted him. We had to. Mom was broke. Insurance was shit. Got turned away so many times—it doesn't matter. Doc left New Mexico, started up the place here on the old base few years ago. We knew what was going on and bought into it, moved Susan out here with him and signed on for everything."

He stared off remembering, went quiet. A minute later he said, "She and I got close there, at the end. Broke my mother's heart to see it. She kept saying how cute we were together as kids. How if she'd known this was coming, she would have made sure we were nicer to each other all along, that we would have been friends, real friends, not waiting until it was too late."

He straightened up, took a deep breath. "You can't make up for lost years. Even though you get old and forget things, you have to have had the chance to build those memories to be able to forget them. Susan used to write home about what they were doing down here. How Doc was a hero. Saving people, changing lives, adding to the list of Survivors, like there was a tally somewhere. I kept every letter she sent. Read them so many times, they're worn out, just creases and faded blue ink."

He handed the picture back to Gator. "It's funny," he said with a laugh, turning toward the window. "How you think you've got it all figured out, and then, ka-boom!"

He said it so loud it startled me. I snuck a look at Gator, sent one of those *Is this guy fucking nuts or what?* looks. Gator gave me the one shoulder shrug in reply.

"Sorry," I said.

Mickey spun around.

"About your sister."

It was his turn to shrug. "Just another statistic. Too fucking young. Beautiful girl. So much to give. Angel in Heaven. Blah. Blah. Blah. Go on. I've heard them all."

Gator, being Gator, jumped in, reining the horse so hard left I almost felt the bit in my mouth. He said, "Tell us about NewGen and Pharmco."

Mickey smiled. "Ah, yes. Fuck sentimentality. Let's get down to it. And you're right, there isn't a shitload of time, and there's a lot you don't know."

Mickey pulled up a chair and began to tell us about H-man, Twitch, Edwin and Doc, and their clinic, which some people were calling a survival camp.

"It's not that kind of survival camp," he said. "This place isn't for doomsayers or girls who want to be better *campers*. This is for people diagnosed with late stage cancer, people who haven't had the best results with chemo, and the ones with the really bad shit. The diagnoses that come with a stopwatch. They offer alternative treatments that aren't always available in the U.S.: sound, light, hypnotherapy, leeches, stuff you don't even want to know. Also, they help make the drugs more affordable."

"By stealing them, right? Drugs that other people need?" I said.

"Not always," Mickey said. "In the beginning, they bought the best stuff, had a wholesaler, worked with clinics, all on the up and up as far as we could tell, but then, maybe they got greedy. I don't know. There have been problems lately, and not just here."

"What kind of problems?" Gator asked.

Mickey hesitated, then said, "You mentioned NewGen. As you probably know, the FDA revoked approval of the drug, due to a few...complications. But some people swear by it. We've seen terminal cases turn around, five-year survival rates increase by twelve percent. For some, it is, forgive the cliché, their last hope."

"I can understand the draw," I said. "But are the risks worth the possibility?"

No one said anything, and in the silence I had my answer.

Mickey took the photo from Gator and tucked it in his pocket.

I said, "So that guy, Doc, he's all right?"

Mickey nodded. "Yeah, I talked to him this morning. It's Edwin I'm looking for now. He's got something they need."

"Yeah, The Baconator guy? You can stop looking for him," Gator said.

"What? Him too?"

I shrugged. *Wasn't our fault.*

Mickey ran a hand through his hair, shook his head. "Where?"

Gator told him about finding the corpse in the woods, how we'd given the information to the cops to keep them busy. They were probably all over it by now.

He shook his head. "How the hell am I going to find it now?"

"Find what?" I asked.

"Never mind, it's not your problem."

"Actually, it might be. Boone and I delivered Baconator's last load," I said.

"And," Gator said, "it was his trailer that your pal Twitch jacked-up, causing the crash that killed Boone. I kind of think you owe her an explanation."

Mickey seemed to agree. He said, "Do you know what was in that load?"

"Paperwork said saline." I shook my head, thinking about the dinged-up, soggy bottomed cardboard boxes coming out of Baconator's trailer at the drop. Eight big boxes that looked a lot like the empty ones in the cold storage room I'd just left.

Mickey raised a brow, tilted his head.

Gator raised his hand. "Can I try?"

Mickey nodded.

"My guess is that the load was really a lot more of the same thing we hauled down here from Pharmco. Vials of NewGen."

Mickey smiled. "And how would you know that?'

"Call it an educated guess," I said.

Gator's hand went to his injured leg, his finger tracing the wound he got when breaking into the trailer.

I stood and stretched. "So, I get it that you're here, working the legal side of things, trying to make things right, so you say. But H-man, I don't see him as a selfless man, running a clinic for those less fortunate, or doing anything for the greater good. What's in it for him?"

"Money, of course. And a certain amount of power. After all, he has people's lives in his hands. He likes to sell to the highest bidder."

"Regardless of need?" I said.

Mickey turned his palms up. It wasn't his burden.

"What kind of money are we talking?" Gator asked.

"Well, there's the clean and the dirty. Trafficking these cancer drugs, real and counterfeit, you're talking about making hundreds of millions. But go bigger, legit, and with everything involved with cancer costs, you're talking getting a stake in the neighborhood of a hundred fifty-eight billion."

"Nice neighborhood," Gator said.

"It's always about the money isn't it?" I asked.

"So they say," Gator added. "Well, that or sex."

"Did you just make that up?"

"No."

"Are you sure?"

"Yeah. Well, pretty sure. What's wrong with sex, anyway?"

I shrugged. "Nothing."

He smiled. "Good."

Mickey watched us, an amused expression on his face.

"So wait," I said, remembering what we were here for. "If the big money is on the legit side, and you've got access to a clinic—which you do— then aren't you on the right track to helping people?"

Mickey see-sawed his hand. "There are other issues, some of the counterfeit meds can make people more sick, some are the same as shooting them up with saline. It's not going to change a thing. And even if the drug is the real deal, if it's not properly stored, it's ineffective. You need medical professionals in these clinics to administer the chemo, to be sure the doses are right, to follow up with additional meds and services."

"That's why people should be in real hospitals," Gator said.

Mickey shrugged. "Same thing. No one really knows what's in every vial. Hospitals don't test what they're buying, or injecting. Think about it, how would you know what medicine you're getting, past reading the label?"

I thought of the images of the stamped colored oval pills on the SD card. All that information for someone to make duplicates. I tipped my head back, exhaled to the ceiling. "Jesus. How deep does this go?"

"The fake drugs? That's been around a while. Cancer? That's been around a while too, but it's getting worse. Look around. I can guarantee out of the three of us in this room at least two of us have lost family or friends to cancer and at least one of us knows a survivor."

No one argued his point.

He pointed to Gator. "You've got a forty-four percent chance of getting some sort of cancer in your lifetime. How do you want to play those odds?"

Gator cocked his head like a dog hearing a faraway whistle, or the sound of a cracker dropping on a wood floor.

I thought about it. Getting cancer, having a loved one diagnosed. Sure, we'd pay out the ass to beat it, but what if we were getting the wrong drugs, bad drugs and got sicker, or worse, died from that, not even the original disease. Who would know? How could they fix that?

The sick would keep paying in, keep hanging on, eating the tiny increments of hope dished out vial by vial.

I said, "When this gets out, when people learn that these drugs need to be tested before you pay seventy-five hundred for a vial of saline, won't this stop?"

"And who's going to test all those vials?" Mickey asked. "Toss out the bad ones, reduce the stock until there's not enough for everyone? Who's going to choose which patient gets cured, which dies? You?"

"They wouldn't let the counterfeits into the system, would they?" I asked. "I mean, they can't. You said yourself, if they're fakes or have been stored wrong, they're no good, maybe even poison."

Mickey didn't answer.

I thought about 9/11—how before a plane crashed into a skyscraper and changed our world—an act like that had merely been a distant threat, a scene from a sci-fi film. Afterward? It was a scary thing that could happen any day at any time. Something we had to protect ourselves against forever—at whatever cost.

Chapter 18

We stood at the lip of the docking bay. Sabrina looked like a black and chrome beast in the murky pre-dawn fog, towering over two black sedans. Mickey explained that while we'd been detained, H-man's crew wiped our electronics. They were very thorough, he assured us. There would be no trail, no evidence, nothing other than our word about any of this. He strongly advised us to walk away and let him handle things, said there were certain protocols that needed to be followed.

H-man's plan was to have us tailed to Louisiana. Mickey said H-man expected us to return to the plantation and hole up for a while. We agreed to keep up pretenses. I didn't want to admit how badly I wanted a shower, a bed, a room, a locked door.

Mickey shook Gator's hand. "You're pretty good, Natoli. You ever think of changing jobs, let me know."

Gator snorted. "Like that's going to happen." He grabbed Mickey's hand in both of his. "Hey, forgot to ask. Where's my Caddy?"

"No worries," Mickey said, disengaging his hand from Gator's vice grip. "I drove her into the trailer for you, left my number in the glove box."

Gator hopped off the dock to go check on his car, calling over his shoulder, "You coming, Jojo?"

Mickey turned to me. "Tell him you'll be right there."

I hesitated, then waved to Gator. "I'll be right there."

I waited until Gator turned around, then looked at Mickey. "What?"

"I just wanted to tell you. What happened with Boone. It never should have come to that. Fucking Twitch was losing it. We all knew it, and no one did anything. I'm sorry. I need you to know that."

I nodded.

"And I need you to know I've got this. There's nothing more for you to do, okay?"

I looked at him, this guy, with all this sincerity oozing from his pores. A dude who somehow, someway was believable, likeable even. *Fuck me.*

I jumped off the docking bay and spun around, saying, "Okay, I'm good with that," then turned and jogged to the rig, thinking, *Or maybe not* as I ran my hand down the side of Sabrina, cherishing the heft of her metal under my hand. I made my way down the trailer to the back where Gator was strapping down the Caddy for transport.

His car seemed none the worse for wear. Centered in the trailer, it was padded, protected and well secured by flat canvas ties ratcheted down. A glance inside showed keys in the ignition and a smiley face drawn on the dusty dashboard. Someone had even made a half-hearted attempt to clean Ivory Joe's blood off the seat.

I told Gator what Mickey had said, about H-man's babysitter in the black sedan, about him handling everything from here on out, and about us following protocol.

Gator nodded as if he was partly listening. He shined up the door handle with the end of his T-shirt, then stood back appraising the Caddy like she was his prom date. I waited for him to pat her fender or sneak in a tire squeeze, but instead he shoved his hands in his pockets and turned to me with a sheepish grin.

"Kind of stupid to care so much about a car, right?"

"Not at all," I said. "Most people don't care enough."

I stared at the Caddy, her wonky muffler that had taken a beating. I said, "If we really cared about everything as strongly as we feel about our cars, then no matter what anyone said you'd have to—"

"Do the right thing," Gator said.

I peered deep into his clear, blue eyes and smiled. "That's right. Which means, we find the NewGen, real and fake and destroy it. Fuck protocol." I jumped off the back of trailer and reached for one of the doors.

"Fuck protocol," Gator said, hopping down and grabbing the other door.

As he slid the bolt across, I could tell Gator wished we had a padlock, or zip ties, or a Siberian tiger to guard his baby. But there was none of that.

I patted his back as we walked around the trailer to the rear of the sleeper unit, stopping only when he motioned me to go first up the metal steps.

Inside Sabrina, a confusing odor of men's cologne hung in the air. It was the mingling of two styles—not unlike Gator and I—except in this case it was ocean breeze meets wet wool, as if we'd had both *Miami Vice* and Sherlock Holmes on board.

I reached into the oven, lifted the false bottom and re-trieved the spare guns.

From the window over the sink we could see a single black sedan idling quietly.

"Remember when Mickey said they thought Twitch was working with someone? What do you think that means?"

"It's something to look at," Gator said. "Come on. Let's get on the road."

Chapter 19

I checked my Kimber, tossed Gator his Glock and asked him to drive. I had some thinking to do.

The whole vibe coming off Highwayman was something I knew well. He was the dude we'd all run into at some point in our lives—unpopular growing up, bullied maybe, not the smartest kid around, but good at something, usually the kind of something that could become a job. Never a great job, never one that would inspire or educate, because he'd never be the best at it. He was destined to live a mediocre life—in all aspects. He would fail at marriage, at relationships, at friendships. He'd have financial problems even when he made a lot of money. He'd spend his whole life trying to get something he wasn't supposed to have. Guys like that were doomed from the start. If this was the Stone Age, and babies were tossed over cliffs for not meeting the standard, for not showing promise, for slowing down the clan? If that were the case? H-man wouldn't be alive and none of this shit would be happening.

But it was, and not just to me. There were millions of people out there fighting cancer. All the fucking kinds of cancer we'd invented. Why couldn't we stop naming them? Père used to say giving something a name gave it power. The last thing this disease needed was more power.

We'd come into this thinking it was just about some missing cargo, some small time crooks getting something over on the trucking community. Gator with his need to create order, to find answers, to close the book. Me, pissed off at the world and thinking it was all about me, my deal, my shit. Now that I knew how Boone died and why, I should be able to walk away. I should want to walk away. What me and Gator had? It was good. Really good. That should be enough.

But, it wasn't. Not yet. Mickey had sold it too hard. He'd done all the things to entice the hunter in me, dangling the big prize, hinting at the trail, suggesting it was unobtainable.

Hunters and truckers love a challenge.

I shut off the computer, pushed it aside, then lay my cheek on the cool, hard table and closed my eyes.

When I was sixteen, I was short on cash and went to a cosmetology school for a free cut and color. I had to deal with a newbie girl whose hands shook, and when she pulled off the towel and spun me around, I had purple hair. They apologized, tried to fix it, but finally had to admit my choices were to stay purple or go bald. Sure I'd saved money, but I ended up looking like an idiot in the end. I hated looking like an idiot.

I moved up front to the passenger seat, and buckled in. "Hey, Gator?"

"What?"

I leaned in and whispered, "Ivory Joe and I had another saying about hunting."

"What's that?" he whispered back.

"It ain't over until the last bird's gone to roost."

I cranked up the volume on the radio, jerked a thumb toward the sleeper area, then pointed to my ear. He must have gotten the message that I thought the rig had been bugged by H-man, because he gave me the thumbs up.

I said, "When I got that weird text from Ivory Joe, about

Paw Paw and hunting two hares from one bush…"

"Yeah?"

"Well, I don't have a Paw Paw. I think he was telling us to look at the someone else, the—"

"One behind the scenes." We finished the sentence together, then fist bumped, like partners do.

A minute later he whispered, "So if we find him, that gets us to the NewGen?"

"You mean, when we find *her*—I knew she had to be involved. I just didn't want to believe it."

"What am I missing?" Gator asked.

I unbuckled my seat belt so I could get close to his ear. Leaning in close, breathing his smell, I wanted to kiss him. I wanted to lick his neck, run my tongue from ear to throat to—but I held myself back. Instead, I showed him the photo of the windblown woman I'd kept from Clayton's office, told him about a certain convertible I knew that was same blue as the one parked next to Clayton's yellow pickup in a photo on the SD card, about a woman who might be blonde now, but…

"Fucking Char—"

I cut him off, clamping a hand over his mouth, then reminded him about the strange call from Charlene when we were on the way to Corpus Christi with the load from Pharmco and how she'd been the one to assign Boone and me at the very beginning.

Gator smacked the steering wheel.

"I know," I whispered. "Remember when H-man said that Dusty and the other drivers had GPS issues? A dispatcher could have done that."

"And a dispatcher can get us back into Pharmco. We need to talk to her, in person."

I smiled. "And by 'talk to,' you mean, beat the shit out of, right?"

"No doubt, Jojo. All I need to know is how do we get rid of him?"

He stared into the side view mirror at the black sedan tailing us.

Traffic was building up on Route 77. Whether we were headed back to Houston or off to Bunkie, Louisiana, we still had to travel the same route—for a while anyway.

I knew that if I was in a sedan behind a rig the size of us, I'd be pissed off and unable to see much. Those two components were in our favor.

"It's going to be tight and I'm not sure I like the odds," Gator said, after I laid out my plan to him—a series of drawings on a pad of paper. We spoke low over an action movie playing on the TV in the sleeper, surround sound speakers up as loud as they could go.

I said, "You just don't like the possibility of your baby getting hurt."

"Which baby is that again?" he asked.

"Don't worry," I said. "I'll be fine. Did I tell you about the stuntman I dated?"

"Here we go," Gator said, making a swift and unnecessary lane change.

"I must have mentioned it," I said.

"No, I would have remembered that. But then again, he might have gotten lost in the sea of actors, professional body builders, astronauts, Navy SEALs, and underwear models."

"Oh, puh-lease."

"What? Did I miss someone?"

"Well, yeah," I said. "A lot of someones, actually. But that's not the point. The point is, I have experience."

"Yeah, you've made *that* abundantly clear."

"What? Oh, really, Gator?"

He sighed, then I sighed, then we both sighed together which made us smile.

"Listen," I said, getting out of the passenger seat. "You're just going to have to believe in me."

"I do," he said. "That's what scares me."

I squeezed his shoulder in the most maternal way I could conjure up, then headed to the sleeper's kitchen where I found an old set of walkie talkies, checked the batteries, then filled a lightweight pack with anything I thought I might need. I slipped on the pack, sent up a brief prayer to the god of dumb ideas, then went up front, poking my head out of the curtains that separated the sleeper from the cab.

I handed Gator one of the walkies and whispered, "Call me right before we hit that hill."

Gator nodded. "Be careful."

I kissed his cheek, then made my way through the sleeper to the back door, glad that we'd be in voice contact with the handhelds. We'd decided to leave the trailer cam off in case our pals were monitoring that as well, though without Gator able to see what I was doing back there and when I was doing it, we'd have to rely on perfect timing—and a shitload of luck.

We hadn't had a chance to repair the hole in the trailer roof from Gator's earlier drop-in escapade, so I was going to attempt a *Reverse Gator*, as my drawings had eluded. Granted it was going to be harder on me, dropping from ceiling to floor, but I did have an expensive vintage Cadillac to break my fall.

The idea was for Gator to sandwich our rig between two trucks in the right hand lane, with the intention of masking my movements and slowing down traffic enough that our escort would do the obvious—pull around the rig behind us and approach Gator on the driver's side, probably wearing his unhappy face.

I'd already set up our rear truck, by flashing a series of signs to the driver of a pretty yellow and orange Volvo. Telling a fellow driver that you had trouble on your tail and needed some help was usually met with a head nod and a thumbs up.

The lead truck had been harder to communicate with. We'd had to compete with his lunchtime followed by a workout routine. But, three signs, one sandwich and twenty curls later, we got his attention and a big hell yeah.

Truckers help truckers. That's what we do.

I tried to not think about all the ways this could go wrong, grabbed the handle and stepped out the back door into the small space between sleeper and trailer. I felt the surge as Gator accelerated, widening the gap between us and the sedan, so the Volvo could slip in behind. A single beep on the walkie told me our rear was covered, and it was time for me to go to work.

Getting on top of the trailer wasn't difficult. Staying on top was. Natural crosswinds on the open stretch of road, plus air buffeting between the big rigs, combined with a downhill angle all added up to trouble.

I hung on, heart pounding, my fingertips turning white, talking myself into step two. "Come on, Jojo. Don't be a pussy."

The roof peeled back easy enough. The opening for Gator was twice the size I needed. I slipped in and let go. The drop to the floor of the trailer was tougher than I'd imagined. The resulting pain in my twisted ankle? Worse than I'd hoped.

I hobbled around the Caddy, began loosening canvas straps, talking the fear down, managing pain the way I'd learned to in the past year. *Suck it up. Breathe.*

Pads and blankets fell away as I worked the ratchets in reverse.

It was hot and almost totally dark in the trailer, except for the stream of daylight coming from the busted roof. Gator's painted cardboard patch dangled and swung, batting the wall of the trailer. I squeezed around the side of the car, felt the vehicle shift as truck and trailer bumped over uneven pavement. With mere inches between me and the metal bumper of the car, between me and the hot metal walls, an image flashed: Jojo Boudreaux, dead, eyes wide open, pinned between car and wall, like something out of a Stephen King novel. As soon as I shook that image away, another appeared—a familiar nightmare—a busted trailer in flames sliding down a highway headed toward a glass strewn cab, a man in black leaning over a body in the road, bright lights flashing in the distance.

Panic slid up my throat, filling my mouth and nose. I gasped for breath, forcing myself down from the ledge I'd created.

After the accident, certain cracks in my perfect veneer had revealed themselves, widening to let in other cracks—of the mental kind. The new claustrophobia was a blessing and a curse, as it forced me to continually seek escape routes. One of the fail-safes I'd installed in the trailer, an interior sliding bolt release, was about to be put to good use.

I checked my watch, took a deep breath and squeezed around the car. I pulled out the last wheel block and was releasing the final canvas strap when Gator's voice broke the silence.

"Hill in fifty yards. We're a go, Houston."

"Roger that." I said as I tossed the strap aside, hopped to the rear and slid the bolt. I gave the doors a gentle shove, letting inertia and gravity do the rest.

As I climbed in the front of the Cadillac, dragging my swollen ankle after me, I felt the incline increase. We were on the ascent side of the hill, and like the rise on a rollercoaster ride, I felt my stomach pull back and away.

I reminded myself this had been my brilliant idea, then released the parking break and started the engine. Behind me, the trailer doors widened. I saw the grill of the big yellow Volvo VN780—too close.

"Pull back!" I yelled, knowing he couldn't hear me, but yelled just the same, "Come on!" We had to be nearing the top of the hill. It was now or never. I shifted into reverse, closed my eyes and floored it. With a shower of sparks and a howling scrape as the undercarriage met metal, the Caddy was free, bouncing onto asphalt at forty miles per hour.

The Volvo, hauling lumber on its flatbed, changed lanes and bore down on the black sedan, forcing it forward as they crested the hill. It felt surreal to be driving in reverse away from them, and into oncoming traffic. For a few seconds everything slowed—my foot moving from gas to brake pedal, my hand reaching for the gear shift to hit neutral, then drive, my mouth forming a giant oval screaming, "Ohhhh, shit!"

Cars in my lane pulled off onto the shoulder, some swerved to other lanes. One passing vehicle raised a cell phone to shoot a picture. Only in America.

Finally gaining control of the car, I maneuvered it toward an exit ramp, caught a bit of grass and air, but quickly felt the tires catch and grab.

I stilled my shaking hands enough to click the walkie twice to let Gator know I was on the road and all was good, then focused on part two of the plan: Charlene.

Chapter 20

Pulling into the parking lot at DeSalena Transport, I was pleased and a bit angry to see nothing had changed—same old office building, broken light hanging from a hinge, same old warehouse with DST trucks backed up to the docks, same old shiny blue T-bird parked in the Head Dispatcher's space. Maybe it was bitter of me to be pissed off that other people's lives had not gotten turned upside down in the past year like mine had, that some might have even improved. But screw it, that was how I felt, and I was all about being true to my feelings—whatever the fuck that meant. Right now, I felt like T-boning Charlene's T-bird with the Caddy.

But that would have meant ruining two beautiful things. Something inside of me just couldn't do it. I pulled into a space as near to the door as I could find and hopped out, ankle throbbing, but forced myself to walk as normally as possible. Hopping down the hall toward dispatch might draw a bit of unwanted attention. First stop was the restroom, one for the obvious reason, and also I remembered that mounted behind the door was a big first aid box.

I left the restroom appreciating the expired Lortab pills someone had donated almost as much as I appreciated the tightly wrapped Ace bandage on my ankle. It was amazing what a long pee and few pain pills could do for one's attitude.

Charlene sat behind her desk, back to the door, flirting with some trucker I'd never seen before. Poor guy looked like a puppy in a cage at the mall, part crazy to be let out and part begging to be scooped up.

"Time for you to go," I said, pointing from the guy to the door, in case he wasn't sure what I meant. He did the dog head-tilt and I repeated my finger motion, feeling like I had the spirit of Boone in me—Ghost Dog-People Whisperer.

Damned if it didn't work. The guy sidestepped me, exited the office, closing the door behind him, leaving a whiff of drugstore body spray in his wake that might have been called, I'm-married-but-that's-just-on-paper-OH-her-daddy-has-a-big-gun.

Charlene swiveled around in her chair. "What the hell? Jojo! You're supposed to be—I mean, come on in, sugar."

She patted her hair, tugged up her neckline, then scooted her chair back into place, as if she'd been on the clock the whole time. I saw flashing lines on her monitor—disrupted calls, unanswered messages, open windows to shopping networks.

"What's going on, Charlene?"

She glanced at the door.

"I'm not talking about him."

Before she could pull her charming country girl routine on me, I said, "I know about Clayton."

She opened her mouth to say something, then seeing the look on my face, and the handgun in my waistband, snapped her lips shut.

"Charlene, do you have any idea what you're involved in?" I said, leaning back on her desk, taking the weight off my bad ankle.

"I'm not involved in anything. I'm just an...interested party."

"I don't know who told you to say that and I don't have enough time right now to explain how wrong you are, or how many people's lives are at stake because of what you've done. What I do have time for is watching you make a few calls and get me into Pharmco." I punctuated the last three words with my well-developed index finger, a finger that got almost as much use as its neighbor finger. Almost.

Charlene stared at me, at my finger on her ample chest, then slowly answered, "I can't help you. They won't let you in unless they invite you."

"What am I a fucking vampire? I don't want them to invite me in. I don't even want them to know I'm there until it's too late."

"How are you going to do that? That place is more secure than my supply of Chunky Monkey ice cream." She tipped her head toward a chained and padlocked mini fridge in the corner of the room.

It was painful to watch the virtual light bulb blink on, her eyes widening as she said, "Wait. Maybe Clayton has some ideas. Here, I'll call him." She reached for her phone.

I put my hand on her arm to stop her. "Clayton's dead."

"What? No. He said that we, I mean, he can't be..."

The tears were real. I let Charlene have her moment, even refrained from glancing at my watch. She gathered herself in a minute or two, then raised her red-rimmed eyes to mine.

"If you knew *things*," she said, "If you had access to areas, knew certain people, and someone came to you and said you'd be helping sick people if you helped them—what would you do?"

"What are you saying, Charlene?"

"Clayton said I was good at finding things out, getting people to talk. DST has been around a long time, seen a lot of companies come and go, a lot of money change hands, you know? I just talked to people, like drivers on the road when they're lonely. And sometimes, other people like the guys in maintenance and the upper level managers—no one wants to be their friend. Clayton told me what to ask about." She looked around, then lowered her voice. "Sometimes I wore a wire."

"Hold on." I started laughing. "Are you saying you're a spy?"

"What's so funny about that?"

"Never mind," I said, shaking my head. "Wait a minute." I pushed myself off the desk and began to pace, bad ankle and all. "Charlene, what do you really know about Pharmco and these cargo thefts?"

"I know we moved some very important cancer drugs for them. They trusted DST, must have figured since we had the Enahel accounts—"

"Enahel? Boone used to drive for them, didn't he?"

She nodded, glanced toward a pack of cigarettes, back at me. "You mind?"

"Go ahead." I waited for her to light a cigarette, produce a smokeless ashtray from behind a plant on her desk, then I asked, "What happened to Enahel?"

"They went under. Filed bankruptcy after their warehouse was robbed. Twice. The first time they took ten million worth of Levemir, some kind of insulin. The next time the crooks were more prepared, brought a tractor trailer, knew exactly when to hit it and where to look. They wiped them out, hauled away eighty million in specialty prescription drugs."

"Holy shit."

"I know, right? There's no coming back from that, even with insurance. Wholesalers stopped calling, drivers became even more leery of taking their loads, some even refused the work. They said Omega Vacs paid better, and they never worried about getting hijacked with an OV load."

"What's Omega Vacs?"

"A sort of sister company to Pharmco, they're owned by the same Houston-based petroleum company." She stubbed out her cigarette, tried to look smart. "I don't know anything else."

She must have seen where I was going next because she jumped in with, "Listen, I had nothing, and I repeat, *nothing* to do with your accident, and what happened to Boone. You gotta believe me."

"I don't have to believe anything you say, Charlene. I have the gun."

Her eyes went from my gun to her desk. I put my good foot on the chair between her legs, pinning her back while I ran a hand under the desktop. Bingo. I pulled out the Colt she'd strapped to the underside.

I said, "Correction. I have the *guns*."

Charlene sunk back in her chair, crossed her arms. "I had a bad feeling something was wrong. I tried to tell you—that day you picked up at Pharmco. Remember? I tried to warn you."

I shook my head. "Warn me how?"

"On the phone, I said, Austin, weather, traffic. You know, clues."

"Charlene, are you fucking kidding me? This isn't a living room game of charades."

Charlene started to cry all over again, blubbering how sorry she was and could I ever forgive her?

She wasn't a good enough actress to be faking. I figured Charlene really had no idea what the fuck she'd been involved in. If I still wasn't so pissed off, I might have felt sorry for her. I told her I wasn't interested in the money she'd socked away or the dirty little secrets of the people at Pharmco, said I'd think about forgiving her on one condition.

Charlene said, "All right then. If you want to get back into that warehouse, you're going to need me." She grinned, clapping her hands like a child. "Hey, I'm used to sending drivers to places they *don't* want to go. This will be new for me."

I slid off her desk, gave her access to the phone. She made two calls, promising both men a future lunch date that sounded like a lot more than a burger and a coke.

"You shouldn't have any trouble at the gate," she said, hanging up. "Look for Gary at the warehouse—this guy," she said, clicking a window on her computer, showing me an image on a Facebook page.

"Got it. Thanks. Now where do you want it?" I asked, waving the gun.

"What do you mean? Jojo, you aren't going to shoot me, are you?"

I looked at the gun, then Charlene's worried expression. "No, course not. I'm just going to knock you out, tie you up and take your car."

She laughed, then saw my face. "Wait. What?" Her hands fluttered over her heaving chest.

"You don't want anyone thinking you helped me commit a crime do you? A big spy like you? Come on."

Charlene stared at the gun.

"Sorry, Charlene. It's not about what you can do for others, it's about making sure others aren't fucking you in the ass when you're bent over cold and naked in the shower reaching for the soap."

She only had a second to reflect on that before I clocked her.

I snagged her keys, hog-tied her with her own belt, then locked the door and hurried down the hall, dialing Gator's number on the phone I took from Charlene with one hand, spinning her Ruger in the other.

He answered as I pushed open the door and stepped out into the Texas heat. "Hey."

"Hey, yourself."

"You okay?"

"Been better."

"Is she—"

"The Caddy's fine," I said, glancing over my shoulder at the scraped and dented Cadillac trailing half a bumper, taillight smashed and hanging from a wire.

I unlocked the light blue Thunderbird, slid inside. It smelled like Charlene—baby powder and bourbon with a glossy nail polish finish.

"How did you leave things with Charlene?" Gator asked.

"We had a discussion, cleared the air. She'll be tied up for a while, sorting it all out," I said pulling onto the highway and opening up the big Ford engine.

"A discussion? Is that right? I thought you were going to beat the shit out of her."

I hesitated before replying. "Charlene and I have a history. As my Grandpère used to say, *Some folks deserve a whole lot of leave alone.*"

Gator grunted his reply.

I left off the words, *and I deserve a sky blue classic T-bird,* saying instead, "So, where are you, now?"

"Not far," he said.

"What do you mean?" I yelled over the noise of wind and road and life. "You should be almost to Bunkie—with your escort."

"Never mind him."

"Gator, don't mess with me. You're supposed to go to the plantation."

"There's been a change in plans," he said.

"Not for me." I pushed the gas pedal closer to the floor. "I'm on my way to Pharmco to destroy some NewGen."

"God, that's sexy," Gator said.

I smiled, trying to not dwell on the way he said *sexy*, yet dwelled just the same. So much that I almost missed his next words.

"I'll meet you there."

"What? Gator. No. I'm—"

But he'd already hung up. I didn't bother re-dialing. He wasn't going to answer. He was too much like me.

Chapter 21

I re-read the information Siri had helped me find on Charlene's sparkly phone. *Medicinal quality of NewGen is dependent on the consistency of cool temperatures during storage. A slight fluctuation is not harmful for short periods of time as long as the temperature does not exceed sixty degrees Fahrenheit. Warning:if the temperature remains plus or equal to one hundred and twenty degrees Fahrenheit for a minimum of five minutes, it will destroy every component and destabilize the drug, rendering it useless.*

It's true. The best plans require two things, things I happened to be born with—fast thinking and creative manipulation. When plans fail it's because people didn't react the way they should in certain circumstances. I thought about Charlene thinking she was helping, doing good things for sick people, but in the end, she was only a puppet, performing her part unknowingly to the benefit of the bad guys, the manipulators, the puppeteers. The ones with the money, power, and control. Greedy fuckers.

I wondered if it was worse to be the bad guy, or the one who enables him. What if you were too weak, kind or poor to be the evil one, and yet, your information or weapon or technology was the thing that helped the bad guy—the thing that gave him the edge, helped him make his evil deeds a reality? Sure, it's not your finger pulling the trigger, but it might as well be. And were you any less culpable in the end?

Growing up in the country, we took responsibility. There

were rules: kill what you'll eat, respect the environment, leave no trace, allow the animal to die honorably, be thankful. Some folks may say hunting isn't a true sport, because in sports both sides know they're in the game. But if you've ever looked in the eyes of a buck before you pull the trigger, you'd know he's been in the game from day one.

Charlene might have started as an innocent, but something changed for her. It wasn't my deal to figure out what that was. Or even to understand it. I had enough of my own baggage.

Less than an hour from San Marcos and Pharmco, I stopped musing on the oddities of life and checked Charlene's phone for a Walmart. I pulled up near the garden center, grabbed an abandoned cart and nodded to the greeter—a Santa lookalike minus the twinkly eyes and most of his teeth. I sidestepped the line of special needs shoppers and their aides, and headed for the automotive section.

Three departments later, I was running my take through a self-checkout lane which suited me just fine. Less chatter and no nosy eyes on my supplies. I fed some bills into the machine, took my receipt and hurried back to the T-bird.

By the time I arrived in San Marcos, I had my pitch down pat. I'd changed clothes in the store parking lot, added a layer of makeup and cowboy hat, fired up the new phone and put together a special disposable camera and my own invention, sort of a twist on my uncle's old freezer temperature control unit he used when he storing venison over the winter—only mine had a few extra wires.

As I exited the highway, the box on the floorboard by the passenger seat shifted, the scratching noise increased.

"Easy, boys," I said, as I raised the volume of the radio and stepped on the gas.

* * *

The gate guard at Pharmco made a show of asking me for ID, and when I tried to catch his eye he leaned in and pointed a lot like he was giving me directions. "Charlene told me to let you in, doesn't mean I have to like it. My name ever comes up? You die. Have a nice day."

The gate opened and he waved me through.

Well, fuck me.

If anyone had asked the men in Warehouse Five, home of the temperature control storage Sector 65B, what they thought was in store for them on this ordinary fall workday, they might have said, "Nothing special. Just moving pallets, loading trucks, taking shit from the supervisor and maybe enjoying a deli sandwich at noon."

Certainly none of them were ready for the arrival of Jojo Boudreaux AKA Cowgirl Candy, The Singing Telegram Delivery Girl.

Hey, it's Texas. Everything's bigger, including our imaginations.

There was enough happening in the warehouse that I was able to park, undo my too tight blouse a few more buttons and slip into the hooker heels with no one noticing. I sent up a prayer to the goddess of strippers, big and small, as I pushed on some dark sunglasses, tucked a lighter in my bra, slung the tote over one shoulder and approached the dock leading the way with my boobs.

I clomped up the dock steps and slipped in the side entrance, stealth advantage zero as the metal door clanged behind me.

Two men cursing and struggling with a crate dropped it and turned around. I recognized the chubby one as Gary, even though his Facebook photo had been a slimmer, younger, less focused version.

He looked at me, then looked away.

I toddled over, calling "Yooo-hoo!"

The other guy grinned and sucked in his gut. "Hey there, sugar. Where you been all my life?"

I held back my regular fist to the solar plexus move and instead dazzled him with my smile as I leaned in and said, "Same place I'll be the rest of your life—in your wildest dreams."

I left the brainless one pondering that and approached Gary, slipped a note in his pocket and announced, "Surprise! You've received a singing telegram from Charlie."

It took him a second, but his recovery was impressive.

"Aw shoot. It ain't for me. It's for him!" He pointed to a guy on a phone, his back to us.

"Oh! Sorry. Here, can you hold this?" I pushed up my cowboy hat, peeked over the top of my sunglasses and handed my tote bag to Gary, staring him down. He broke into a sweat.

"Read the note," I whispered.

I readjusted my hat and glasses, toddled over to the man on the phone. Just before I tapped him on the shoulder, he spun around, grinning.

Mickey.

He spoke through gritted teeth. "Not exactly my idea of following protocol, Boudreaux."

He'd managed to reduce me to the errant child. I didn't like that.

Before I could explain or reply through my own gritted teeth, though they were less gritted, more slack-jaw incredulous, he skimmed my body with laser eyes, spoke to my cleavage. "Not that I'm complaining. Yet. Go on. Sing for me. We've got an audience."

I glanced behind me. Brainless was in the exact position I'd left him, probably still trying to figure out if I'd slammed him or given him a compliment. Gary's lips moved as he read my note.

I spun back around, a bit more wiggle to my toodle and put on my best Marilyn Monroe pout adding a country flair as I sang the birthday song, easy on the vocals and heavy on the tits and ass. On the last note, I reached in my back pocket, grabbed the disposable camera, careful of the dangling wire.

"Sorry, Mickey," I said, zapping his neck with the homemade taser. It incapacitated him enough for me to zip-tie opposite hand to opposite ankle, twice.

I kicked off the hooker heels and tossed the hat as I ran past the slumped body of Brainless to the cold storage unit. Gary had pried open a small vent at the back.

"Hope that's what you wanted. Hard to read your writing," he said.

"Yeah, thanks," I said, taking my bag from him. "You're sure this is where the NewGen is?"

Gary nodded, hovering. "You'll tell Charlene, right? That I helped you?"

"Course," I said, giving him the dazzle. "Course I will. She'll be real pleased."

Tying a rag to the tail of a mouse might seem crazy. Doing it to two mice? Definitely. So what would you call me if I then doused the tip of the rag in lighter fluid and lit it on fire?

I could tell you and PETA that I'd taken a few extra minutes to fashion tiny fire retardant mouse suits from baby PJs. But I'd be lying. Hey, after watching documentaries of cancer testing, I was pretty sure I was giving these mice a kinder death.

Gary's beady eyes teared up.

"Don't you judge me," I said, as I tossed one, then the other into the vent. "Close it up."

I ran around to the front of the unit and used my new multi-tool to open the face of the temperature gauge. Through the small window, I could see the mice skittering, flames shooting up. Three cardboard boxes began to smolder. Within seconds, two more were on fire, the storage alarm light clicked on. Before the sensor could send off a signal, I used my jerry-rigged remote control, closed down the circuits, sending up a little prayer to the Virgin Mary for introducing me to that hot electrician/bomb maker in Ohio years ago. One more twist of the wire, and I had convinced the computer panel in the unit hot was cold and cold was hot. The temperature gauge read one hundred degrees. Twenty degrees to go.

"Is it working?" Gary asked, leaning over my shoulder.

I almost got the words, *Think so* out of my mouth before Gary's co-worker whacked him across the back with a pipe, taking him down.

"Shit!"

I dropped the controller and rolled away as Brainless smacked the concrete beside my head. *How do people always seem to come up with random pipes in fights?* I scurried into the rows of shelving, tried to dodge and run, but the ankle wasn't cooperating. I dove between two pallets, rolled out and came up in the next aisle—right in front of Brainless and his pipe.

He grinned. "Well this must be my wildest dream."

I heard the fat lady sing.

Then, I heard a more beautiful sound. The flutter of a helicopter followed by the crash of a skylight and the zip of a descending line, man in black attached.

Brainless did the old duck and cover as glass and warehouse roof rained down. I rolled back under the shelves until I heard a familiar voice.

"Back off, asshole. Drop the pipe."

Gator hung above me, gun trained on Brainless, who dropped the pipe and stepped back, hands in the air.

"You okay?" he asked over his shoulder as he slid the last few feet to the floor.

"Yeah," I said, staring at the busted ceiling, the bottom of a helicopter, my dangling hero.

"Come on. Let's get out of here," he said.

"Hang on."

"Kinda have to," Gator said, pointing to the rope.

I jogged back to the cold storage unit, retrieved my bag. The temperature gauge read eighty-six degrees. It was enough.

I took another ten seconds to run back to the dock, where I'd left Mickey. The zip-ties were sliced, lay in pieces. Mickey was gone.

"We need to be done here, Jojo," Gator called.

I hurried back. "We're done. Oh except this one thing."

I kicked the pipe away from Brainless and stepped in close, faking the punch I'd contemplated earlier. When he dodged, I grabbed his balls with my other hand and twisted until he screamed.

"Be nice to women," I said, getting another quarter turn. "Nobody likes a douchebag. Got it?"

He squirmed, sweat breaking out on his forehead, then nodded. "Yeah. Got it."

I opened my hand, let him drop to his knees as I returned to Gator.

"Feel better?"

"I do, thanks."

Gator adjusted his harness and handed me a length of rope ending in a foot loop.

I stepped in and held unto his back, strong, broad, warm.

He spoke into his wrist and we began to ascend.

Chapter 22

Getting a helicopter ride to Bunkie was interesting. Not just for us, but for three surrounding towns. Gator told me not to worry, folks would probably just think it was the cops looking for an escaped convict, or Hollywood scouting another location to shoot a heartwarming backwoods hick reality show.

He introduced me to the pilot, a rich Texas neighbor who collected aircraft like Gator collected cars. I knew how it could be with buddies and favors, so I didn't ask for details, just thanked the guy best I could.

We flew away from Pharmco, Gator and I strapped into helmets with mics. Gator explained how after I'd left in the Caddy, the sedan tailing him in Sabrina had suffered a bit of an accident, apparently thinking he could fly when he drove off an overpass. There was a lot more to say, but it was tough enough to hang on inside the chopper, without trying to figure out the nuances in someone's words, words that were cut in half, breathy and buffeted about in the air. We chose instead to be mostly quiet. I might have dozed off at one point.

I did manage to tell Gator about seeing—and tazing— Mickey at the Pharmco warehouse.

"He didn't seem surprised to see me," I said, remembering how he'd been on the phone when I'd come in.

"Huh," Gator said before looking away.

We approached the plantation house, whining and

whirring over the bayou like a huge mosquito armed with a searchlight instead of a stinger. Lights glowed in almost every room of the plantation house. It looked like a misshapen jack-o-lantern, or one of those places on a cheesy Lifetime TV show, where the war widow is waiting for her man to come home. *I'll leave the light on, Johnny. Forever.*

I knew I was super-tired when I started thinking in Lifetime TV mode.

Our headsets crackled, orders barked out as the helicopter descended, landing us in the field nearest the house.

I pulled off the helmet, then attacked the cords and straps holding me in as Gator exchanged words with the pilot before pushing past me and jumping out. I took his offered hand, landed mostly on my good ankle. We ducked as the copter ascended, blades whirring faster, kicking up grass and dirt. Leaning into Gator as he moved us toward the house, the thudding and whomping shook my bones. I slowed.

"Can you make it?" Gator yelled. "I can carry you."

"I'm fine. Don't go getting all soft on me," I yelled back.

The helicopter became a speck in the sky, then disappeared. My hearing returned. Sounds of the field and bayou took the place of the copter's whirring blades and staccato engine.

"Get soft? Well someone ought to be," Gator mumbled.

"What's that?" I said.

"Never mind. Let's just get inside."

I glanced toward the house in time to see a dark form rise up beside the front porch and take off running, heading straight for us. Gator pushed me behind him, drew his weapon, took aim.

"Wait!" I yelled, sinking to my knees. "Don't shoot!"

The familiar baying howl of a pleased coon dog filled the air, seconds before Elvis launched himself, knocking me down.

I rolled with him, scratched him behind the ears, trying to keep his slobbery jowls at arm's length. "Good to see you too, boy."

Gator scanned the yard, then slipped the gun in his waistband.

"What are you so nervous about?" I asked.

"Old habits die hard," Gator said, forcing a smile as he bent down to pet Elvis. "Come on, let's get some ice on that ankle."

He helped me inside, fed me a shot of whiskey and some extra-strength ibuprofen, then poured some kibble for the dog. Downright domestic.

I was settled into a chair on the porch, icepack on my elevated ankle, beer in hand, Elvis splayed at my side, snoring and farting in his sleep, when Gator poked his head out the screen door.

"This computer's been chiming like crazy, looks like your father's trying to get hold of you." He held out an open laptop, the video chat screen beeping and flashing with my father's image.

"Here," I said, swapping out my empty beer bottle for the laptop. "I should have called him by now. He's going to be mad."

"Get you another?" Gator asked, gesturing to the beer.

I nodded as I settled the computer in front of me and logged in.

Seconds later, we were connected. My father sat in a wood paneled room, rows of books behind him.

He said, "Shâ, where you been? I've been trying to—"

"Père, we're here and everything's good." I tried to not focus on the bags under his eyes, his unshaven chin, the stammer in his voice. "How are you and Pilar?"

"She fine. Little bit mad on me." He shrugged. "Nothing going to change that but time."

I smiled. "You know she loves you. And so do I."

His face changed from worried to relieved. I could tell he was holding back equally on the joy of seeing me safe and the desire to cuss me out.

He said, "Gator, he got a nice place here, all these books, all them fancy cars, but it ain't home. Me and Pilar, we're going to pick up Ivory Joe at the hospital tomorrow and drive back. You know I always carry a spare key for Mercy."

I wasn't sure how Ivory Joe was going to feel about that, playing back seat driver to Père in a 1967 Fastback Mustang.

"Why don't you catch me up," I said. "What happened when the cops got to the warehouse?"

We spent the next twenty minutes detailing—or avoiding the details, as it might be—of the events of our day. Quite different from the how-was-school-today talks of my youth, but just about as honest on my end. There was no reason to worry the people I loved by speaking of dangerous things that had already happened. When I finished with the heli-copter ride and Elvis's welcome, Père laughed, his grin putting new creases around his eyes.

"Some day, huh?" he said, leaning back in his chair.

I could see his face clearer, farther from the computer screen. He looked older and smaller, as if recent events had shrunk him.

"Some year," I said.

"So..." we both said together, then laughed, in that stilted way you do when things feel awkward. The elephant was still in the room, possibly resting on my chest.

"Père, I'm really sorry," I said, apologizing for whatever needed apologizing for—from feeling awkward, to putting him and Pilar in danger, to not being the daughter he needed, or the son he'd wanted—the list was endless.

"Nothing to be sorry for, Shâ. What you going to do? Say you're sorry for life? There are some people out there who did bad things, not you, Shâ. There are always people doing bad things. That's why you need to be doing good things. You see, someone's got to even it out, make things level. Maybe that's you."

I shook my head.

Père said, "It's like those scales." He turned his palms up, shifted one high and one low, saying. "You got good and you got evil." He moved his hands again until his palms were even. "If it's like this, we got a chance. But if it do this?" He shifted back to an exaggerated high-low. "We screwed."

The clomp of Gator's cowboy boots on the wood floor announced his arrival before he came through the screen door butt first, a fresh bag of ice in one hand and two bottles of beer in the other. He handed me one, let the door slap shut, took a swig then asked, "What did I miss? Who's screwed?"

I pushed my thumb against the tiny laptop camera and whispered, "Might be you, play your cards right."

Gator grinned and leaned in for a kiss.

"Hey," my father yelled. "Just 'cause I can't see you, don't mean I can't hear you."

I pulled my thumb off the camera. "Sorry, Père."

"There you go again. Get some rest, Shâ. Talk at you tomorrow."

Before I could say a proper goodbye, Gator closed the laptop, scooped up me and my bad ankle and carried us inside, pausing long enough in the doorway for Elvis to slink by and me to leave the computer on the foyer table. I kissed him hard and long, stealing his breath from his warm mouth, pressing myself against his chest, clinging heart against heart all the way to the bedroom where the last thing I did was rest.

* * *

Lying in bed beside Gator in my father's house, the home of my childhood, I felt equally nostalgic and a little uncomfortable. Not just because Gator took up eighty percent of the bed, but because I still had leftover guilt. I hadn't completely let go of Boone, and here in the same bed I'd shared with him I couldn't help feeling I was somehow cheating on my dead fiancé.

Sinking into the gentle slope of the bed under Gator's weight, matching my breathing to his rhythm, it should have been a comfort to me, coupled with the sounds of crickets, night insects and the occasional bullfrog, the lullaby that city people bought in electronic devices and mounted beside their Sleep Number beds. In Bunkie, we just opened the window. But, even with all that, I couldn't sleep. Another glance at the bedside clock showed I'd made it through ten more minutes of lying passively, waiting for that sweet emptiness. My brain wouldn't shut down, my ankle throbbed and then my bladder joined the chorus.

I rolled over, creaking the bedsprings, pulled on a T-shirt and slipped from the bed, putting cautious weight on my wrapped ankle.

I hobbled to the bathroom, found some ibuprofen in the cabinet and a pair of sweats in the hamper. Maybe Elvis would be up for some company in the kitchen.

I made my way downstairs thinking about what Père had said. I knew where he was coming from. Most of the good old boys in Bunkie lived by the rule of *laissez-faire*, and that's all well and good in the swamp or the woods, but out in the real world, things were different. You can't always just walk away and let things be. That balancing of good and evil? It was a constant struggle. Like a fat lady in a cupcake shop with a pocketful of laxatives. Something shitty was bound to happen.

Boone used to call me a pessimist, said I could find

pinprick holes in a sterling silver lining. I preferred to think of myself as a realist, whose decisions and judgments were based on real life circumstances, fueled by fucking awesome instincts. Like when my instincts told me to grab that switchblade letter opener as I passed Père's office, I did.

She sat in the dark kitchen, one foot on Elvis, the other on a side chair. The yellow glow from the light over the stove was strong enough to illuminate the gun in her hand.

"Aww, can't sleep? Should I make you some warm milk?"

I palmed the letter opener, shoved my hands in the pockets of the baggy sweats and shrugged, as if it was every day some bitch appeared in my kitchen in the middle of the night.

"What do you want, Shannon?" I asked, stepping closer, ignoring her, focusing instead on Elvis and the half-chewed steak by his muzzle.

"Not much of a watchdog, is he?" she said, pushing the heel of her boot into Elvis's side, rolling him over. His mouth hung open, tongue lolled, but his chest rose and fell evenly.

"Is that what you came here to talk about? Dogs?"

She shook her head slowly. "Nah, I came here to settle a score."

"If this is about Ivory Joe, I—"

She swung her feet to the floor, leaned her elbows on the table leveling the gun, squinted one eye and took aim. "That loser? Yeah right. I wouldn't waste a bullet on him. Well, maybe one, just for kicks."

I braced myself on my side of the heavy wooden table, amazed at the transformation of the woman in front of me. The sweet Southern girl was gone. No longer the prissy white sandals-wearing debutante I'd met in town, this was a black leather and chains ponytailed biker broad with chiseled biceps, at least one skanky tattoo and a shitload of eyeliner.

She cocked her head, smiled. "You really have no idea why I'm here?"

"No clue."

"Here's a clue for you. Edwin. Dorsey."

Baconator?

I shrugged. "Nope. Not helping."

Shannon shook her head, then raised the gun, leveling the sight. "Fucking bitch. It wasn't enough you had to steal the SD card, fuck with our shipments, turn all those eyes on Pharmco? But you had to go and kill him? Edwin was my man. He was my everything. Now you're going to pay for his life."

I sighed. "You got the wrong girl. I didn't kill anyone. I think you know that. Why are you really here, Shannon? Wait. Don't tell me. You want...world peace." I moved closer, waving one distracting hand, babbling. "No, that's not it. That's far too noble. Let me see. I think you'd ask for something closer to your heart, like a diet pill that really works, or maybe greater compassion for the limitations of bikers in assless chaps?"

"Shut up!" Her shoulders shook, the tip of the gun dropped.

I laughed, pushed a little harder. "What's the matter, Shannon? Can't take a joke? I mean look at you, don't you own a mirror?" I laughed harder. "Skull tattoos? Holy shit, that's so...nineties of you."

I leaned in as if to get a better look, gripped the edge of the table and flipped it, throwing her backward off the chair. Her gun skittered across the floor like a hockey puck.

The crash was loud enough to wake Gator and neighbors if we'd had any. But all thoughts of my man rushing in to gallantly save me—if I'd had any such thoughts—quickly went out the window when I heard gunfire and shouts from upstairs.

It was Shannon's turn to laugh. "You didn't think I'd come alone, did you?"

"Actually," I said, "I bet you do all the time."

"Bitch!" she yelled, lunging for me, hands at my throat.

I held her off, pushing at her ribs, scratching at her wrists. When she took one hand off my throat to grapple, I leaned in, throwing her off balance, jamming my head into hers, thinking she'd be smelling country blonde, fresh soap and herbal essence, but up close, she was stale beer, cigarettes, cowhide—emphasis on the cow. I slammed my skull into her face, heard something pop. My head spun. I dropped to my knees.

"Fuck!" Shannon yelled. She touched her fingers to her bloody lip, ran her tongue across a newly chipped tooth, then took a step back, set up and kicked me hard—boot to ribcage. Calculated and well-executed.

When I recovered I yelled, "You fucking whore!" and charged her, throwing wild punches, putting in the small hurts while avoiding her spike toed boots. I got in a nice jab to the ribs before she pulled a knife.

I faked left then came in hard with my favorite elbow to the temple move, then stood back to watch her fall. She didn't.

What the fuck?

Shannon regained her balance and straightened up, smirking, tapping her head. "Metal plate, Mexico City, 2010."

She raised her knife and pounced, getting in a swipe to my thigh.

I scored a few scrabbles and jabs, lost a second in time and when I looked up, she had a blade at my throat.

"You really want to keep doing this?" Shannon asked,

pulling on the neck of my T-shirt, winding it around her hand.

"I got all night," I said, as she pushed the knife deeper, drawing blood.

"Me too," she said, her words bloody spittle on my chin.

I leaned away from the blade, putting weight on my bad ankle as stars filled my vision. I swallowed hard, fueled by the pain, shifted my weight and rammed my knee into her pelvic bone. She yelped, dropped the knife and crumbled. I grabbed her by the ponytail, stomped on her hand, kicked away the knife. She yelled, slapped and clawed with her one good hand at mine wound deep in her hair. I tugged harder, pulling her to her feet, then backed up against the kitchen wall, holding her off me, eyes blazing, jaws snapping like a nasty bog turtle, her broken hand flapping uselessly.

I dragged my foot across the floor until I felt the ridge, the place where the rotten boards had been replaced with new. One more step left. Yanking Shannon's ponytail, I jerked her head back. She fought, straining her neck, spitting at me. Veins popped in my forearm, as I tugged against her. My other hand found Père's letter opener in my pocket, clicked open the blade, then reached around and slashed the clump of hair clenched in my hand as I ducked.

Shannon's head snapped forward, connecting perfectly with Memaw's wall-mounted cast iron frying pan.

"That's for calling my friend a loser, you bitch," I said, as she slid unconscious to the floor. "And *that*," I said, dropping the foot-long blonde mane. "Is for drugging my dog."

I turned at the sound of a cheering whistle. H-man stood at the entrance to the kitchen, a shiny, long barreled revolver at Gator's temple.

Chapter 23

I tried to look past the weeping bloody gash on Gator's pretty forehead, the slice of brow dangling over one eye, the pain radiating through his grimace. Tried to center myself, stuff my emotions into a tiny pocket with a thick lead lining, the mere image bringing to mind a fist full of bullets, a trigger-happy finger, exploding skull, bone shrapnel, blood spatter.

I knew I would kill for this man. I just wasn't sure who'd be first.

"Never mess with someone's dog, I always say." H-man grinned.

I raised the ridiculously small blade in my hand. He lifted one hand in mock surrender.

"She dead?" he asked, tipping his chin toward Shannon.

"Not yet," I said.

"Good," he said.

"I don't think I'm done with her," I said through gritted teeth.

He laughed. "You think we're done with you?"

"Define done," I said, catching Gator's eye. I slid mine toward the bottom of the stove, where the butt of Shannon's gun protruded. He blinked his acknowledgement and I drew my attention back to H-man, thinking he was more muscle than fat, but not wanting to give him any credit.

I shifted my weight off the bad ankle, raised my knife

hand and was about to lunge when salvation came from an unlikely source.

Angels might have broken into song, a slice of heaven might have slipped through the gray cloudy sky of Bunkie, Louisiana. Whatever it was, I now believed in divine intervention. And his name was Elvis.

A coon dog who lives on kibble, beef scraps and baked bean leftovers is a happy dog. A gaseous, happy dog. The sudden odiferous flatulation that emitted itself from the sleeping dog's ass was both frightening and glorious.

"Jesus fucking Christ," H-man yelled, clamping a hand to his nose. "What the hell is tha—?"

Gator slid across the floor, snatched up Shannon's gun, aimed and fired with a click. H-man spun, gun arm sighting Gator, taking aim as I jumped on his back, circling my arm around his throat in my version of the cop chokehold. It was effective—more so with the addition of the heel to the balls move—something I called The Bunkie Twist and Shout.

He shot the ceiling. Twice.

"Fuck! Gator?" I yelled, twisting H-man's barrel sized neck, jabbing with my heels. "Little help here."

"I know. I know," he yelled, ejecting the magazine, slamming it back into place, while I rode H-man, him grabbing my legs, spinning like a bull in a ring.

He slammed me up against the fridge, rattling the bottles inside. I hung on, waiting for Gator to take the shot, aware he might miss, equally aware my grip was slipping and H-man wasn't tiring—at all.

The first shot passed through the fabric of my baggy sweats, ripping into H-man's thigh. He roared, then bent over, grabbing his leg. As I vaulted off his back, Gator's second shot hit paydirt. Chest. Heart. Down.

I stood slowly, ears ringing and made my way to Gator.

"Thanks," I said, leaning down to kiss him, lingering,

moving my lips to his ear. "Next time, don't wait so long, darlin'."

He kissed me back, hard then harder.

The front door slammed open.

Gator pushed me behind the overturned table, rolled on top of me, pinning me with his this-is-not-the-time-eyes then turning his attention to the kitchen doorway.

There were shouts, the tell-tale stomp of boots on wood, up the stairs, down the stairs, then silence.

Gator stood, gun at the ready, as I pulled myself together, smoothing my hair like I was welcoming someone's momma, before I rose to my knees behind the table.

Mickey walked into the kitchen unarmed, grabbed an apple from the bowl on the counter, tossed it in the air, caught it and took a huge bite.

"Wasn't sure they'd come," he said, speaking around a mouthful of apple.

"But you thought they might?" I said, working myself upright. "And you let us come back here anyway? Are you fucking kidding me?"

Gator lowered his gun, clipped it to his belt. I looked at him, then Mickey. "You used us for bait, didn't you?"

Mickey shrugged.

I lunged. Gator grabbed my arm, stopping me mid-swing as Mickey's crew appeared in the doorway dressed like ninjas and armed to the gills.

"Easy, Jojo," Gator said, hugging me tight, whispering in my ear. "There'll be time for that. Not now."

I stopped struggling, looked at him closer, the furrowed brow, pursed lips.

"Were you in on this, Gator?"

"I'm sorry, Jojo."

I shook off his grip, squared my shoulders.

He reached for me saying, "Most of it I put together. Mickey just confirmed it."

I didn't know if I was more upset at Gator for keeping a secret, or at myself for not figuring it out.

I ignored him for the moment and addressed Mickey. "So, who is she? Really," I asked, tipping my chin toward the unconscious Shannon. "Said she knew Edwin, The Bacon-ator."

"She did. She also knew H-man and Clayton—Twitch— they moved stolen and counterfeit drugs from Texas to Miami. We thought she was behind the Pharmco cargo thefts, just needed the proof. Meet Ava—Mrs. Edwin Dorsey," Mickey said, taking another bite of apple. "Former head of security at Omega Vac, a leading vaccine developer that's transitioning into the oncogenic biomarker field."

I must have looked as confused as I felt because he finished chewing then added, "Also called cancer biomarkers, they're used to diagnose the progress of disease in patients or monitor response to specific drug treatments. The biomarker market is expected to reach revenues of—" He tossed the half-eaten apple over his head. "—forty-point-eight-billion."

The room was quiet enough to hear the soft landing of an apple in a gloved hand.

I turned my head to see one of Mickey's crew zip the fruit into a pocket with one hand, his weapon never wavering.

Leave no evidence behind.

Before I could ask what any of that had to do with me or Boone or Gator or Pharmco or Corpus Christi, he said, "Turns out the SD card they wanted so badly was encrypted with a detailed list of new biomarkers, quantified on the molecular level. Access to this information could revolution-ize our healthcare system, change the way we treat cancer forever, for better."

As if on cue, Ava/Shannon came alive in the back of the

room, coughing, cursing, spitting blood and broken teeth. She sat up, squinting, poised to attack.

"Hello, Ava," Mickey said. "Sorry about your partner. Or should I say partners?"

Ava stared at the bloody body of H-man, then scanned the room, slowing her gaze on me and Gator.

If eyes were lasers, I'd have a few less freckles.

Mickey grinned. "Seeing as you're on your own now, you might want to rethink that deal we discussed."

She spit a bloody stream. "You might want to go fuck yourself."

Mickey raised a hand, two beckoning fingers. Half his crew moved in, one with a very large gun, the other with thick black zip ties.

"Wait," I said. "Can I ask her something?"

Mickey nodded.

"How can you do it? You're playing Russian roulette with people's lives, and they don't even know they're part of your game. Medicines that might have worked are going to be forever questioned, maybe even revoked, because they didn't perform the way they should—because they weren't the real thing. You stole NewGen and repackaged it. You took the drug that someone dying needed to live and sold it to someone else with more money. How the fuck can you do that?"

Ava smiled, crooked, gap-toothed. "Because. I. Don't. Care. It's just business."

"So it was all for the money?"

She tipped her head, remorseless.

"You're a piece of shit, Shannon, Ava whoever the fuck you are—"

Mickey put his hands on his hips and stretched. "It doesn't matter what you call her. After today? She doesn't exist."

"Well that makes it easy," I said, grabbing the gun on Gator's belt, taking position.

"Afraid I can't let you do that." Mickey said, stepping in front of Shannon.

I held my ground, moving the firearm to aim around his head.

Gator touched my shoulder, a light tap, then heavier. "Jojo."

His hand felt good, warm and reassuring. He squeezed and I relented, dropping my arm, sliding my finger from the trigger.

Gator caught my eyes, looked through me.

"Bang, bang?" I said.

He gave me a half smile, the blue in his eye glinting in reply.

A chin tip from Mickey and the two guys wrestled Ava out the back door as the third righted the kitchen table, and the fourth produced an aerosol can and sprayed a dispersing solution over the bloodied floor and walls.

Mickey held out his hand for the gun. I spun it once then gave it to him, butt first.

"What now?" I asked, watching the one-man cleaning committee.

"Come on." He led the way to the front of the house.

We stood shoulder to shoulder on the porch as the sun rose over the fields. The birds took up their duties as critters settled into the high grass.

Mickey broke the silence. "Sorry I was late."

"Yeah," Gator said. "You ought to work on your timing."

"Well, where I'm from we're never late to the party because of goddamned alligators in the road."

I was about to tell him he was lucky it wasn't Carnival season, when I heard a car door slam. A few seconds later, a white minivan pulled up from the barn. The side door slid open. Mickey's crew had swapped out their ninja jammies for T-shirts and ball caps.

"I still have questions, you know," I called to his retreating back.

"He knows where to find me," Mickey said, nodding at Gator.

He paused beside the van. "Like it or not you're one of us now. And we always take care of our own."

Gator and I watched until the van's tail lights faded. I was too tired to ask him anything else, too afraid of the answers I might get, and too unwilling to start a conversation that would delay my head hitting the pillow.

I thought I would be relieved, happy even to have this behind us, to have that oh so necessary closure. But could this ever truly be behind us?

There are times when we should be able to hold up a hand and stop information from pummeling us, where we can put our fingers in our ears and sing *lalalalala* while the big bad world rushes by. We should be able to enjoy days in which we choose to not turn on the news, to not read the biased newspaper, to not engage in noise, in things we can't change. Instead, we should give ourselves a gift. Walk outside, or sit in a quiet room. Sip hot tea, or listen to, no, *hear* music. Throw a stick for an eager dog. Say nothing. Enjoy a moment of simple pleasure, of beautiful blissful ignorance, honor the gift of life.

Was that possible?

Gator must have read my mind. He wrapped his arms around me and rested his chin on the top of my head. "At the risk of sounding like a Broadway orphan, there's always tomorrow."

Chapter 24

Gator was more than forthcoming when he joined me in my morning bath. I was almost certain he would have been just as open had I not offered to...scrub his back. But a girl could never be sure.

He apologized for not telling me about the set up with Mickey, how he'd told him I was headed to Pharmco to destroy the NewGen, and how they planned to draw Shannon/Ava and H-man to the plantation.

"It seemed like a good idea at the time," he said.

I had to remind him this wasn't a showdown in the Wild West, and he wasn't a real cowboy. "You do know that, don't you?"

"Course I do," he scoffed. "Don't be so dramatic. It all worked out for the best, didn't it?'

"Sure. I mean, look at us."

"I'm looking," Gator said, definitely not focusing on my cuts and bruises.

I sunk lower in the tub splashing an armful of water his way. Pillow fights got nothing on a good old-fashioned tub rumble.

Later, we sacked out on the couch, nursing our aches and bruises, swollen eyes and lips—like celebrities recuperating from a trip to the plastic surgeon—without the big bill or promise of beauty.

"Thanks again for cleaning up," I said, settling back into the cushions as Gator tossed me a frozen bag of peas.

"No problem," he said, scooping a handful of corn niblets from a hole in his veggie bag.

"Hey, you're supposed to put that on your eye, not in your mouth."

He grinned. "I'm applying from the inside out."

"Anything else you want to tell me before Père gets here?" I asked.

"Nope."

"Sure?"

"Well, there might be *one* thing," he said.

"Oh shit, here we—"

"I love you, Jojo Boudreaux."

Sometimes the least expected thing is the most needed thing. After all, I was, despite the layers of camo, still a girl. And there's no girl in the world who will admit to hearing someone say the words *I love you* too much. And no man in the world who would hesitate in saying those words if he knew the kind of thank you he'd receive in return.

Ivory Joe took the news in stride. It was his way. He didn't want to accept that he'd been tricked by Shannon, but there wasn't much sense of denying it. He tried to apologize for putting me and Père in danger, but I stopped him.

"Ivory Joe. Look at me. Bad shit finds me. Always has, always will. I just need enough people like you around when it gets too deep."

He shook his head. "You know who you sound like, don't you, Jojo?"

"Who?"

"Crazy Sonny."

I laughed, raised my beer bottle and clinked his.

Gator joined us in the kitchen, trying to get in on the laugh.

"Who's Crazy Sonny?"

I smiled. "Old friend. You'll have to meet him sometime."

Ivory Joe reached out and patted Gator's shoulder. "Good luck with that."

We sat around the dining room table, a hodgepodge of people who might not belong together, but after what we'd been through would never grow apart. It felt like someone had gotten married, or graduated, or been offered the dream job/house/trip that no one thought would happen. It was one of those big sigh moments, where you touched hope, slid your hand down its back slow and easy, until the fur ruffled the wrong way.

I let Gator do the majority of the explaining. He was a better liar than me, at least to my father. Ivory Joe jumped in with some cancer statistics, adding inside information only a survivor knew, while I kept my head down and worked my way through a few cold ones and a big plate of chicken and rice.

We couldn't change the pharmaceutical industry. We couldn't heal cancer patients or reduce the cost of medicine. We couldn't change healthcare or doctors or hospitals or clinics, but we could stop thieves from robbing our cargo, and we could make sure it was stored and delivered properly. We could do that much.

And we could hope that *most people*—cancer fundraisers, research specialists, medical professionals, pharmaceutical salespeople, drug distributors, cargo haulers, wholesalers, end market salesmen, oncologists and nurses—were good people, honorable people.

Even though we knew how that *most people thing* worked. Sort of like a magician waving his right hand in the air, while his left hand stuffed a rabbit in his pants.

* * *

The TV had been playing low in the other room. We'd glanced at it occasionally, but when Pilar pointed at the screen and said, "Manny, turn that up," we all turned in our seats.

"The FDA is looking into allegations that fifty lots of NewGen, formerly called 'the miracle breast cancer drug' has made its way back into circulation. NewGen was revoked by the FDA due to complications in cancer patients, including such side effects as kidney failure and lymphedema.

"This announcement comes on the heels of a recent rash of pharmaceutical cargo thefts from Texas to Miami in which certain drugs may not have been properly stored. Law enforcement has alerted hospitals, clinics and pharmacies to decline all deliveries from Pharmco and its subsidiaries until further notice."

Ivory Joe gave me the thumbs up, mouthing "Good job." Gator squeezed my thigh under the table and I silently thanked Mickey. Maybe he really was one of the good guys.

When the broadcast went back to the studio, the cheerful, large-eyed anchorwoman spoke of a generous, anonymous donation made to the St. Christopher Truckers Development and Relief Fund which would re-open the naval clinic on the abandoned base in Corpus Christi, Texas. While dedicated primarily to research and development of cancer biomarkers, one wing of the facility would be dedicated for the medical care of truck drivers with cancer, and the families of truckers in need.

"Well, look at that," Pilar said.

"Yes," I said, reaching for Gator's hand. "Look at that."

* * *

We healed. It's what we do. Ivory Joe moved back to his place, promising to keep in touch and Pilar and Père dug into the hunting business. They made plans to close in the back porch for more sleeping quarters and started calling breeders for dogs they planned to buy.

Part of me wanted to stay right there and raise puppies, but the best part of me, the part that was almost perfect again, that part was ready to hit the road and see what life had in store this time.

Down at the barn, Sabrina had been tuned up and cleaned inside and out. The trailer roof was fixed and new back doors installed. She looked as good as new, better even with more lights and chrome—you could never have too much chrome.

I ran a hand over the warm hood of Gator's repaired Caddy. It had taken a hell of a lot of sweet talking, not to mention hours scouring replacement parts, dropping welds and calling in favors to return her in short order to her pretty shiny self.

If only people were as simple to put back together.

Gator and I took one last walk down to the bayou. We cut through the fields, crunched our way through dead brush and downed limbs at the edge of the woods, then pushed through salt meadow grass to stand at the edge of the water. This was home, a place I knew well, a place that had never failed to comfort me.

I told Gator how lately I'd been feeling that nothing was predictable anymore. Growing up, we used to be able to plan ahead knowing when the rains were coming, when the weather would be cool enough to be called enjoyable. We knew the lifecycle of certain biting insects and what would ward them off. We knew the habitats of woodland creatures and the widths of streams in spring, summer and fall.

But in recent years, the whole world had gone topsy-turvy. Asteroids and meteors, shifting plates, flash floods, wild fires and dying breeds—new cycles that followed no pattern, and new troubles we couldn't ward off. It wasn't just Mother Nature who had taken a detour, the whole world was fucked up—people, governments, fashion, music, technology, communication. If I thought about any of it for too long, my stomach started to hurt.

"You okay?" he asked.

I said, "I don't know. This whole thing we just went through? Who knows what really happened? Who even cares?" I shook my head. "Do you think anything will change?"

"Hey, it made the news. Well sort of."

"*Sort of* doesn't leave me with the warm fuzzies, if you know what I mean," I said.

Gator smiled and reached for my hand. "Never took you for a warm fuzzies kind of girl."

"What's that supposed to mean?"

"What it sounds like. Probably the only time you get warm fuzzies is when you win."

I stopped and looked at him. Did he want a warm fuzzies kind of girl?

"One time at the range shooting Père's .357, I got a hot casing down my shirt. Does that count?"

"No," he said laughing.

He pulled me close and nuzzled my cheek working his way around to my lips. Before he kissed me he whispered, "But I wouldn't have you any other way."

We left two days later, with a plan to work the west coast, spend Christmas in the mountains. Charlene had offered additional apologies by hooking us up with a high paying job running from Sedona to Napa, and I couldn't find anything not to like in that.

We said our goodbyes to Pilar and Père. Pilar suggested I take it easy for a while, maybe give karma a day off. Before I climbed up into Sabrina, she tucked a small white bag into my pocket. "For protection. Don't open it."

As Gator drove us off the plantation, I pulled the bag from my pocket, held it to my nose. Sage, rosemary, something musty. I tossed the bag in the glove box and turned up the radio as we passed through downtown Bunkie, then I went to lay down in the sleeper.

It still bothered me, how we place all our hope in a medicine to fix us, heal our hurts, return us to normal—tiny pills, syringes of promise—and in the end? They might be counterfeit, watered-down versions of the real deal, or poorly stored, mislabeled prescriptions—an expensive poison—that kills.

The idea that this truth would never come out—probably not in my lifetime—only made me think about all the other hidden truths. Not the small ones, like closet smoking, or midnight snacking, or even stolen kisses—but the doozies, things we'd always believed to be true. Things we planned our lives on, our faith on. Even the way Pilar had offered that bag of herbs to protect me.

What did she believe? Whose truth? And is it the actual truth that drives us? Or the pursuit of such a thing?

I thought about that for a long time. Maybe across two states. It was a lot to think about.

When I finally went up front to join Gator in the cab, he barely looked at me. The road was jammed with cars, the kind of traffic that suggests there's an accident far up the highway, one that will be reduced to road debris and odd stains on the shoulder by the time you pass. In the meantime, all you can do is wait and wonder. Something we both sucked at.

When one more car slid into the small space in front of Sabrina's grill that Gator had left free for safety reasons, his knuckles turned white on the wheel and his teeth clenched.

Sensing a storm on the rise, I tuned in the Spa channel, patted him on the shoulder and left the passenger seat, drawing the curtain between cab and sleeper.

In a short while, I was elbows deep in the kitchen—cooking noodles al dente, heating a quart of frozen homemade marinara, browning a loaf of garlic bread—all the while thinking, *It's going to be fine. After all, how much trouble could he possibly get into up there?*

You know that thing about famous last words?

They're called last words for a reason.

ACKNOWLEDGMENTS

To Eric at Down & Out Books who took a chance on Jojo—and me. Thank you for seeing through the steam rising on the asphalt and not demanding the answer to the question: Where would we shelve this? Independent publishers have changed the way I write and more importantly the way we read. Thank you, Lance, for going above and beyond to birth this baby in record time. You guys are the best.

To the truckers who told me their stories and showed me their rigs, from MATS to GATS to IOWA 80, you had me sold on your kindness, loyalty and sense of humor from the moment Granny Smith won the Volvo and gave her old truck to Hershey Bar to the gathering in the parking lot for a Native American wedding where the bride and groom were encircled by rigs of all colors and sizes and a man in a gorilla suit passed out cake.

None of this story would have made it to the page if it hadn't been for the amazing support of my family, the encouragement from my writing pals and the infinite grace of God.

Linda Sands is the award-winning author of five novels. Her short stories and essays have appeared in *The Atlanta Journal-Constitution*, *The Walton Sun*, *Skirt! Magazine*, *Dogplotz*, *Moronic Ox*, and a bunch of defunct lit mags and various anthologies. Most recent awards include Georgia Author of the Year for Mystery/Detective novels and two Killer Nashville Judge's Choice Awards for Best Neo-noir and Best PI novel.

Linda splits her writing time between the Gulf Coast of Florida, the Mountains of Georgia and the suburbs of Atlanta where she and her husband cheer on the competing colleges of their children.

OTHER TITLES FROM DOWN AND OUT BOOKS

See www.DownAndOutBooks.com for complete list

By J.L. Abramo
Chasing Charlie Chan
Circling the Runway
Brooklyn Justice
Coney Island Avenue (*)

By Trey R. Barker
Exit Blood
Death is Not Forever
No Harder Prison

By Eric Beetner (editor)
Unloaded

By Eric Beetner
and Frank Zafiro
The Backlist
The Shortlist

By G.J. Brown
Falling

By Angel Luis Colón
No Happy Endings
Meat City on Fire (*)

By Shawn Corridan
and Gary Waid
Gitmo (*)

By Frank De Blase
Pine Box for a Pin-Up
Busted Valentines
A Cougar's Kiss

By Les Edgerton
The Genuine, Imitation,
Plastic Kidnapping
Lagniappe (*)
Just Like That (*)

By Danny Gardner
A Negro and an Ofay (*)

By Jack Getze
Big Mojo
Big Shoes
Colonel Maggie & the Black Kachina

By Richard Godwin
Wrong Crowd
Buffalo and Sour Mash
Crystal on Electric Acetate (*)

By Jeffery Hess
Beachhead
Cold War Canoe Club (*)

By Matt Hilton
Rules of Honor
The Lawless Kind
The Devil's Anvil
No Safe Place

By Lawrence Kelter
and Frank Zafiro
The Last Collar

By Lawrence Kelter
Back to Brooklyn (*)

(*)—Coming Soon

OTHER TITLES FROM DOWN AND OUT BOOKS

See www.DownAndOutBooks.com for complete list

By Jerry Kennealy
Screen Test
Polo's Long Shot (*)

By Dana King
Worst Enemies
Grind Joint
Resurrection Mall (*)

By Ross Klavan, Tim O'Mara
and Charles Salzberg
Triple Shot

By S.W. Lauden
Crosswise
Crossed Bones (*)

By Paul D. Marks and
Andrew McAleer (editor)
Coast to Coast vol. 1
Coast to Coast vol. 2

By Gerald O'Connor
The Origins of Benjamin Hackett

By Gary Phillips
The Perpetrators
Scoundrels (Editor)
Treacherous
3 the Hard Way

By Thomas Pluck
Bad Boy Boogie (*)

By Tom Pitts
Hustle
American Static (*)

By Robert J. Randisi
Upon My Soul
Souls of the Dead
Envy the Dead

By Charles Salzberg
Devil in the Hole
Swann's Last Song
Swann Dives In
Swann's Way Out

By Scott Loring Sanders
Shooting Creek and Other Stories

By Ryan Sayles
The Subtle Art of Brutality
Warpath
Let Me Put My Stories In You (*)

By John Shepphird
The Shill
Kill the Shill
Beware the Shill

By James R. Tuck (editor)
Mama Tried vol. 1
Mama Tried vol. 2 (*)

By Lono Waiwaiole
Wiley's Lament
Wiley's Shuffle
Wiley's Refrain
Dark Paradise
Leon's Legacy (*)

By Nathan Walpow
The Logan Triad

(*)—Coming Soon

82984240R00163

Made in the USA
Middletown, DE
08 August 2018